A
PLACE
OF
SAFETY

EMMA SALISBURY

Copyright

BOOKS BY EMMA SALISBURY

THE COUPLAND AND MORETON DETECTIVE SERIES:
FRAGILE CORD (Book One)
A PLACE OF SAFETY (Book Two)
ONE BAD TURN (Book three)

THE DAVY JOHNSON EDINBURGH GANGLAND SERIES
TRUTH LIES WAITING (Book One)
THE SILENCE BEFORE THE SCREAM (Book Two)

Dedication

For Dave, for encouraging me to carry on when the
Corrie omnibus and a family sized bar of chocolate
seemed the better option

Prologue

He always knew one day he'd get mixed up with guns. It was only ever going to be a matter of time, given the company he kept and the lifestyle he aspired to. You can't go about in the circles he moved in without needing protection, needing to defend your own corner once in a while, but what he hadn't expected was this.

'Go on,' a deep voice behind him urged as the car slowed down a second time, a hand snaking along his thigh in case further encouragement was needed.

He'd thought it was some sort of test, some elaborate initiation to prove he had bottle, could be trusted to follow orders. So he'd gone along with it, waiting for the moment they'd yank the gun away from him, pissing themselves because he'd been daft enough to fall for it, slapping his back and shaking their heads, telling him he'd had 'em going for a minute.

Only that didn't happen.

Instead a hush descended upon them as they watched him and waited. 'Go on,' the voice behind him repeated once more, the hand gripping him harder.

Sweat dripped between his shoulder blades as the car window lowered. His hands felt clammy and he wished more than anything he had the balls to say no.

Oblivious to the music thumping from the stereo, he swallowed, pausing just long enough to eyeball his target.

Then he fired.

Chapter 1

There was nothing quite like the anticipation of going out on a Friday night. Best day of the week, no question. Made sense of the endless shitty filing and data processing that filled Abby's working days since leaving school and joining the accountancy firm Rogers and Black as a trainee Finance Clerk. She looked at the time on the bottom of her computer screen and sighed; why did time drag when you had plans?

Through the office window the early rush hour escape had begun, workers pouring out of buildings onto the high street, eager to catch the early bus home, or failing that get a seat on the regular one. The evenings were still light, although cooler now; passers-by wore jackets and woollen scarves, young girls marking the transition by wearing thick tights under skimpy shorts. It seemed to Abby that Salford took on a life of its own once the offices had shut, the people milling around its centre over the next few hours did so because they wanted to, going out on a bender they'd slogged all week to pay for, a top night out in reward for keeping their heads down, going with the flow for another week.

Angela, a wiry bespectacled woman in charge of the firm's finance staff smiled kindly in Abby's direction.

'You got your tickets then?' She asked. Abby nodded, trying not to let her eyes slide up to the wall clock above Angela's head.

'Queue was massive! They wouldn't let you buy more than two tickets at a time, so I had to text Dixie and tell her to get her backside down there soon as. But yeah, got mine and Becca's tickets OK.'

Angela pushed back from her desk to reach down for the elegant leather bag by her feet. 'I'll give you the money for Becca's ticket now,' she informed Abby as she rifled through the contents, 'she can owe it me rather than you.'

'You sure?' Abby asked, already on her feet as she made her way over to Angela's desk. Rebecca wasn't the best at settling her debts, good job she had a mother always willing to bail her out.

The older woman's eyes twinkled as she studied Abby. Tall and slim like Becca, but there the similarity ended. Whereas her own daughter was quite studious looking, some would even say plain, Abby's shock of red hair and dazzling smile catapulted her into a league of beauty that she seemed blissfully unaware of. Both girls had been best friends since primary school, virtually inseparable; she frowned as she remembered that was all going to change. She broached the subject once more:

'No regrets then, Abby, about coming to work here?'

'You mean regrets about not going to uni?' Abby corrected her. She paused, her eyes staring into space as though searching for an answer that would finally satisfy everyone; convince them all she was doing the right thing, that she hadn't been influenced by the situation at home. 'Look, I didn't get the grades, it happens. I wasn't prepared to do resits...' She smiled at Angela's concerned frown.

'...don't look like that, Angela,' she soothed, 'Becca was always the bright one. I just ambled by scraping through. But I don't want to carry on scraping through. A mediocre degree today is no good to anyone, besides, the graduate route isn't the only way into a career – you should know that – and who knows, if I get the experience here, maybe in a couple of years I'll study for the diploma, see where that takes me.'

Angela smiled sadly, 'You know, Becca was

heartbroken at first, when you said you weren't going with her, wanted to turn Bristol down...if Salford had run a similar course...'

'I know,' Abby conceded, 'and I'm cool with it, really. The way I see it is it just wasn't meant to be. Besides, we'll have more to talk about when she comes home.' A further glance at the corner of her computer screen told her it was a quarter to five, if she didn't catch the next bus...

Tonight was a big night in many ways, the opening of a new nightclub in the centre of town and Becca's last night out before leaving for Bristol in the morning. It had to be special; Abby had choreographed every minute of it a thousand times in her head. They were starting out at her house for drinks at six, which left precious little time to get ready as it was. She turned her pleading eyes towards Angela. 'Haven't even made up my mind what I'm going to wear yet.' She confided impishly, 'Becca's bringing over a couple of tops...'

Angela glanced at her Longines watch. Stifling a smile, she made a wafting motion with her right hand. 'I can take a hint,' she said good-naturedly, 'off you go then,' her last words carrying over to Abby as she hurried towards the lift: 'Just don't do anything I wouldn't do...'

'You still gonna do this?'

'Yeah, I'm still gonna do this, what choice do I fuckin' have?'

'It's drugs though bruv, Mum brought you up better than that.'

'Like that stopped you from bein' sent down?'

Aston curled his lip, sucked air through his teeth and slapped his hand against his younger brother's shoulder. 'I'm only lookin'out for you Earl, no need to disrespect me.'

Earl looked up at his older brother, wondered with a pang when it was he'd actually stopped looking up *to* him. Round the same time as Aston's stint in prison, he reckoned, leaving Earl to take care of their mother and sister. Their fathers were long gone.

'Look,' Earl reasoned, 'all I need to do is pull off this last job, then Pauly'll leave me alone and I can go back to school.'

Aston pulled a face and smacked his right hand against his own forehead as though he'd remembered something crucial, 'So that's how it's done…' he muttered slowly, 'shit man, why didn't you say? I can see now where I went fuckin' wrong…' He shook his head in frustration, 'roundabout the time I used to believe what Pauly says and what Pauly does were the same ting…' he shook his head in disbelief, 'and to think we all thought you were the smart one in dis family.'

'I'm smarter than you man,' Earl retorted, 'I ain't been inside for handlin' stolen motors -'

'That was a long time ago, bruv, and I learned my lesson. Look at me, I've turned my life around, I got a girl, a job-'

'Yeah, under the thumb and always broke. Smart move, man.'

'I know what I want now. I don' wanna be lookin' over my shoulder for the rest of my life, and I don't want that for you…'

'*Very touching.*'

The temperature in the flat plummeted as a sinewy black man with a shaved head entered the room behind them. 'Why you here, Aston,' he drawled, his Mancunian accent peppered with third generation patois, 'dis is no place for a *pussy*.' Earl suppressed a smirk. Aston was bigger than him when all said and done. 'Why don'tcha run off back to your mamma,' Pauly taunted, 'leave Earl to take up where you left off.'

'Shut your mouth, Pauly.'

'Who you orderin' around, man?' Pauly moved forward with confidence; Aston might be taller and well built, but the older man had the benefit of his henchmen playing on the X box in the next room if needed. Aston took a step back, tried a different approach. 'Just lookin' out for ma family, man, you know the score.'

It was hard not to notice Pauly's 'chib', a scar from a knife slash that ran from the right side of his mouth, curving down below his jaw line. A memento from a turf war ten years earlier, in the days when he travelled alone, fought his own corner. He'd moved on since then, got himself a reputation and the muscle to protect it.

Pauly stretched his lips into the widest smile; put his arm around Earl's slender shoulders, drawing him closer. The sight of the gangster pawing at his brother like that turned Aston's stomach but he knew how intoxicating it was to hold Pauly's attention. 'C'mon Pauly,' he placated; arms open to show he'd not give them any trouble, 'you can't blame me for watchin' his back.'

Pauly seemed to give this some thought. 'He's a big bwoy now,' he said in his defence, 'and if he wants to work for me that's his choice...but...' he paused as though working out how they could come to an agreement without him losing face, 'him do this last job for me and you have my word I'll leave him alone.'

'You sure?'

'I'm fuckin' sure man.' The grin was starting to slip. 'Now leave him, he's got work to do.'

Aston paused, looked back at Earl, who, at fourteen, was six years his junior. Fourteen going on forty.

'You OK with this bruv?'

Earl nodded. 'Yeah man, just *go*.' Aston tutted; sucked his teeth once more before slamming out onto the tower block landing.

'Pussy.' Earl snarled after him.

Pauly patted Earl on his back, nodding his approval, his smile returning to its Cheshire Cat grin. At that moment one of his foot soldiers, all seven feet tall and shoulders as wide as the Hulme Flyover, entered the room carrying a package wrapped in brown paper. He paused in the doorway, waited for Pauly to grant right of entry before approaching them, stopping just in front of Earl. They both turned to look at Pauly, waiting.

'Empty your pockets.' Pauly instructed.

Bewildered, Earl did as he was told; removing the parcel of puff resin he'd been instructed by Pauly to pocket an hour before. A look of confusion flashed across his face.

'I thought you wanted me to deliver…'

'Tings have changed.' Pauly said abruptly, nodding at the Hulme Flyover to unwrap the parcel he was holding, careful not to touch the contents directly, holding the paper's edge so his prints didn't transfer onto it.

A 9mm semi-automatic.

He wrapped it up again before holding it out for Earl to take. Pauly's arm around Earl's narrow shoulders tightened in a vice-like embrace. 'An important job has come in.' he breathed low into Earl's ear, inhaling cheap body spray and teenage boy sweat.

'And when I heard what was needed, I knew juss de man for de job.'

The queue was already snaking round the block by the time the taxi pulled up at the kerb outside Ego, a long line of over made up girls in skimpy skirts and young men in knock-off designer clothing waited patiently to be let inside. Abby counted out the cab fare and included a tip, thanked the driver once more for waiting longer than was decent while she and Becca had run round the flat in a flurry of excitement collecting bags and purses, performing last-minute make-up retouches as they'd said their goodbyes to Marion, Abby's mum. The cab was Marion's treat; she'd given them money for the return fare too:

Won't have to worry about how you're getting home then – or if, ;) Her typewritten note had read, hinting at a humour almost forgotten along with the sound of her voice.

'Seriously she's really cool your mum, Abby,' Becca gushed, 'bet she was a total honey when she was younger. I think my mum was *born* an accountant.' It was true that Abby's good looks had originated from her mother, going by old photos and the comments her dad used to make before the emphysema took him – and a stubborn streak to go with it. Sadly, two years into Motor Neurone Disease her mother's mobility had deteriorated, along with the ability to carry out most tasks – she relied heavily on Abby now to dress her, do her hair and make-up and help with her two younger brothers. Abby had been in the process of speaking to social services to ask for help with caring for her mother once she'd left for university, so in many ways not getting the exam marks she'd needed had been a relief, besides, she wasn't quite sure she was ready to leave home yet, in some perverse way she enjoyed being needed.

Findlay and Jordan, her younger twin brothers were at that impossible stage – most days they did something that made her want to explode, like pouring her best perfume into their bedtime bath, or lathering themselves in her designer body lotion – a birthday present from Angela - but at the end of each day they would look at her with their big round eyes and little boy grins and all would be forgiven. She was like a second mother to them, how could she, in all conscience, leave them while she went away to study? Besides, there was another altogether selfish reason she was happy to stay put…

'What are you plotting now?' Becca giggled, already in the party spirit thanks to the bottle of sparkling wine they'd shared before leaving. Abby had wanted them to have some time alone, a chance to reflect on their friendship before they met up with the others and got off their faces. The first couple of hours after Becca had arrived at Abby's flat they'd stayed in her room, laughing and joking as they did each other's hair, swigging from bottles of Smirnoff Ice that Becca had brought with her. Afterwards, they'd shared a takeaway with Marion, the twins dispatched to their room to watch a film.

The taxi had arrived early and Abby still hadn't given Becca her gift, so hurriedly she'd thrust the simply wrapped parcel into her friend's hands. 'I'd got a speech prepared and everything,' she admitted shyly, 'but all I really wanted to say was good luck.' She waved her hands in front of her face as she felt the tears begin to well, 'I'll miss you,' she gasped, 'and whenever you wear it I hope it'll remind you of me.'

Becca tore into the parcel and opened the velvet jewellery box inside to reveal a silver chain with a small diamond chip pendant hanging from it. Lost for words, she rushed towards Abby to plant a kiss on her cheek.

'And don't go bloody losing it either,' Abby warned, 'I'll still be paying for it after Christmas.' The sound of a car horn beeping spurred them on, Becca handed the necklace to Abby to fasten around her neck, then with a flurry of hugs and handbags and a puff of perfume they were gone.

The blast of cool air and cigarette smoke as Becca held the cab door open for Abby in front of the nightclub brought her back to the present. Abby smiled as she answered her friend's question with a white lie. 'Just wondering if the men of Salford know what's gonna hit 'em tonight.' She replied, linking her arm through Becca's as they strolled towards the end of the queue.

'Here! Bex, Abby, over here!

They followed the voices until the unmistakable shape of Dixie and Kristin came into view. Dixie, at six foot three, had always been the tallest girl in high school, Kristin, at four eleven, suffered from a growth hormone deficiency that resulted in her having rods inserted into her legs to stimulate bone growth. With killer heels she was a reasonable height, although forever overshadowed by her towering best friend who wore ballerina pumps to compensate. Waving, and ignoring the filthy looks and tuts from the crowd behind them Abby and Becca slipped into line some ten yards in from the back of the queue.

Later, Abby would look back at their decision to push in with regret. The defining seconds that formed a fork in their future, taking them on a path from which there could never be a return.

The car travelled south across the city, a heady mix of rap music and adrenaline causing the chassis to vibrate in time to the MC's lyrics. Earl wiped the front passenger seat window with his sleeve for the third time, his over-breathing causing it to steam.

'You sure you don't want some o' dis?' Pauly asked, taking the reefer from Kester, his driver, offering it to Earl before taking it himself. Earl shook his head. Despite moving drugs around the city for Pauly, he'd never actually taken any, had seen up close what it did to the losers who bought from Pauly's men at the several trading posts across the estate, not long out of school but hooked on a substance that reduced them to nothing. Yeah, so it hadn't stopped him keeping the supply chain going but drugs would always be around, and while there were buyers there would always be someone like Pauly, ready and willing to cash in on other people's misery.

The stench of the reefer was beginning to make Earl feel light-headed. The atmosphere in the car was cloying, the leather seats giving off their own particular odour. He pressed the button on the passenger door to open the electric window.

'What the fuck-?!' Pauly kicked the back of Earl's seat, swore at Kester, his driver to close the fucking window, disable all the other fucking windows while he was at it.

They'd reached the main street that snaked its way through Salford's city centre, parallel to the new club that had once been a Casino, stripping the residents of hard earned money long before on-line gaming saved them the trouble of leaving their homes to be fleeced. Kester slowed, looked in his rear view mirror at Pauly, a baffled look on his face.

'Drive!' Pauly barked, pissed that Kester couldn't read his fucking thoughts, that he had to spell out everything. No wonder he was the main man, the one they looked up to, the rest of the crew couldn't find their arseholes with two hands and a mirror. Pauly sucked air through his teeth, leaned forward between the two front seats to turn the radio down. 'Round the block one more time, man.' He said to the back of Kester's head, and then, staring at the scalp between Earl's cornrows, instructed: 'I'll let you know when we're ready.'

It was the blast of loud music that caught her attention. The blare of Dizzee Rascal, full on and close up, that made her turn, glance at the car as it slowed down behind them before cutting the sound and moving on, foot down to beat the lights, engine revving, tyres screeching as it shot across the junction before turning left into the one-way system. Abby felt a flash of recognition, so quick she couldn't place it before it flew out of reach, moving deep into the corners of her mind where it evaporated, leaving a notion of unease in its wake.

At the start of the road leading up to the club Kester killed the engine, sat grim-faced, while Earl urinated in a side street. 'S'all we fuckin' want,' he moaned, 'im gettin' pick up for pissin' in public while we sit around in a stolen-' the nozzle of the gun at the base of his skull stilled his tongue. He stared solemnly at Pauly in the rear-view mirror, planning how to back-pedal. 'Look man,' he placated, 'I know he's cool, but he's young, s'all I'm sayin'.' He tried to laugh but it died in his throat.

'How ol' were you when you join' me?' Pauly asked.

'But that was different, man. I had nobody else, I had to look out for myself, I was hungry...' His words tailed off as he recognised the glint in Pauly's eye, felt he was back on comfortable ground. 'You were always hungry,' Pauly soothed, 'always willing to please...'

Pauly sat back in his seat as the car door opened and a sheepish Earl climbed back in. Handing him the weapon, Pauly removed his gloves, his hand dropping to the boy's thigh giving it a playful squeeze, leaving it there longer than was necessary.

'S'all right, pretty bwoy,' he drawled, 'everyone get nervous their first time...'

The moving line had picked up pace, the doormen letting girls and couples enter without a second look, the groups of men held back, pockets patted, bodies frisked, questions asked and accusations made, pressing buttons until they got a reaction, refusing entry providing the only entertainment in the evening's proceedings.

They'd reached the entrance to the club. Dixie, after flirting outrageously with the man on the door had jumped the queue claiming she needed the toilet, dragged Kristin along with her, promising they'd get the drinks in. From where she was standing Abby saw the car that had driven past earlier approach a second time, pausing as it drew level with the club's entrance once more, no music this time as the passenger window lowered. From the corner of her eye she saw an arm, gloved, holding something steady.

Blink.

Her brain went into go-slow as she tried to make sense of what she was seeing, of what it could mean...the arm pointing out of the window…the boy in the passenger seat, the flash of gold around his neck, his face turned towards her, the fear in his eyes.

A gun.

Everyone around her oblivious, laughing, stamping feet to keep warm as they waited in line; the doormen, speaking into their mouthpieces as they jostled with a couple of chancers, unaware of the danger approaching.

Abby swung away from the gunman's aim, pulling Becca with her, but the force of her movement wasn't enough to remove them both from his range. Becca had an arm outstretched, as though she'd seen him too and was warding off the impossible. The shot when it came sent them reeling back, legs buckling beneath them, falling hard. The bullet entered Becca's neck, above the silver necklace Abby had given her for luck.

An arc of blood sprayed into the air turning everything red. There was a moment's hush, then pandemonium as the car sped off and the extent of Becca's injuries became clear. Abby's scream died in her throat. Her mouth tasted of metal. She bent double, swiping a hand over her eyes as she spat out clots of skin and tissue.

Chapter 2

'Once more unto the breach...'
DS Coupland had parked some distance from the nightclub, watching the clear up operation unfold. During the initial seconds following the shooting all hell had broken loose, mass panic, girls screaming, splashes of blood on onlookers' clothing spread fear that there were numerous casualties, several ambulances had been despatched. Those standing further back in the queue ran screaming into the nearest bars along the road, others close to the entrance yelled at the club's doormen to let them inside; those already in, on hearing a rumour of a drive-by shooting scrambled to get out, see the extent of it.

The doormen were doing their best, some had seen action in Helmand Province, knew how to deal with terrified crowds, others, new to the game, wanted to get the fuck away as soon as they could. Squad cars had arrived; officers contained the crowd already inside the club, taking the names and addresses of those standing nearby when the shot was fired. One shot. A single shot and a seriously injured girl. Message from a rival gang? Or a domestic vendetta?

A young PC had been given the task of securing police tape around the immediate vicinity, awaiting the arrival of CID. A couple of police vans circled the perimeter in case of any trouble from tanked up passers-by. Coupland took his time, watching the scene unfold until he felt he'd got the measure of it. Time for one last cigarette.

A man in a smart suit walked over to the constable

securing the police tape, asked him something that had the officer point in Coupland's direction. *They know I'm here then*, he muttered; *better get this show on the road.*

'Thought you'd have got here before me.' DCI Mallender commented as Coupland drew near. A good ten years his junior Mallender was a newly promoted Chief Inspector replacing DCI Curtis after the powers that be had seen fit to elevate the former DCI to the rank of Superintendent. Even now Coupland grimaced at the thought, felt as though he should make the sign of the cross every time Curtis' name was spoken aloud.

Coupland regarded the senior officer with a smile. He'd seen enough of them come and go over the years to know their observations weren't personal, just a way of marking their territory, making it clear they were the boss of you whether you approved of them or not. To Coupland it was white noise; he wasn't an ambitious man, had joined the force at a time when all you needed to do was sign your name. He had no time for the politics and the standing on ceremony, all he wanted was to do his bloody job.

'I did,' He replied, his blue eyes raking through the crowd outside the club. 'but I wanted to check out the rubberneckers first, see if anyone lurking on the sidelines was showing a particular interest in proceedings.'

'Shooter returning to the scene?'

Coupland shrugged, 'Possibly, or sending an errand boy to report back.'

Two young men standing by the club's entrance had the audacity to call out to Coupland, asking if he could get them in. 'I can do better than that, Sonny Jim,' the sergeant replied dead pan, 'I can get you bed and breakfast an' all at no extra charge.' His warrant card explained the joke and the lads moved away sharpish, swearing under their breath.

'What I don't get is why they asked me,' Coupland wondered aloud as he followed the DCI into the nightclub. 'Probably thought you were a bouncer.' Mallender replied, taking in Coupland's heavy frame and his reputation as someone with a very short fuse.

'*Charming.*' Coupland mouthed at the DCI's back.

One of the security staff held open a door for them to pass through and they found themselves entering a hallway covered floor to ceiling in red velvet, a desk at the far end, another doorway to the right of the desk, a flight of narrow stairs to the left. The place reminded Coupland of an elaborate knocking shop.

The doorman made the mistake of trying to pass them without drawing any attention to himself, staring at the floor as he did so. Coupland kept his smile in check, recognising the signs. Broad and squat with dark cropped hair and a swarthy skin, the arms of his black jacket had ridden up his wrists to reveal a heavy gold bracelet on one arm, an imitation Tag Hauer on the other.

'Warby!' Coupland greeted the man warmly, patting him on the arm like a long lost friend. 'Glad to see you're putting your skills to good use, this being a recession an' all.' Then, turning to back the DCI, 'I told him time would fly by, and here he is, not even twelve mo-'

'Sir,' a uniformed sergeant standing in the club's main entrance called out to Mallender, 'Crime Scene Manager wants a word.' Mallender nodded, making his way towards him.

'I'll do the honours upstairs,' Coupland said to the DCI's retreating back, his words drowned out by the drone of voices coming from the main dance floor which was now a makeshift interview room with uniformed officers questioning witnesses, taking statements, establishing where in the line each person had been standing when the shot was fired. The staff had to be interviewed too, even those who were inside at the time and didn't see anything.

It was going to be a long night.

Coupland climbed the carpeted stairway which led to a VIP area containing a cluster of leather sofas that looked like beds and a private bar. The area was empty save for a young bartender leaning against the counter top wiping glasses that hadn't been used yet. Two ashen faced girls perched on bar stools as they clung onto half-drunk glasses of brandy they didn't have the stomach for. Brought up in the age of alcopops they were unused to the sour taste of a real drink.

'Are you Rebecca's friends?' Coupland asked.

The girls nodded.

'One of the policemen said we could wait here,' the taller one informed him, pointing to the officers milling about on the floor below, 'while we wait for a lift home.'

Coupland nodded. 'Did he take your statements?'

'We told him we didn't see anything.' They shrugged in unison. Coupland nodded, making a mental note to read through what they'd said anyway, sometimes the smallest detail had the greatest significance in a case like this.

He called over to the bartender: 'Can you tell me where I can find the head honcho around here?'

'That'll be me.' The voice, coming from behind him was dark and accented – Turkish perhaps. Coupland turned round, held his warrant card out for inspection: 'I'm DS Coupland sir…and you are?'

The man standing before him was tall and olive-skinned, designer stubble with shoulder length black hair like an extra from a Francis Ford Coppola film. A good suit concealed a wiry frame.

'My name is Ashraf Zadawi,' he took a step towards Coupland extending a hand, all genial. Coupland shook it.

'Please, come through to the office.'

Zadawi pushed open the camouflaged door, led the way into a small room containing a desk and a chair, a small sofa and very little else. He slumped into the chair behind the desk as though he'd been on his feet all night, wiped a hand through slicked back hair.

'This is a terrible, terrible business.' He sighed, offering Coupland the chair on the other side of the desk. Coupland refused, preferring to stay on his feet. Reaching for a bottle of Remy XO perched on the corner of his desk, Zadawi held up a glass. Coupland shook his head.

'You don't mind if I do? I expect, in your line of work, you're hardened to this kind of thing.'

Coupland tried not to let his irritation show. 'I never get used to one person taking chunks out of another one for no apparent reason Sir.' He tried to soften his words with a smile but the sting was there.

'You must forgive my poor command of English.' Zadawi offered up in mitigation, 'sometimes it seems I say the wrong thing.'

'Do you think that's what's happened here, then?' Coupland asked.

Zadawi looked bewildered. 'I don't understand.'

Coupland sighed. They were obviously going to have to go the long way round. 'Have you any enemies, Mr Zadawi? Someone you might have crossed recently who thought that shooting at young girls on your opening night would teach you a lesson.'

Zadawi shook his head, taken aback. 'You think that is what this is..?' he paused, before adding: 'I'm sorry to disappoint you, but this is not the way I do business. My associates are not the type to resort to violence if an invoice isn't paid on time.'

'So you owe people money then?'

'Doesn't everyone?' Zadawi countered. 'Times are hard, if you hadn't noticed.'

Coupland stared him out.

'This is a new business venture for me; of course I owe money-'

Coupland glanced around the sparsely furnished

office before turning his attention back to Zadawi, 'Then I want a list of all the people you owe money to.' He demanded. 'Names, addresses, telephone numbers,' Zadawi made a show of looking for a pen but Coupland found a chewed Biro in his jacket pocket which he passed to him. 'Here,' he said amiably, 'We aim to please.'

The new DCI was on his second cigarette by the time Coupland found him standing on the pavement across the road from the club. Overweight and over forty Coupland had tried to give up smoking, had tried to give up most of the things he enjoyed that were bad for him, including the donner with extra chillies that he signalled to the kebab shop owner to prepare for him now. He lit a cigarette while he waited.

'You know boss,' Coupland began, the way he did whenever he felt the need to justify his action, 'seems to me the government's got it all wrong. This healthy eating lark isn't all it's cracked up to be.' Earlier in the year he'd given up packing in smoking on the basis you've got to die of something. 'Lynn's father is ninety and bedridden, was the only one left from the car factory making brake pads during the seventies who hadn't contracted Asbestosis. His reward for living so long? Spending his final years in a convalescent home, unable to leave his bed to take a dump in private.' Coupland shook his head quickly as though ridding himself of the thought. 'If that's living then I chose dying any day.'

Point made he returned to the business in hand. 'The girls didn't have much to tell, by all accounts,' He observed, nodding his head in the direction of the club. 'I spoke to the officer who took their statements but they were already inside when the shot was fired, didn't even click it was their mate until the others didn't show.' He pulled his notebook out of his anorak pocket to check a couple of details. 'Rebecca Louden. Eighteen. No previous form, leaving to go to Bristol in the morning, studying something fancy I don't doubt over at the university.'

Mallender inhaled the nicotine as far as it would go. Held it there. Maybe Coupland had a point.

'Word from the hospital,' Coupland added, 'Rebecca's undergoing emergency surgery to stem the bleeding. Touch and go from what the registrar was saying.' Mallender exhaled slowly, just because he could.

'How's your wife?' he asked awkwardly, 'Never seems the right moment to ask.'

Mallender's question surprised Coupland. The new DCI seemed as preoccupied and uninterested in the lives of his team as his predecessor, yet here he was showing if nothing else that he'd read through Coupland's personnel file, saw his leave of absence several months earlier - and the cause of it.

'She's responding to treatment.' Coupland said evenly, as though no other explanation was necessary. It was the phrase his wife's oncologist used whenever Coupland tried backing him into a corner, daring him to admit the truth of it.

He shook his head. Words were not his strong point, he'd never found the vocabulary to express how Lynn's illness made him feel, the sheer bloody enormity of it. When she'd been diagnosed with breast cancer earlier in the year it had felt as though someone had ripped his heart right out of his chest before stamping all over it.

'She's got more wigs than Joan Collins, now.' He quipped before turning away, clenching and unclenching his fists.

It was amazing how time could be so elastic, one minute stretching out so slowly you could remember every second, another contracting and colliding into the next so that events became a blur, a hazy kaleidoscope of all that had taken place. It was as if the scenes in Abby's mind were on a loop: images of Becca back at the flat, opening the present she'd bought for her and giggling in the taxi flashed by over and over, interspersed with freeze frame stills of her suspended in time, her hand outstretched, the shock at being hit, knowing it was serious but not realising why.

Becca had been taken straight in for surgery on arrival in A&E, Abby ushered to a cubicle with a female PC. A police car had gone to Becca's home, brought her parents to the hospital, blue lights flashing, Angela at this moment holding a vigil in the relatives' room while she waited for Becca to come out of surgery, her husband working his way through a packet of cigarettes just beyond the fire exit. Abby had asked the policewoman not to worry her own mother; she wanted to know the outcome of Becca's operation before she made the call home.

'Would you like me to call anyone love? The WPC had asked, and she'd hesitated just for a second before giving her his number. It was true their relationship had got serious very quickly, that he was no longer a stranger in her home, let alone her bed, but even so she felt self-conscious using the term boyfriend, as though calling him that made her needy somehow, staking a claim on him that she had no right to make, not yet anyway.

Calls made, the WPC returned to Abby's cubicle with a coffee which she accepted, sipping at it cautiously until it cooled. Her mind was in overdrive. 'Was this an accident?' she asked, before correcting herself, 'But then no one gets shot accidentally do they?' She thought for a moment, remembered the case of the schoolboy in Liverpool, of other cases, in London, that punctuated the news from time to time, innocents in the wrong place at the wrong time.

'What I mean is,' she continued, 'no one accidentally shoots someone do they? Whoever did this -' she paused, gulped back a sob with a mouthful of coffee, 'he set out to hurt someone from the outset otherwise he wouldn't have had a gun – but who'd shoot *Becca*, or anyone for that matter? We were just standing outside a nightclub, minding our own sodding business.'

The WPC put a hand on Abby's shoulder. She'd spent a couple of years in Moss Side, had seen the aftermath of gun crime more often than she'd care to acknowledge.

'That's the way of it sometimes, love, I can't deny it. Look, when you've finished that cuppa how about you start from the beginning, see if we can't piece together the evening from beginning to end, right up to, you know-' her tone was soft but they both knew she wouldn't budge until Abbey gave her what she wanted.

Abbey sighed.

Earl leaned against the cold brick wall, his body shaking involuntarily. Shock, he supposed. The spasms when they came made him double over and wretch, the contents of his stomach long since emptied, he spat bile onto the floor of the ginnel. He wiped his mouth with the back of his hand, wincing at the smell of dried vomit on his sleeve. The shirt had cost him a packet. Not that it mattered now. Now that he'd gone and fucking shot someone, nothing fucking mattered.

He'd been about to drop the gun right after pulling the trigger but Kester had managed to grab hold of his arm, yank it back into the car before speeding away while Pauly prised the weapon from his fingers, giving it a wipe before wrapping it back in its cloth. The mad bastards were laughing, like they'd just been taking part in their favourite sport. He hadn't anticipated *that*. The pleasure in Pauly's eyes.

They'd dropped him back at the estate, told him to go straight home. By now the car would be torched and the gun would have been made to disappear, all courtesy of local kids like him, young boys eager to impress Pauly and his crew.

He closed his eyes; wished he could go back in time, back to the point when Aston had asked if he really wanted to work for Pauly, if he understood what he was letting himself in for.

The point where his life jack-knifed into two.

How could he tell Aston the reason he allowed himself to be at Pauly's beck and call? He'd promised to keep his mouth shut, didn't want a reputation for being unreliable. But this? He hadn't anticipated this…

He could still see her face, looking right at him, stunned, like he'd pulled a fucking gun on her. Only yeah, he *had* pulled a fucking gun on her. And fired. He rubbed at his eyes with the heel of his palms and let out a long, slow breath. He always knew that one day he'd get caught up with guns; you can't work the streets without stepping on someone's toes or needing to defend your own corner, but what he hadn't expected was this. A girl. Unarmed. Going about her own fucking business. She wasn't even wearing gang colours; he didn't even know her. Had it really been a test to prove how far he'd go? He knew the others had done stuff, sat some kind of initiation to demonstrate their loyalty but this was way off the scale. Earl sighed, long, like his lungs had a puncture. Pauly promised Aston that after this job there wouldn't be any others, so why bother setting him a test? But then a knot tightened in his stomach as it dawned on him that his brother was right – this was never gonna be the end.

This was just the beginning.

It had all happened so suddenly. Abby replayed the events in her mind trying to put them into some semblance of order. She'd been standing close to Becca, hadn't really paid much attention to what was going on around them. The notion they were in danger came in a miniscule flash. Not quite a premonition but a feeling; a warning; not fear but something like it. Every fibre in her body putting her on alert, telling her to move – and quick

– if she hadn't, it occurred to her that she would be the one on the operating table now – and it would be Becca pacing the floors.

Bittersweet reasoning.

The WPC kept pressing her for details even though she complained her head was hurting. 'Not unusual if you've been close range to a gunshot.' The officer reassured her, as though that made it alright.

'When will you go and check about Becca?'

'Soon,' Was all she'd say.

'What time did you arrive at the club?' The WPC persisted.

'I told you. It takes about twenty minutes by car from home; we'd booked the cab for half past eight, so...about ten to nine.'

'Are you sure you didn't see anything unusual?'

'Apart from my best friend getting her fucking head blown off?' Abby didn't usually swear, living on an estate where swearing was the native language she tried to set a good example in front of the twins, but they weren't here right now and she was losing her patience.

'You're doing really well Abby,' the WPC soothed. *Please, call me Linda.* 'I know it isn't easy.'

Abby dropped her gaze and studied the floor between her feet. *Linda* didn't know the bloody half of it. Failing your A levels on purpose wasn't *easy*. This...this *nightmare*, was in a league of its own. Abby stretched her legs out in front of her and rotated her ankles, as she drew them back blood from the soles of her shoes smeared across the lino.

'And the car,' Linda prompted, 'you're sure there were two passengers in the car?'

A nod.

'And the gunshot came from the front passenger window?'

'*Yes!* Now please, can you find out how Becca's doing?' Abby was cold, tired. Her clothes were matted in blood and other stuff she didn't want to think about. She couldn't believe it but she was hungry too. Weren't people supposed to lose their appetite in times of crisis? She wished she could turn back the clock, made sure they'd jumped into the taxi the moment it arrived, maybe they'd have been further up the queue at the time of the shooting or further back in the line if they hadn't pushed in. They should have argued to be let inside with Kristin and Dixie, but she'd never been blessed with the gift of the gab. If she'd read out the speech that she'd written for Becca, or not given her the necklace until later.

If, if if…

Abby thought of the twins tucked up for the night. She'd arranged for a neighbour to help her mother to bed, she'd be reading in her room, oblivious. She couldn't reach to switch off her bedside lamp anymore, would be waiting for the sound of Abby's key turning in the lock before she came through to say goodnight. Abby glanced at her watch. It wasn't even midnight yet, she had a couple of hours' grace before she needed to phone home. No one was missing her.

Yet.

The WPC got to her feet, moved around the room to stretch her legs. 'Please,' Abby began, 'can you *please* go and find out how Becca's doing?' The policewoman turned and Abby could tell from the set of her shoulders she wasn't finished yet, that she wanted to crack on with her endless bloody questions. Just then the curtain pulled back and a black man wearing G-Star Jeans and a zip up Superdry jacket strode into the cubicle.

'Can you step outside please?' The policewoman began, moving towards him, 'you're not allowed-'

'Yes he is.' Abby butted in, moving quickly to his side. 'You rang him earlier - he's my boyfriend.'

Ignoring the WPC's disapproval at the interruption, Abby threw her arms around him, burying her face in his chest. After a moment she drew back her head to look into his eyes, the first smile she'd mustered in the last couple of hours.

'Christ Almighty,' she said, relieved to have him with her. For the first time in what seemed like hours she felt safe. 'What took you so long, Aston?'

Chapter 3

Even in the early hours of the morning the corridor was busy. An incident room was being set up in a side room next to CID. Two uniforms were manoeuvring a table through the door, Chuckle Brothers' style, negotiating the legs through the narrow space.

Coupland walked into the open plan office, flicked on the light before flopping into his chair. His desk was cluttered with ongoing case files and post-it notes stuck around the top of his PC. He read one of them now: CHECK EMAILS it said. He rubbed his hand over his face, the stubble beneath his fingers sounding like the rustle of sandpaper. He looked at his watch. Gone midnight and a report to prepare so Mallender could brief the Super first thing. He needed caffeine, felt around in the pockets of his jacket but couldn't scrape enough change together for the vending machine in the corridor. Christ, he muttered. It comes to something when I'm narked at not having enough money for a crap coffee. He searched in his desk drawer, found a bottle of flat coke that'd have to do instead.

Their flat was in darkness. Earl's mother, asleep on the sofa. She'd been watching a documentary, a group of teenagers being interviewed by a reporter about the effects of underage drinking and the related increase in crime. She loved these shows, devoured them with an appetite of someone warding off evil. Earl turned off the TV, covered his mother with the crocheted blanket she kept over the back of her chair. If only she fucking knew. He had a sudden urge to wrap his arms around her, to ask her to hold him like she had when he was little, but then she'd know something was wrong. He pulled his mobile out from the back pocket of his jeans. No messages. Pauly'd said he mustn't call him, no texts, nothing. He was to keep away from Pauly's place as well, hang loose for a while, keep his shit together.

Moving through the flat quietly he checked on Arlene, his baby sister, or Surprise from God as his mum referred to her. He tried to imagine how he'd feel if someone put a bullet in *her*, had to shake his head to rid himself of the image.

'What have I done?' he whispered.

He felt drained. He was exhausted, but it was the kind of exhaustion sleep wouldn't fix. He went into the room he shared with Aston, closing the door behind him. He stared at the rug that acted as a demarcation line between two foreign states, his own bed unmade, clothes scattered across the floor like he'd upended a laundry bag just for the fun of it. Aston's bed was neatly made, his clothes folded and put away. Earl used to mock him for being so tidy, for doing everything he could to be Mum's blue eyed boy. It used to make Aston mad, 'It's about respect, bro,' he'd say in reply, 'respect for our mum and respect for myself. It's about time you started thinking like that.'

Earl swallowed hard. Yesterday all he'd had to worry about was picking up a few lousy socks then today he goes and shoots someone. He felt his legs go weak; he lowered himself onto the floor into a sitting position, lay his head on his knees. If someone had told him this was going to happen he would never have believed it. He wasn't stupid, he knew right from wrong. To pick someone out then gun them down for no reason…He clamped his eyes shut trying to block out the girl's face as she locked eyes with him. 'Please don't die…' he whispered into the void.

There was a flurry of activity on the observation

ward as Angela Louden asked to be taken to see Abigail Marlowe. Abby rose to her feet pushing back the curtain round her cubicle and practically fell into Angela's outstretched arms. Aston had gone in search of a vending machine that worked, the policewoman, finally relenting, had gone to look for the nurse she'd spoken to earlier.

'Is there any news?' she choked, before burying her head in the woman's shoulder.

Angela shook her head in reply; squeezing Abby so tightly she felt the air push out of her lungs. 'I just wanted to be sure you're alright.' Angela stepped back a little, continuing to hold Abby at arm's length while studying her, seeing the blood and registering where it came from.

'Did you get a look at him?' Angela asked, once Abby had replayed an edited version of the moments leading up to the shooting. Abby nodded slowly. She wished people would stop asking her, the more they asked the more she felt the details slipping away, like when you try to remember a phone number you use all the time that you don't need to write down as it's etched in your brain and then someone asks you to say it out loud and suddenly it's gone up in smoke. She could still see his face but the features were diminishing, as though he'd already been relegated to *evil bastard*, therefore further description wasn't necessary.

'Do you think he knew you?' Angela asked next, which Abby thought was an odd question but before she could say this they were interrupted by frantic shouts beyond the cubicle.

'*Ang!*' Becca's father was calling out for his wife.

'I'm here, John!' Angela cried, her hand flying to her mouth as though suppressing the scream that was to come.

'Oh, Jesus,' he moaned, taking hold of Angela's hand, leading her back to the relatives' room, barely giving Abby a second glance. His skin was grey, like a cadaver.

Abby swayed in their slipstream, hands covering her ears, already knowing but not yet ready to hear it.

Chapter 4

The incident room was crowded. Some of the uniformed officers coming off shift had decided to stay on. A teenage girl had been murdered on their patch; several officers had youngsters the same age. It was an unspoken fact that until this case was solved no one would be getting much sleep.

'So, Rebecca Louden and Abigail Marlowe take a cab from the Tattersall Estate, arriving at Ego between fifteen and twenty minutes later, which takes us to eight forty-five, nine pm, tops. Abby pays the driver before both girls join the line with two other friends. The queue moves slowly and as they near the front a car slows alongside them and Rebecca falls to the ground.'

Coupland paused as he looked around the officers assembled at the briefing. The faces that stared back at him were alert, each one visualising what they'd do if they caught the bastard away from prying eyes. A young girl gunned down on a night out while celebrating what should have been the start of a new life. The adrenaline in the room was palpable; Coupland knew he had to keep them focussed, make each officer feel he or she was doing something productive, playing a key part in catching a killer.

'Alerted by the sound of gunfire the security manager runs to the front of the building, calls emergency services then administers CPR. Rebecca and Abby are taken to hospital by ambulance, Abby is released several hours later with minor cuts and bruises, Rebecca Louden was pronounced dead at sixteen minutes past three this morning after surgeons failed to repair the damage to her carotid artery.'

Beside him Mallender made hand written notes on the report Coupland had prepared for him the previous evening. Due to the intense media interest that serious crimes generated, Superintendent Curtis liked to be kept in the loop and this case would generate more interest than most. Salford was becoming a hotspot for gun crime in its own right; half of all Britain's firearms offences occurred in just three major forces: Greater Manchester Police, the Met and West Midlands, and the press seemed to thrive on it, dredging up previous incidents and dedicating centre pages to a roll call of the dead, printing row upon row of victims' photos, lined up side by side like some macabre yearbook. Curtis had already made it clear that he alone would handle the press; Mallender was to keep him up to speed with all new developments. No wonder the DCI looked hard done to.

The officers were shifting in their seats, keen to crack on in what was for some, their first incident involving a drive-by.

'Our priority is tracking down the gunman.' Coupland continued, 'I want everyone in the vicinity traced, interviewed, eliminated. A sketch artist will work with Abby Marlowe, the friend who was with Rebecca when she was shot, see what they can come up with. In the meantime I want the CCTV outside the club checked – Alex, can you go through the footage, cross-check with the ID of the clubbers interviewed, any known faces – you know the drill. Robinson, check through the statements taken from the shop owners that were open for trade at the time of the shooting, go talk to them again if you need to, see if anyone noticed someone staking out the place, hanging around for no apparent reason.'

Robinson snorted but said no more, could see by the set of Coupland's jaw now wasn't the time for wise-cracks. Coupland acknowledged the DC's reticence with a nod, knew exactly what was churning through that head of his. 'I know it's asking the impossible,' he acknowledged, 'that the centre of town on a Friday night is always mobbed but we have to start somewhere. I want everyone questioned that was in the vicinity of that club, even if the only reason they paused was to tie their bloody shoelaces.' Robinson squirmed in his seat, unable to resist adding: 'No one ties their laces any more, didn't you know that?'

Abby had no idea what time of day it was. She rubbed at her eyes; they felt gritty as though she'd slept with her mascara on. Her mouth tasted foul too, as though she'd been sick several times in succession. She looked around her room, looking for clues that could explain the growing unease in the pit of her stomach. Then it dawned on her. Slowly, almost cruelly, her brain began to step up a gear, began to playback the events of last night as they unfolded:

Laughing with Becca in the back of the cab. Standing with Dixie and Kristin as they queued to get into the club. The car slowing down; the barrel of a gun pointing straight at her.

The taste of Becca's blood.

Abby lurched out of bed, steadying herself against the bedroom window as a low growl erupted from deep inside her. Outside, the square below was quiet, milkmen didn't stray here, the only movement came from shift workers stepping out, or revellers returning home, going about their day like sod all had changed. 'No!' Abby moaned, over and over, as the realisation that Becca was dead hit her like a fist.

The bedroom door burst open and Aston rushed in. 'It's alright babe,' he soothed, scooping her up in his arms and holding her close, his hand stroking her hair as she sobbed against his shoulder. 'C'mon,' he coaxed, taking her by the hand and leading her into the living room, 'I've made you some toast.' Abby wasn't hungry but she let Aston take control, watched as he plumped up cushions and brought the quilt through from her bed before easing her onto the couch and placing it over her legs.

Abby looked gratefully at Aston. Aware Marion's wheelchair couldn't fit through the door to her room he'd done the next best thing and positioned Abby where Marion could reach her. She'd been losing the power of speech for some time, her words beginning to slur when she was distressed or in pain. The hospital had given her equipment enabling her to type out instructions, preparing things she wanted to say to friends in advance. This morning her thoughts were in turmoil, no one could have prepared for this.

'Abbeee.' Was all she could manage right now, a single tear pooling in the corner of her right eye.

Abby didn't know which was making her feel worse. The effort Aston was putting in to make her feel better or her mother's struggle to offer her any comfort.

Abby was trapped between two timelines, how everything was before she and Becca had set out for the club and after: an oncoming train loaded with confusion and grief. When she closed her eyes she was standing beside Becca, arm outstretched, pulling her to safety; when she opened them, Becca was dead. Shame washed over her like an incoming tide.

'You read about people doing heroic things,' she said aloud, 'running into burning buildings, lifting a car with one hand to reach someone who's trapped, showing that mind really can win out over matter.' Even while the shooting was unfolding there was a part of her brain that was recording every second, congratulating her on keeping a cool head as she reacted to the situation. But still it hadn't worked. Becca was supposed to *live*.

'I thought I could pull her to safety.' Her voice, cracked now, sounded as though it belonged to someone else. 'We should have been laughing over this, pouring over an article in tonight's Evening News: *Friends So Close a Sniper's Bullet Couldn't Part Them.'*

Except it hadn't worked out that way. The one time in Abby's life when her action really *mattered*, she hadn't made the slightest difference at all. She squeezed Marion's hand. Stress could worsen her mother's condition; she needed to keep strong for her sake. 'Shall I make us a cuppa?' she asked, surprising them as she pushed herself to her feet, all the while wishing this was some elaborate 3D nightmare she would eventually wake up from. Marion nodded slowly, trying to convey a range of emotions in that one gesture. Abby took her mother's hand, gave it a reassuring squeeze. Marion was tired, her head lolled slightly to the side as though pondering an exquisite work of art. Her muscles were getting weaker; she'd recently been fitted for a neck brace to hold her head upright although she fought against wearing it.

Aston checked through the messages on his phone. He hadn't been allowed to keep it on at the hospital and by the time he'd brought Abby back to the flat it seemed pointless checking through it then as it would have been too late to call anyone back.

'I've got two missed calls,' he informed her, 'both from Earl. Funny he only speaks to me when he wants something.' He looked at his watch: the last voicemail had been left at two in the morning, over four hours ago. 'Well I guess he conned some other mug into into helping him out,' he muttered, slipping the phone back into his pocket, 'whatever it was'll be ancient history by now.'

Coupland pulled up outside the red brick Victorian semi separated from the busy main road by a bank of trees along a grassy verge. The exterior of the house was freshly painted; windows gleamed in the autumn sun. The lawn, having been mown recently was trim, with just a few fallen leaves of the season making the property look homely rather than picture perfect. Inside, however, was an altogether different scene.

Angela and John Louden sat side by side on an oversized sofa that seemed to swamp their shrunken bodies. They and several family members were gathered in the artificially dark sitting room, it was daylight but the curtains had been drawn, blocking out the sun. 'Press keep driving by,' the female Family Liaison Officer said quietly as she opened the door to Coupland, ushering him through to the large room at the back of the house. 'Couple of them have even come knocking but don't hang around when they see me answer the door.'

He followed her along a wood panelled hallway. Coupland glimpsed a state of the art kitchen, granite worktops laden with gleaming chrome appliances, a downstairs loo that resembled a Zen retreat. Yet already it was changing; the smell of tragedy now hung in the air; burning candles and wilting flowers, the sourness of boozy breath.

Coupland introduced himself to Angela and John, asking them both if they wouldn't mind stepping into the adjoining dining room where he could ask them questions in private. His request seemed to startle them, as though he was the first person to ask them to do anything since their daughter had died. Whatever medication they were on had dulled their motor skills; they moved towards him as though wading through treacle, their faces deep in concentration.

He helped them into chairs around a large oak table, dragged his own round from the other side of it so he was closer to them. 'Can you think of anyone who had a grudge against your daughter?' He began. He thought at first they hadn't heard his question, both seemed to ignore him, staring straight ahead as though in a competition to see who would blink first. Slowly, Angela turned her head in his direction.

'She was perfect.' She answered simply, 'Everyone

loved her.'

'That's right,' John agreed, 'No one who knew her would do this.'

'What about either of you?' Coupland asked, 'has anyone made threats against you, even if it didn't seem important at the time-'

'How could it not seem important?' John challenged, although his face remained impassive.

'He's only doing his job, love,' Angela soothed, placing her hand on her husband's arm, 'he didn't mean anything by it.' Whether he needed to wait for the medication to take effect or to work its way out of their system Coupland couldn't be sure, but he knew he'd not get much more from them.

'Can I look in Rebecca's room?' he asked instead.

Angela pushed herself to her feet, nodding her permission. 'I'll show you up.' she offered, moving into the hallway. 'She didn't even have a boyfriend,' Angela muttered regretfully, as though this milestone was socially significant. 'She's never known what it's like to be loved by someone other than her family.'

Coupland clenched his jaw as he thought of his own daughter Amy, who never seemed short of finding boys to practice on. He followed Angela up a carpeted stairway to a narrow landing where she hesitated in front of one door.

'You don't need to come in, Angela,' he said gently, 'All I need to know at this stage is if there is anything unusual about Rebecca's room.' *Apart from the fact she's no longer in it,* he left unsaid.

As he held the door open they were met by a cacophony of smells – hairspray and perfume, nail varnish and body mist. The room looked as though it had been left in a hurry. Shoes tried on then discarded lay at angles to each other in front of a built-in wardrobe. An array of skirts and tops lay draped across the bed, circles on the dusty dresser indicated an assortment of bottles and tubes had been removed. 'She'd taken her make-up to Abby's,' Angela informed him, 'they were getting ready together.' The computer on Rebecca's desk was turned on; Coupland pressed a button on the key pad to reveal a Harry Styles screensaver had been saved onto the desktop.

Apart from her taste in boy bands there was nothing here to ring alarm bells, nothing to be gained by going through her possessions with a fine tooth-comb.

He'd seen enough.

Chapter 5

Memory can be a funny thing. It plays tricks on you so that a story you've been told so often from being small becomes real – Abby didn't really remember playing an elf in her infant school play but the tale of how she burst into tears and ran off stage because she didn't like wearing green had been retold so often at family gatherings it became part of her own consciousness, her own story to tell. In the same way memory can be re-written: by constantly wishing that something is so, it's possible to believe that it *is*.

Over the past 24 hours she'd been asked to describe the events leading up to the shooting in so much detail it seemed as though Becca was still alive, but then the questions that followed were about the shooting itself which catapulted her back to reality. She'd described the car and its occupants so many times she felt on trial herself, as though the officers who traipsed through her flat with their sketchbooks and notepads didn't really believe her.

'The better the description, the more chance we have of making a positive ID,' the detective who'd pitched up earlier explained, 'it's more than likely the gunman or his accomplices will have a previous conviction – first offenders tend not to start off with firearms, chances are they'll have a record for something else – and if there is some form of history we can go on, we can begin the process of tracking them down.'

She'd nothing to go on to make a comparison but the detective seemed decent enough, though he too seemed hell bent on making her re-live the whole incident again. He took copious notes even though the WPC with him tapped everything down into her electronic notepad. They were sitting in the cramped kitchen, Aston had popped out to pick up some food they didn't need. He couldn't escape quickly enough, nodding curtly as he'd shown the detective in, not pausing long enough for Abby to ask him to stay. He'd told her he'd been in prison the first time they'd gone out together so she could understand him being jittery around cops.

Her mother was in her room having a nap. The twins, quiet as church mice, were watching a Disney video Aston had brought round from his flat earlier on.

Abby hadn't been out since Aston had brought her home, hadn't had a proper night's sleep since she'd been back. Lots of catnaps punctuated by well-wishers calling round, neighbours, concerned friends, she was beginning to feel disorientated.

This cop was different from the others who'd been round; he seemed less officious, less intent on ticking a box then moving on. Despite appearing at the door an hour earlier, he'd made no move to leave even though she'd answered everything he'd asked her.

She pushed back from the table and pointed to their empty cups, 'Can I get you both another?'

The WPC shook her head but Coupland pushed his empty mug across the table towards her.

'Go on then, you've twisted my arm.' He said, making Abby smile.

'My Dad used to say that.' She told him, before her eyes filled with tears once more. Coupland slipped a hand into the inside pocket of his jacket, pulled out a cleanish tissue which he handed to her. 'I live in a house full o' women,' he said good-naturedly, 'I spend most o' my time telling one or the other to cheer up.' When he smiled the corners of his eyes crinkled up and she thought he'd be the kind of Dad you could run rings round, if you had a mind to. She wondered unkindly if the women he lived with ever tried to smarten him up, he didn't dress like the detectives she saw on TV, his clothes were like her own, catalogue bought and cheap looking. He glanced up at her sharply as though he could tell what she was thinking.

Abby refilled the kettle, moving around the kitchen while she waited for it to boil, adding fresh teabags to the pot she'd made earlier, topping up the detective's mug, tipping away her untouched drink before replacing it with another she'd probably leave.

Coupland had taken the opportunity while Abby's attention was elsewhere to look around the kitchen, scanning the cereal boxes lined up on the work-top, the crockery on the draining board, two mugs decorated with the boys' hand prints. The shoes Abby had been wearing on Friday night had been thrown beside the kitchen bin. They were special occasion shoes, high heeled; the price tag was still visible on the sole, as were the flecks of blood and God know what else caked around the sides. He asked the WPC to put them into an evidence bag.

There were parts of his job that he hated the most, and this was one of them. Picking over old wounds like an obsessive lover, unable to let even the slightest detail go. He had more than enough information regarding Friday's shooting, what he needed now was an insight into Abby's friendship with Rebecca. If he chipped away long enough, he wondered what cracks would show.

'I can see how upset you are,' he began, 'but you must understand I have to ask this…do you know if Rebecca was in any kind of trouble?' he let the question hang in the air for Abby to think about.

'What do you mean?'

'Had she been acting out of character lately, seeing new friends?'

Abby laughed. 'She was my best friend, we tended to hang out exclusively, y'know?' she explained, 'Which was why it was such a big deal that I wasn't going to Bristol with her.'

The detective darted a glance at the kitchen's tired décor and Abby found herself seeing her home through his eyes. Shabby, there was nothing chic about it. The teak furniture wasn't so much distressed as bloody knackered, but it was her *home* and she'd thank him not to look down his snotty nose at it. She felt a spark of anger.

'Can't work out why a girl from an estate like this doesn't jump at the chance to escape?' She spat defensively. Startled, Coupland shook his head, raising his hands palm outwards as though shielding himself from her outburst. 'Not at all,' he began but she stared him out. 'OK,' he said, self-consciously, his cheeks flushing, 'Maybe a little…I grew up on an estate like this, I just remember being so glad to get away…'

'Depends what you're leaving behind.'

She had him there. Coupland thought of his bullying father, how he couldn't wait to put some distance between them.

He picked up his coffee mug, blowing across it while Abby pondered her own question. 'When Dad died we were devastated, Mum'd just had the twins, wasn't able to return to work until they started nursery. She found herself a part time job cleaning the big houses in Worsley, money was tight but we managed, but then she started getting pins and needles down her arms and legs, found it harder and harder to swallow. By the time we had a diagnosis she'd already been laid off and I'd started doing more around the house for her. Becca's mum stepped in – got me a holiday job at her place – they've been good like that – work as and when I need it so I can be around for mum and the boys. Can you see now why moving away was never really an option for me, more a dream that you know is never going to happen?'

'I'm sorry.' Coupland said simply.

'Becca wasn't a wild child,' Abby persisted,

'otherwise she wouldn't have been hanging out with someone like me. She was a book worm, would've trounced uni...' And then the tears came, quietly, controlled, so as not to worry anyone in the neighbouring rooms. Coupland glanced at the WPC beside him, signalled it was time to go.

'I'll be in touch.' Was all he said.

Chapter 6

The third time the foot met with her ribs DS Alex Moreton changed position, placing her hand over her side as though trying to lessen the impact, readying herself for the next blow. Struggling to keep her face in neutral, she tried to follow the argument going on around her, the raised voices as each opponent tried to make his point. Animated, the two men squared up to each other, both convinced that he alone was right, that the other was talking utter bollocks.

Coupland was perched on the end of Alex's desk where he'd lit the touch paper half an hour before and watched it go up. Turning sharply as she groaned he eyed her with sympathy. 'Little fella playing you up again?' he asked.

Alex pulled a face. 'Something like that.' She responded, shifting her weight from one buttock to the other, rubbing her swollen belly absentmindedly.

'Come on Sarge,' Robinson called out, 'you've got to have an opinion – breast or bottle – which is best?'

'All I said,' Coupland repeated when Alex shot him yet another dirty look, 'was breast feeding is fine in the early days, but if a dad wants any chance of bonding with the baby then he needs to be involved at feeding time too.'

'Christ, Coupland,' Alex interjected, 'you make it sound as though having a family's like living in a zoo.' She paused for a moment as a thought occurred to her, before catching his eye and smiling. Both already had one child each, had experience of daily family bunfights. 'Point taken.' She conceded.

'It's better for the mother too,' a passing DC interjected, not long back from paternity leave. 'Helps her lose weight.'

'Fat good that does if she won't let you near her,' another added with such feeling many of the men looked away, too close to home to dissect further.

'Come on, Sarge,' Robinson persisted, 'you're the only one qualified to answer this properly, what are you gonna do?' Alex shook her head in exasperation as every eye in the room fell upon her, waiting for female words of wisdom. She'd never quite known a bunch of men like them, wondered if they were like this at home. She remembered feeding Ben herself, the pride and pain in equal measure; the breast pump she never quite got the hang of whenever she needed to leave him. Cabbage leaves stuffed in her bra.

She shuddered, aspects of motherhood she'd relegated to the past suddenly began to loom ahead of her now she was halfway through her final trimester, two weeks of desk driving to go before her maternity leave kicked in. Whatever plans or fears she had about child rearing, she certainly wasn't going to share it with these jokers.

'I take it you've got time on your hands then, Robinson?' she asked, creating a diversion, 'Only there's been a report passed through from traffic of a car being stolen a couple of hours before Friday's drive-by, it matches the witness description of the car at the scene of the shooting – I'll let you do the honours.'

She handed him a slip of paper detailing the owner's address, shooed him out of the room. She looked around at the rest of the congregation:

'Anyone else not got enough to do?' The team were already moving away; returning to desks piled high with files, grabbing jackets and car keys, slipping out of the CID room as quietly as they could in case they were allocated more tasks.

Coupland clocked her squirming in her seat and chuckled. 'Piles as well?' he

asked, ducking at the hole punch that flew his way in response. 'Seriously though,' he said as though the thought had just occurred to him, 'it's gonna be quiet round here without you.'

Alex pulled a face: 'Only because you'll have no one to take the piss out of.'

'That's not true.' He replied, looking hurt.

She thought about it for all of five seconds. 'No you're right. You take the piss out of everyone; I'm just the mug who drags you out of shit street if you cause offence.'

'I rest my case.' Coupland beamed as he performed a mock bow. 'Anyway, how did you get on with the CCTV?'

Alex pulled a face. 'Nothing out of the ordinary. A couple of dealers doling out their tricks, mainly local kids, all known to us. I sent uniform round to question them but funnily enough no one saw a thing.'

'That it?'

'Cameras are pointed down the side street and back alley, nothing front of

house – the security guys are there for that.'

'Talking of which, bumped into an old lag by the name of Warby when I attended the scene at Ego on Friday, Ian Warburton's his proper name, I'd put him away eighteen months before.'

'Did he know the owner previously?'

Coupland shook his head. 'Saw the job advertised in the paper.'

'He didn't pick up on anything though, hadn't been brought in because Zadawi needed extra muscle for anything else?'

Coupland shook his head. 'Front of house duties only. *Look hard, don't leave a mark on 'em*, that's all he'd been told.'

'And there'd been no prior altercation?'

'Nada. The club was brand spanking new.'

'Is it really a turf war?'

A shrug. 'S'all we have at the moment…'

'What do we know about Zadawi's other business interests? What about the rest of his family?'

'He's not appeared on our radar before, but I reckon it's family money he's using to fund the place. I'm going back over there to speak to one of the shop owners who reckons he got a glimpse of the car used by the shooter. I know him, as it happens, seems a good enough sort.' Coupland's voice brightened at the prospect of a between-meal snack, a mixed shish on pitta, hold the salad, extra chillies on the side. He could feel himself salivating. 'I can do a bit of digging,' he added, 'see who really pulls the strings.'

Alex nodded.

'Amy didn't fancy it then,' she asked, 'What with it being the opening night and everything?'

Coupland grimaced, the way he did with increasing regularity whenever he thought of his daughter. 'She's not old enough,' he replied, 'not that that would stop her. As it happens she'd been grounded for coming back from a party pissed.'

He suppressed a shudder as he recalled how he'd felt when news of the shooting came through. He'd been at home, not been due on shift for another eight hours but with Alex confined to desk duties control had called him instead. He recalled how he'd run to Amy's room to check she was there, that she hadn't sneaked out anyway like she'd done several times before. She'd been lying across her bed, fingers tapping across the screen of her smartphone like they'd taken on a life of their own. An incoming beep and the grin that met it told Coupland some boy was on the warpath, accessing his daughter by invisible means. Lighting up her face in a way he hadn't managed since she was five years old. How the hell could he compete with that?

Amy's smile had faded when she saw him in the doorway, her face adopting a look that signified she'd heard it all before, didn't need a repeat of it just because he was bored. 'I've just taken a call,' he'd said, his voice all over the place as his throat constricted at the sight of her.

Beautiful. Feisty. Safe.

'And why would I care about that?' she'd replied belligerently, as though her interest in his job would be preposterous. He'd been about to tell her about the shooting, when a shadow in her eye told him she already knew, that the jungle drums of social media had brought the details to her quicker than any news team ever could. She was shocked, he could tell, and maybe a little bit scared that she could have been caught up in it if her old man hadn't kicked off the previous night. She knew what had happened all right, didn't need her bloody nose rubbing in it.A thousand words passed unspoken between them. 'Goodnight, Love.' Were the only ones he'd said aloud.

'Night Pappy,' She'd said to his retreating back, and he'd grinned like a cat as he'd let himself out of the house.

'Must be hard,' Alex sympathised, 'finding sanctions that work when they're virtually an adult.'

Coupland rolled his eyes, 'she's been virtually an adult since she was seven years old.' He shook his head as though trying to rid himself of some barbaric thought. 'And who said anything about it working?'

Mallender walked by the entrance to the CID room, on his way to Curtis by the scowl on his face. He carried a file clamped under his arm; striding down the corridor he was oblivious to the two detectives studying him.

'So, come on then,' Alex looked at Coupland impatiently, 'what gives?'

Coupland shrugged. 'What do you mean?'

'Don't give me that!' Alex folded her arms over the top of her stomach. 'We get a new boss drafted in and you're the only one that's been on a shout with him, so…'

Coupland stared at her non-plussed.

'Come on Kevin! Stop being so bloody coy, I can see you're dying to spill the beans.'

'There are no beans to spill.' Coupland said honestly. 'He doesn't say much, then when he does he asks stuff you don't expect, like he's done his homework on your personnel file.'

'There's nothing wrong with that.'

'Didn't say there was.'

'And?'

Coupland shrugged.

'I give up on you sometimes, I really do.' Alex rolled her eyes in frustration, 'Does he have a wife? Kids? Mad aunt in the attic? C'mon, for a guy who spent an hour this morning arguing the toss about the pros and cons of breast feeding-'

'-Yeah but that's 'cos I know you.' Coupland protested.

'-you can be really backwards in coming forward!' Alex continued, ignoring him.

'S'always better to let these guys do the talking in their own sweet time.' Coupland said wisely.

'So you're saying you didn't find out anything about the new boss because you were being polite?'

Coupland squirmed. 'Something like that.' Alex glanced at him sharply but she could see his straight face was starting to crack. 'You know, you women are all the same,' Coupland summed up, 'when he came here last month all I got from Lynn that evening was "How's your new guv? What's he like?" I mean, how the hell would I know? The few times I've gone out with him we've been too busy surveying a crime scene to find out his inside leg measurements.' Alex winced. 'Rub it in, why don't you.' She hated being confined to desk duties, felt the other officers respected her less now she wasn't working at the coal face.

'Well, you know what I mean.'

He was right about that. She knew what it was like to be so immersed in a case that it was hard to return to the day to day minutiae that made up people's lives. But still. 'C'mon Kevin, you and I talk loads in the car, you must have learned something about him.'

Coupland thought about it. 'I know he smokes Marlboro Lights,' he said flippantly.

'And that's it?'

'S'all he's admitting to at the moment.' Coupland replied.

Chapter 7

The polystyrene tray contained slices of donner, some shish, cubes of chicken marinated in spices and chilli oil, 'The Works,' as Coupland referred to it, 'but hold the bloody salad.' Satisfied with the meat feast before him he stabbed each piece with his plastic fork like a pathologist performing an autopsy. 'Go on,' he urged, nodding his head in encouragement at Osman Afram, the kebab shop's owner, as he relived the night of the shooting.

'We don't get busy till people have had a few scoops.' He began, watching as Coupland bit into a spicy bell pepper. 'When it's quiet I stand by the entrance to the shop,' Osman explained, 'to have a smoke.' As if the mere mention of it was cue to light up he wiped his hands down the front of his apron, picked up a packet of cigarettes by the till. He walked around to the front of the shop, stood inside the doorway out of the wind that carried a chill with it. He inclined his head in the direction of the nightclub across the road.

'There were queues around the block.' He said, extending his arms to emphasise the width as well as the length. 'Young girls, dressed up to the nines,' he glanced quickly at the beaded curtain at the back of the shop that separated him from his living quarters and a wife Coupland was certain shaved more than he did.

'Does no harm to look.' Osman shrugged, like it was an involuntary act. Coupland wasn't so sure. He'd fucked up once, had an after work fumble with a civilian from the station and before he knew it his life had gone into freefall. He blinked several times. Even the memory of it shamed him.

'So you saw the car pull up?' Coupland prompted.

'Well no,' Osman shook his head, 'I mean, I saw it all right, but I didn't really pay any attention till I heard the shot, you know?' With all those fake-bake legs on display Coupland understood him very well. 'Then I realised it had come from a car which had just slowed down. I was leaning just here,' he indicated the doorway he was slouched against now, 'watching the queue get longer. I'd shouted through to Fatima to give me a hand, looked like we'd be mobbed later. Anyway, there was a sound, like a car backfiring - I already told your colleague this – and then the car drove off noisily, like the driver was crunching through the gears too fast. There were raised voices, shouting. Someone was screaming. I ran across the road; saw the girl on the ground, her friend leaning over her trying to stem the flow of blood. It was then that I realised I had seen the gunman's car.'

Coupland wiped his mouth with the heel of his palm, aimed the empty container at the bin behind the counter. He joined the Turk out front for a post meal cigarette.

'You heard raised voices?' he prompted, cupping his hands around the end of his cigarette while he lit it.

'Yeah,' Osman nodded, animated now. 'From inside the car…shouts, whoops, like they'd done a *good* thing.'

'They?'

'There were three of them. Black. They had scarves around their necks pulled up to cover the bottom of their faces.'

'Recognise any of them?' Coupland asked. He could live in hope.

Osman threw his arms in the air like he'd already given up on that one. 'Sergeant, I see a gun, I see scarves around faces, you think I'm going to keep on looking?' Osman shook his own head in reply to his question. 'Not bloody likely,' he muttered into his chest. 'I like cars,' he added, 'most men notice the cars that they like – in the same way they admire pretty girls,' another glance towards the back of the shop.

'The car, I can tell you about in great detail. It had my attention when it drove past the first time.'

'The first time?' He had Coupland's attention now.

'Yeah, it was a flashy blue Subaru, artwork down the side, a boy racer's car but good to look at, you know what I mean?'

Coupland nodded.

'Anyway, I see the car, think: "Nice looking motor." Then quick as a flash it is gone.' He paused, absentmindedly scratching his chin. 'Actually no,' he corrected himself, 'I noticed the car as it passed me here,' he explained, 'but then it slowed down, in fact the more I think about it, it slowed alongside the pavement by the club.' He looked at Coupland as it dawned on him, 'Maybe they were looking for their victim?'

Coupland took out his notebook to record Osman's description.

'We'll need you to make a statement.' He said, hoping his eagerness didn't frighten Osman off. The shop owner stalled, as he saw the prospect of living a quiet life slip through his fingers. 'I'm not sure I want to get involved, Sergeant,' he reasoned, avoiding Coupland's eye.

'You know what it's like, these guys hear there's a witness, they'll remember me, the guy from the kebab shop eyeballing their car when they drove past...'

'She's dead.' Coupland said quietly, hating himself but knowing it needed saying all the same. Sometimes it made all the difference.

'Then I don't have any bloody choice do I?' Osman sighed.

Mallender's mother was sleeping in the chair by the fire. Beside it an Adam style fire surround displayed a series of photos: his sister's first steps, her first day at school, sports day. Above the fireplace, an oil painting took centre stage, copied from the last photograph taken of Joanne before her abduction.

No pictures of Mallender were in sight. These, he knew, were displayed in his father's study, his old man's well-intentioned attempt at minimising the snub.

Mallender knelt beside his mother, using the muslin cloth draped over her shoulder he dabbed at the saliva that had pooled on her bottom lip. It had been seven months since the stroke, seven long months since she'd had the capacity to reduce him to nothing simply by staring straight past him. She could do it now without trying.

'Coffee?' His father hovered in the doorway before returning to the kitchen to make a fresh pot anyway.

Mallender brushed a strand of blonde hair from her forehead. At 58 Dorothy Gibson's hair was still strong and thick, his father paid a local girl who worked in a smart salon in town to come and style it twice a week. Her face was pale, make-up free; the left side of it now sagged making her look permanently sad if you only saw her from one angle. The sound of clinking coffee mugs as John returned to the sitting room began to rouse her. Her one good eye focused on Mallender and for a moment he saw a spark of recognition.

'The doctors are pleased with her progress, Son,' John held out a mug of steaming coffee, 'They always said it would be a long road to recovery.' His voice trailed away and Mallender wondered if the doctors were referring to his mother's medical condition or the state of her broken heart.

'You working on the shooting?' His father asked, as though he'd been building to it. Reluctant to tear his eyes from his mother Mallender nodded. John made a sound like a tyre losing air, a big tyre. 'Time was when a community wouldn't stand for that.' He hissed. 'Didn't need coppers to root out any trouble, would've dealt with it ourselves.' *Great,* Mallender grimaced, *Just what I need right now, a trip down memory lane.*

But then, as ever, the temptation was too much. 'So what do you suggest then?' he challenged, angry with himself for rising to the bait once more, 'Leave it to the local vigilante groups to go off into the night pulling in every stranger whose face doesn't fit?'

'Maybe,' John replied agreeably, 'at least it would be sending out the right message, *Don't mess on our manor.*'

Mallender felt his teeth set on edge as images from his childhood flooded his vision. His father holding court, Don Corleone style, granting favours and calling in debts, a nod here, a glare there, plenty of ambitious young men to do his bidding.

Apart from his son, of course.

On his mother's insistence he'd been sent to a boarding school some ten miles away, close enough to come home at weekends, far enough away not to be involved in his father's firm.

'*Manor?*' Mallender repeated hotly, 'You think we haven't already ruled out whether it's a-' he lowered his voice so as not to startle his mother, 'bloody turf war. We're not sodding amateurs.'

'No,' John answered slowly, 'but you do have to work within the law.'

Mallender snorted. 'I'm a policeman Dad,' he said tightly, 'it goes with the job.'

His father smiled in a way that implied he'd heard it all before. 'Come back and say that in 10 years.' he retorted.

'Look, I know you mean well,' Mallender glanced at his mother, checking for some sign - disapproval even - that she could hear what they were talking about, swallowing back disappointment when her eyes remained vacant. 'But times have changed. There's no honour amongst thieves like there was in your day, no brotherhood to bail you out. It's every man for himself; there are no rules of conduct anymore.'

'Went to the dogs when the drugs took over.' John conceded. 'Too many wise-boys jockeying for position. That's the problem you see, drugs bring an instant wealth that make ordinary toe rags get ideas above their station. They take over territories but don't give a shit about the communities who live there.'

Like most things his father said, there was a logic that Mallender found alarming. He was glad the part he played was rounding the buggers up; he didn't envy the jurors' job of having to make sense of it.

It was obvious he'd trodden on a nerve; his father wasn't for letting it go.

'You think I don't know what's going on in my town?' John challenged, his voice raised several octaves louder than before. 'You think when I retired I lost touch with the men who'd worked for me since boyhood?'

Mallender shrugged.

'You think I don't still have my ear to the ground?'

A vein protruded in his father's neck whenever he was angry. Mallender sighed; he didn't want to consign him to the other side of the fireplace dribbling into his designer shirts. He raised his hands in mock surrender.

John Gibson had built up a business empire based on protection rackets and extortion, had progressed into nightclubs and gambling when Mallender was a child. After his daughter's murder, and his stretch inside for killing the man blamed for her death, he decided to go legitimate, moving into property development, where he could put his connections to local councillors and MPs to good use.

'You've never really forgiven me have you?' Mallender challenged. 'Are you ever going to let it lie?' He pointed to his mother, 'Will she?'

He watched as Gibson backed away, defensive. 'Did I want my only boy to become a copper?' He shook his head as he spoke. 'You know how I felt about that.' He shrugged, 'but its behind us now, what's done is done.'

'She still thinks I'm a failure,' Mallender knew he sounded petulant, but that mirrored how he felt right now, 'That I don't pull my weight as a son, but you know why I have to keep my distance. Some journalist gets wind that a local DCI pays more visits than necessary to the home of the former head of Salford's largest crime syndicate and they're going to start digging around.'

It was one of the reasons he'd changed his surname, reverting to his mother's maiden name so that he'd pass the selection process to get in the force. That, and the fact it made him feel as though he shared something other than a tragedy with her.

'She doesn't think you're a failure, son.' His father moved until he was positioned behind Dorothy's chair. He looked down sadly at the woman who had stood by him for nearly 40 years.

She had been Dorothy Mallender when his father had swept her off her feet in a fairy-tale-style romance, living in blissful ignorance of her husband's many business interests until their daughter was murdered by a disgruntled associate.

Mallender's twin sister Joanne. 12 years old when she was taken from them, his last memory of her was Joanne placing a finger to her lips as she was bundled away, warning him not to make a sound.

Or he'll come for you too.

It was as though she'd known it was the last thing she could do for him, that it was in her power to save her brother, an act his mother had never forgiven him for. '*You should have run after her Stuart!*' she used to scream at him when she'd reached her lowest point, rejecting the notion that if he had she could have lost both of her children that day. As though in some way his actions would then have been honourable, rather than the reality of what he had done, waiting until her kidnapper was out of sight before raising the alarm.

Mallender offered up an olive branch: 'I know you still have connections Dad,' he said simply, 'I just don't want to know who they are.'

His mother continued to stare at him so he smiled back encouragingly, reaching for her good hand, holding it between both of his own.

He wondered if there was a way back for him, whether she'd ever be happy *enough* with the child she'd got left. To give a damn, or not give a damn, that was the question. He just had to work out the answer.

'It's me, Mum,' he said softly, willing her to react in some way, even her customary look of disappointment that it wasn't his sister would be *something* at least.

She didn't respond.

Coupland sat in his car in a lay-by off the East Lancs Road, the front seat covered in police reports and witness statements, trying to find a link between Rebecca Louden and her killer. The temperature outside had dropped; he kept the car engine running because right now he cared more for his circulation than his carbon footprint.

After leaving the kebab shop he'd spent the rest of the afternoon canvassing the perimeter of Ego, the scene of Rebecca's shooting. He slowed at the entrance, nodded at the officer still standing inside the taped off area, then drove away in the direction of the main road out of town. He called into a couple of pubs and wine bars along the way, showing photos he'd downloaded of a vehicle similar to the one Osman had described he'd seen during the shooting, asking the regulars if they'd seen anything suspicious on the night in question. No one saw the car with its gun-wielding passenger. In the end Coupland had questioned two dozen drinkers all suffering from boredom, amnesia, indifference.

If it didn't impact them directly, most people didn't give a toss.

He decided to call it a night, but not before driving through the Tattersall Estate, passing the block of flats where Abby Marlowe lived with her mother and brothers. Pausing long enough to locate the second floor window, a light on behind it indicating someone was in the kitchen clearing away the dishes after eating a meal, life returning to some sort of normality, at least for a while.

Chapter 8

After a fitful sleep Coupland had risen early and was in the station before the dayshift had started. Mallender found him sniffing a carton of milk. 'Thing's bloody run out o' creamer again.' He grumbled, 'What's the point of having a vending machine if you've still got to add basic ingredients? All it's bloody done is add hot water, no different than a bloody kettle, albeit a bloody giant one you have to walk down the corridor for...'

Mallender was getting used to Coupland's tirades. He may not recognise the social niceties like *good morning* but he was as straight as a die and always spoke his mind. It must be tough though; he couldn't imagine how he was coping with a sick wife and a teenage daughter. It was no surprise that sleep evaded him too.

'How did you get on with the guy in the kebab shop?' he asked, returning to business, 'reckon he got a good look?'

'Tiny bit o' headway,' Coupland offered, 'He corroborates Abby Marlowe's statement that the car drove around the block twice. He was having a smoke when the car came round the first time, fancies himself as a bit of a petrol head so was able to provide a detailed description which matches the vehicle ID Abby gave us, same colour, same shape – reckoned it was a pimped up Subaru. Also agreed on the number of passengers.'

'Have we checked-?'

'-Car belongs to a James Doughty, Ellenbrook, reported it missing early Friday evening.' Alex interrupted, calling over from her desk by the window. 'Taken from a parking bay at the back of where he works – didn't notice it missing till he left to go home.'

'Time?'

'Sixish.'

'No security? CCTV?'

'Never been any need – until now.'

Mallender nodded.

'And what does he do then, this James Doughty?'

'I'll be sending Robinson over to find out, Sir.' Alex informed him. 'Will let you know as soon as.'

Mallender looked at his watch. 'So what's your excuse for coming in early?'

'Couldn't sleep, Sir,' Alex frowned, placing her hand protectively across the top of her stomach, 'little bugger kept me up all night.'

'I think I need to have a word with Carl,' Coupland quipped, 'doesn't he realise that's how you got in that condition in the first place?'

'Ha, bloody ha,' Alex replied good-naturedly, 'I won't miss your witty repartee when I'm knee deep in nappies.' Yet even as she said it, she knew it wasn't true. Coupland could be a right old pain in the backside but he was *her* pain in the backside and she had to confess to feeling slightly green-eyed that for the foreseeable future he'd be winding someone else up.

Mallender was mentally preparing for the next update with Curtis: 'Has someone been over to Tattersall, surveyed the landscape?'

A sprawling overspill estate separating Salford from Manchester's city centre, Tattersall was a magnet for burnt out cars. In the same way that other cities commissioned iconic statues to decorate their streets, the vandalised vehicles abandoned along the length and breadth of Tattersall represented the lawless – a sight so familiar that locals could be relied upon not to bother calling the police – the residents had more pressing worries than a stripped-out motor blighting their view of the tower blocks opposite.

'Turnbull's doing a tour of duty just now,' Coupland informed him, 'will send up a flare if he finds anything.'

Mallender nodded. 'This nightclub owner, is he the front man for someone else?'

Coupland shook his head. 'Doesn't seem to be. Just a spoiled little rich kid by all accounts. I asked around - his father runs a string of fast food restaurants and cafés in Manchester. Clean track record, been the odd brush with environmental health but nothing major, Ashraf is the eldest of four sons, turned his nose up at joining the family business, Dad indulged him by paying for the lease on the club, financing the building work.'

'Sibling rivalry?'

Coupland smiled: 'I'm on it.'

'Does no harm to keep the pressure up, let him know he's still on our radar.'

Instead of returning to his office Mallender moved further into the CID room until he stood beside Alex's desk. He found it impossible these days to look at her without staring at her bump, found himself resisting the urge to place his hand on her stomach, feel the life growing inside her. He caught her eye and smiled.

'Is everything alright, sir?' she asked him, alarmed.

'I should be asking you that.' He said cautiously, he hadn't yet got the measure of her.

'I'm fine,' she beamed, 'the little so and so has been going hell for leather recently, par for the course at this stage.'

'Can't help you with that,' Mallender said warmly, 'but let me know if you need anything…?'

'As long as it's not hot water and towels,' Coupland chimed in, 'you know what the higher ranks are like about getting their hands dirty.' He left before Mallender could retaliate by assigning him a shitty job.

An awkward silence enveloped the room for a couple of minutes. Alex, conscious of her swollen ankles and lank hair no longer felt as confident around men as she used to, and this new boss was harder to fathom than most. She felt as though there was a barrier between them, increasing in line with her expanding stomach.

'I miss being out there,' she said, indicating in the direction of the two large windows overlooking the station car park, further still the East Lancs Road and beyond. 'all the statements in the world don't replace the things you learn just by staring into the whites of someone's eyes; it's hard trusting others to have that same sixth sense.'

'Welcome to the world of delegation.' Mallender acknowledged, then,

'Actually, there is something you can do for me, something that'll break the monotony of cross matching data entries all day.'

'Go on.'

'Coupland went to see Abby Marlowe – the witness to Friday's shooting. She's going out with an Aston Baptiste, new relationship by the sound of it. Find out what you can about him, Coupland said he was pretty keen to make himself scarce when he turned up.'

Alex raised her eyebrows in mock surprise. 'Isn't that par for the course? On a popularity poll we're right down there with paedophile DJs and HMRC, can't blame the guy for giving us a body swerve.'

'No,' Mallender conceded, 'but we can find out why – or rather you can.'

'Leave it with me,' Alex acknowledged. 'Will be good to leave this desk for a while.'

'Just ask around Alex,' Mallender cautioned, 'no getting backs up, I don't want the union saying I put you at risk.'

'I hear you.' She replied, but she was already reaching for her car keys and coat.

The drive to the Tattersall estate took less than ten minutes. Alex could close her eyes and get there on auto pilot, such was the frequency she'd been called out there over the years.

A pebbledash atrocity would be the best way of describing it. Row after row of giant breeze block style maisonettes standing at the feet of a concrete tower block. The council had poured hundreds of thousands of pounds of ratepayers' money into regenerating the area, which amounted to replacing the military style grey wooden doors and window frames throughout the estate with military style brown wooden doors and window frames. The damp and the dirt on the interior remained the same. Councillors had come to the community centre for a photo-shoot following the major refurbishment, but left early when residents lambasted them about the local school which ranked bottom of the league table with no sign of improvement. Was it a coincidence that Tattersall had the highest level of unemployment in Salford? The terse response before they'd climbed back into their chauffeur driven cars was that under their leadership parents had the right to choose which school to send their children, so if they were dissatisfied with their children's education they could vote with their feet.

All well and good if the residents had the resources to send their offspring to the only other comprehensive school in the area, but it was two bus rides away and most of the residents couldn't afford cars. Three hundred housing units and a space for twenty-nine vehicles. Go figure.

Aston Baptiste lived in Byron House, the last tower block left standing following the area's regeneration. The other high rise flats had been demolished in favour of luxury apartments for the wealthy incomers working in Salford's Media City. No one seemed to give a toss that the local residents were being side-lined, moved to other areas, other poverty hotspots, only now they were disconnected, no longer part of the social fabric that used to make up a town. Regeneration? Alex shuddered, more like social cleansing.

Parking the vehicle as close to the block as she could Alex regretted bringing the squad car, might as well have covered herself in red rags. Too late now, she chided herself, locking the doors with a clink, clamping her shoulder bag against her side with her left elbow.

Byron House had not been part of the regeneration programme, its bleak exterior shaming the architects who had long since retired, moving to farmhouses in Provence for their rustic appeal. There was nothing appealing about a neglected block of flats, unless you counted the opinion of the stray dogs who roamed around its base, assembled like guard dogs protecting the manor. Kids gathered too, wearing the uniform of the local crew: baggy jeans slung low enough to display branded designer underwear, zipped up hoodies with red and green scarves announcing their allegiance to one of the local tribes.

Alex knew when Mallender had said ask around he'd meant at the local community projects where youth workers spent their time getting to know the kids – they could have given her a heads up on Abby's boyfriend without him being any the wiser. She also knew she'd get the sanitised version because social workers and counsellors hated to lose their street cred by bleating to the police unless it was absolutely necessary. Spurred on by the fact that according to CRIMMINT Aston didn't have a history of violence - he had a record for car theft, which by Tattersall standards was positively law abiding - Alex decided to seek him out herself.

Chapter 9

Earl stood on the corner of the tower block landing, watching the police car three floors below as it drove along the ring road, occasionally pulling into the side roads, pausing along stretches of wasteland as though looking for something. He wondered where Pauly'd dumped the car, wondered what he and Kester were doing right now.

The girl was dead. He'd stayed up all that night to listen to the news, hoped to God he'd only scratched her. When the newsreader announced there'd been a fatal shooting his insides had turned to jelly, he'd had to run to the toilet as his bowels went into over-drive.

He hadn't meant to kill her, just to prove to Pauly that he could follow orders. Step up when needed. It was unreal; impossible to comprehend he'd caused so much harm to someone he didn't even know. A complete fucking stranger. Now, with her photo plastered across every news bulletin on every channel he was finding out things about her he'd rather not know: She'd been leaving the following morning to go to university, was having a last night out with her friends.

She was an only child.

Pictures of her devastated parents leaving the hospital flashed across the TV screen, followed by footage of friends lighting candles in her memory, placing them beside flowers and teddy bears at the scene. He'd found out far more than he'd bargained for - she was no longer a test, a challenge to prove his loyalty to Pauly, she was a walking talking person, and he'd wiped her off the planet without a second thought.

He looked at his watch, guessed that Aston must have stayed the night with his new girlfriend, would be in no hurry to come back. He couldn't blame him, he'd made it clear he didn't want his older brother meddling in his life any more, that he was old enough to stand on his own two feet. Earl pulled a face. Who had he been trying to kid?

He'd been happy enough hanging around on the periphery of Pauly's gang, doing menial tasks, fetching and carrying for those further up the chain of command, then Pauly got it into his head he was better than that, could start moving up the levels if he got more involved. Guns though, guns at this stage of the game had thrown him. He'd half expected Pauly to piss himself when Kester gave him the package, tell him that he was only having a laugh, just wanted to test his bottle. But Pauly hadn't laughed, so he'd put the gun in his pocket like it was no big deal.

Aston was gonna kill him. When he finds out what he's done he'll remove his head from his shoulders without so much as stopping to draw breath, yet even with the threat of his reaction it was better he heard it from Earl rather than from someone else. Pauly might be confident that the police wouldn't find anything to pin on him but that didn't allow for the local grapevine where the name of the shooter would be handed down like folklore. He might not be able to turn back the clock but he could minimise the damage. He needed to get to Aston first, tell him his side of the story, beg him to help him, tell him what to do next. Yeah, he'd be pissed, but he'd help. He knew Aston's girl lived on the floor below them but didn't know which flat exactly. Short of working his way along the front doors knocking on each one like he was selling religion he figured the best thing to do was keep watch; see which door his brother finally emerged from. He positioned himself at the corner of the landing, opposite the lift which no one used anymore;

bided his time.

'Did you get a good look at him?'
'Kind of.'
'Would you recognise him if you saw him again?'
Abby shook her head in frustration, combing her fingers through her hair in an attempt to control it; she hadn't looked in a mirror since getting ready to go out on Friday evening. Aston banged his fist on the kitchen table in frustration, 'When I find out who's fucking behind this, I'll-'
'What?' Abby demanded, 'Kill 'em? Like that'll bring Becca back? Make anything better?'
Aston shook his head like a wild man, pacing around the tiny kitchen like it had become his prison. He turned to look at Abby's bowed head. 'It could have been you.' The words caught in his throat, he hurried to where she'd slumped forward in her chair, sank to his knees and wrapped his arms around her waist, laying his head on her lap. His eyes were shiny, his mind alert, picturing the scenario if she hadn't been so fast on her feet. It was an awful thing to think, and it would be some time before he'd have the guts to say it out loud but as he clung on to Abby he couldn't stop thinking how lucky he'd been, that he was glad it had been Rebecca and not her.

Alex tramped along the walkway, regretting the smart smock style maternity dress she was wearing, wishing instead she'd got changed into something more casual – albeit uncomfortable – waistbands were so a thing of the past. She worried that her appearance on the block may cause trouble for Aston. She hadn't bothered trying the lift, decided instead to get her blood pumping. She'd continued at the gym for as long as she could, had only stopped when her expanding bulk prevented her from fitting into the resistance equipment. Alex shrugged. From rowing machine to vending machine, that just about summed her up. She placed her hand over her bump in time to feel junior practice a drop goal. Coupland still managed to do the job with his weight, she reasoned, didn't seem to hold *him* back. But then he was jammy enough to get teamed with raw recruits more often than not, either that or men who went running for fun, a pastime Coupland would never get his head round in a month of Sundays.

A teenage boy stood on the far end of the landing, leaning into the concrete balcony as though waiting for someone. Fourteen maybe, hard to tell with the oversized sportswear and baggy top, baseball cap pulled low over his eyes. Aware for the first time of her vulnerability, Alex avoided eye contact as she continued up the stairs, pulling out her notebook from the side pocket of her bag to check the flat numbers against the address she'd scribbled down back at the station.

The flat's exterior was tidy; its door and windowsills had been repainted white by someone who gave a damn and stood out against the bulk purchase brown of the rest of the row. Alex knocked on the door. After waiting a couple of minutes she tried again, louder this time though she knew it was fruitless. She consulted her notepad once more, decided to try Aston's girlfriend's address, which she was relieved to see was only one floor below.

'You took your time!' Earl hurled at Aston the moment he emerged on the landing, hood up, hands deep in pockets despite the wind dying down. 'I've been trying to reach you.'

Aston bit back his irritation at Earl's constant self-interest; he supposed that's what happened when your older brother constantly bailed you out.

Something about Earl's dishevelled state alarmed him, the ruffled hair between each cornrow, clothes that looked like he'd slept in them - 'What's up?' he demanded, 'Mum and Arlene, are they OK?' Without waiting for an answer he pushed past Earl, heading for the stairwell to the floor above.

Earl sprinted to keep up with him, gripping onto his arm. 'They're fine! Aston, wait…' Relieved, Aston spun round, staring at his brother but his relief soon turned to confusion.

'What's going on?' He demanded, sinking back against the stairwell wall, running his hands over his scalp. 'I could do without any hassle right now, the night we've had…' He indicated in the direction of Abby's flat, shrugging helplessly, 'It was her mate that got shot. You know, the one on the news?' He looked at Earl for acknowledgement, saw his head jerk just a fraction. 'She was *there,* bruv. Fucking right beside her, saw it with her own fucking eyes…'

Aston turned and threw a punch at the stairwell wall, barely flinching when his knuckles cracked. 'So I'm sorry I didn't come running when you called me, only I'm sure even you can see I've been up to my eyes in it.'

Earl backed away, his mouth slack, eyes bulging as though he had a thyroid problem. Aston eyed him suspiciously. 'You OK bruv?' and then, more insistent, 'You been taking something?' he moved in closer trying to get a look at his eyes.

'I ain't no fool, bruv.' Earl responded defensively, wishing it were true. He backed away anyway.'Dealing's one ting, taking the stuff? I don't wanna know.'

Satisfied, Aston nodded, then, shyly this time: 'Her name's Abby. Would you like to come and meet her?'

Earl backed away, as though Aston had suggested something indecent, 'You gotta be kidding, right, you think I want to watch you playing happy families? I got better things to do with my time.'

He turned into the stairwell, pulling the hood of his sweatshirt as far over his head as it would go. In the parking bay below a police car slowed before coming to a stop, two uniformed officers climbed out, heads tilted back, hands shielding eyes as they regarded the tower block. Earl leaned into the shadows. 'Hey bruv.' Aston called after him. 'What did you want me for?'

Earl turned to look at his brother, all the while conscious of the cops' muted conversation as they waited for the lift. He needed to be away from there – and fast. He pasted on a pretend smile. 'It's sorted now.' Was all he said.

Alex passed the boy from the landing below as she went down the stairs; he bounded up them two at a time barely giving her a second glance. She'd heard voices coming from the stairwell, both male, had expected to see someone follow behind him, instead another youth, taller and stockier built, was stomping off in the opposite direction.

She located Abby's flat and pressed the buzzer. A sad looking girl with bedraggled hair told her Aston had just popped out; she'd catch up with him if she was quick enough, her voice tinged with doubt when her gaze fell on Alex's bump.

'Shit.' Alex muttered, scolding herself for thinking legwork was anything to be missed. The lift at the end of the walkway spluttered to a stop and two uniformed officers from her division stepped out onto the landing. 'Thank you, God.' She mouthed, before bellowing at them to hold the bloody lift for her.

The young black man she'd seen walking ahead of her on the second floor exited the stairwell just as Alex made her way out of the lift. As usual, her condition attracted well-meaning attention.

'I can't believe you've just been in there.' He observed, indicating with his hands the stench that had enveloped her, all of it human. She pointed to her bump good naturedly as they walked out of the block together, 'Beggars can't be choosers.' Within seconds his demeanour changed, the expression on his face telling her the police car was in his line of vision, that he'd worked out she hadn't been making a social call.

'Haven't you lot finished with your door knocking yet?' he growled, turning his body so that he faced her full on. 'Isn't it about time you went looking for whoever did this?' he persisted.

'I take it you're the boyfriend then?' Alex asked, although it wasn't really a question. The anger in his eyes and the protective note in his voice told her the investigation mattered to him more than most.

'It's Aston, isn't it? Look, I didn't come here to speak to Abby, or anyone else for that matter.' Alex reassured him, 'I came to talk to you. 'Aston regained his composure quick enough, but not before Alex had clocked a look that fitted across his face. Mistrust, or something like it.

'Is there somewhere we can talk?' she asked hopefully. Before turning into Byron House she'd passed a row of boarded up shops, concrete retail units with rusted metal shutters in permanent lockdown.

'There's a community centre round the corner,' Aston offered, 'Can go there if you like?' Alex nodded, stepping aside to follow him round the perimeter of the block.

The community centre was in a purpose-built concrete unit, no bigger than a couple of lock-ups knocked together. The back room contained a drinks machine that offered more choice than the one at the station by the look of it.

'I don't like hot drinks.' Aston muttered; Alex shrugged, fumbled in her pocket for the correct money for an herbal tea, punched in the relevant numbers.

'I don' wanna leave her for too long.' He began, inclining his head in the direction of Byron House, 'She's finding it hard to deal with.'

'I'm not surprised,' Alex agreed, 'must have been horrific.'

Aston nodded. Slowly, but a nod all the same. 'Any idea who did this?' he asked.

Alex shook her head.

'Then why are you here?' he demanded, 'You should be out looking for them.'

Alex stared pointedly at her stomach, 'They won't let me go anywhere at the moment,' she explained, 'Against union rules.'

'So why *are* you here then?' he persisted.

'To find out more about you. To see if you have any idea who could be behind this.'

'You mean I'm black so I must have gangster friends, or at least friends who carry.' He made a sucking noise through his teeth, slapping the side of his leg in frustration. Alex shook her head impatiently.

'Look,' she reasoned, 'I could try and pacify you and tell you that policing isn't like that anymore, that we weeded out institutional racism root and branch following the Lawrence Inquiry. I could give you the names of all my black friends, or try to make out that I play Tu Pak on my stereo at home but I'd be insulting you and you deserve better than that, in the same way I deserve better from you.'

'What do you mean?' he asked suspiciously.

'You saw a white woman, a cop at that; you projected your own prejudices onto me: That I'm a bigot; racially stereotyping you before we've even spoken to one another. Why is that?' she asked, searching his face for a clue, 'To avoid disappointment later when you're proved right? Well, newsflash, we're not all the same, some of us get up in the morning and just want to do our job, yeah? Do the best we can. Now, in answer to your accusation - do I think you have gangster friends?' she paused, searching his face, '…I can't say for sure, but I think a guy from this estate probably hasn't got to your age without knowing who not to get on the wrong side of and that's all I'm asking for right now,' she reasoned, 'a couple of names to work with.'

There was a moment when she thought she'd lost him, when her outburst might have pushed all the wrong buttons, but then he stifled a smile as he conceded her point. 'For your information I don't go about with anyone who's carrying,' he responded, 'but I can probably tell you a thing or two about the main players around here.'

'Do us a favour and pull over one of those chairs,' Alex interrupted, 'My feet are bloody killing me.'

Chapter 10

By the time Alex returned to the station Coupland was working his way through the ballistics report Mallender had left on his desk with a note to follow up before that evening's briefing. The bullet, which had penetrated Rebecca Louden's neck had been passed onto the Forensic Science Lab.

'I'm on my way over to the mortuary now, see what else your ex can dredge up for us.' Alex went pink at the reference to Benson, the pathologist she'd gone out with during a break up with Carl a couple of years before. 'Jesus, Coupland,' she reminded him, 'it was a couple of bloody weeks, that's all, you've had dinners last longer than that. What are you, my Dad?'

'Hey,' he retorted sounding hurt, 'More like a concerned older brother.'

'Older brother from a first marriage that ended twenty years before I was born.' she corrected.

His eyes widened at the rebuke, the tell-tale mischievous grin spread across his dough-like face. 'Did I tell you your bum looks big in that?' he retaliated, before dismissing her with a middle finger as he headed for the door.

And your paunch is still bigger than my bump, she said to herself, sitting down quickly in an attempt to deprive anyone the opportunity of checking her rear end out for themselves.

A young man standing close by had been following their conversation. 'We love each other really.' She reassured him.

'I think you look great, Sarge,' he stammered, as

though some sort of validation was required on his part. Alex's spirits soared in a way they hadn't since she'd stopped being able to see her feet – and other body parts – in the shower some four months earlier.

'For your age.' He qualified.

Alex had been typing up a report of her meeting with Abby Marlowe's boyfriend when DC Robinson returned balancing two vending machine cups on a file he carried like a tray. 'They've restocked the hot chocolate,' he explained, gesturing for her to take a cup before perching on the end of her desk, nursing the other.

'Thought I'd treat you to one before word gets out.'

Alex smiled appreciatively, glancing over at the new DC. *That's how it's done, Sonny,* she tried to signal telepathically.

Robinson had driven out to Ellenbrook, an upmarket development on the outskirts of Worsley, to interview the owner of the stolen Subaru involved in Friday's shooting. He opened his file, pulled out photographs of the electric blue vehicle before and after it was torched and found abandoned by Turnbull on the ring road of the Tattersall estate. He pointed to the metallic flame motif stencilled down both sides of the car.

'Classy.' Alex observed dryly.

'It matches the witness statement the victim's best friend provided,' Robinson began, 'even down to the alloy wheels.'

'And the owner?' Alex prompted, 'The car was taken from his place of work?'

'Yeah, one of those cash converter places on Pendlebury Road. James Doughty's the manager, didn't notice his car was missing until he locked up at six.'

Alex shrugged her shoulders. Some people it was hard to feel sympathy for and people who made money out of the hard-up were right at the top of her list.

'Had anyone suspicious been seen around the place in the days leading up to the car theft?' She asked, although the answer was contained in the question. Most people skulked into a pawnbrokers, either through the shame of it or the fact they were trying to palm off something they shouldn't.

'No one out of the ordinary.' Robinson replied. 'But it faces onto a busy main road. It wouldn't have been that difficult to observe which cars belonged to shoppers and punters and which were stationary all day. Plenty o'cafes along that top road, decent ones too.'

'And this bloke's distinctive choice in motor made it pretty easy to keep tabs on.' Added the young DC, who had been following the conversation between Alex and Robinson like a spectator at Wimbledon. Alex, who'd been trying to forget the kid's earlier faux pas by ignoring him completely found herself irritated by his presence. 'Still here?' she accused; eyebrows arched as high as they could go in what she hoped was a menacing stare.

'Why wouldn't I be?' he asked brightly, and then, 'You did get the email right?'

Alex prided herself on her admin skills, was way ahead of the others when it came to filing reports and updating stats. She responded to any correspondence promptly with courtesy and an adherence to grammar Coupland could only dream of. But she wasn't a saint, and like most people she ignored messages she was copied into and anything sent out by Human Resources. She vaguely recalled seeing a message in her Inbox, had right clicked on the attachment to print it out to read for later. She was buggered if she could remember where she'd put it, but wondered with a sinking feeling if that memo and this joker were connected in some way.

'I'm your maternity cover, Sergeant.' He said eagerly, 'I've been assigned to shadow you over the next couple of weeks, so I can hit the ground running when you go off on leave.' *Hit the ground running*, did he just say that or was she hallucinating? Just great. Now she felt fat *and* sidelined. He was acting up out of uniform too; she tried not to be insulted by what was simply an exercise by Superintendent Curtis to provide cheap cover. She wondered if DCI Mallender had known, he hadn't said anything when they'd spoken earlier.

'Is there a letter as well?' she asked. The rookie shook his head. 'It was all in the email, HR copied everyone in.' So, Mallender would be none the wiser then.

Alex let out a sigh. 'So,' she began, trying to pour enthusiasm into words she didn't feel. 'What's your name, Kiddo?'

'Oldman.' He chirped brightly, failing to see the irony,'Todd.' He held out a hand causing Alex to stifle a smile but she grasped his anyway and gave it a shake. She wasn't so long in the tooth that she couldn't remember the fear of making a good first impression, the excitement at the prospect of working in plain clothes, trying to win the respect of men who'd seen far more than was good for them. A silence settled upon them, and she tried with all her heart not to be peeved that Todd's arrival signalled her imminent departure, that he was here to step seamlessly into her tight fitting shoes.

She wondered if he'd started shaving yet, his skin was pale and free from any kind of stubble. He had brilliant white teeth too, as though he only ever drank water, either that or he'd paid a visit to one of those laser whitening clinics. His smile was wide and boyish and compared to her colleagues he looked so damn *clean*, like an Ivy League graduate in a Hugo Boss ad. More Mallender than Coupland, she decided, plus he smelt nice too.

'I suppose you'd better pull up a seat then,' she said grudgingly. 'Don't worry if it feels like everything's going over your head, you'll get up to speed once we start assigning tasks to you.' She stifled a smile; she'd already decided he could clear everyone's filing.

'So, why take such a distinctive car?' She sipped at her hot chocolate which was already lukewarm. 'Why not take something that doesn't stand out from the crowd?'

Robinson shrugged in reply.

'It was already dark, remember?' Oldman butted in, 'The paint job wouldn't have been that noticeable.'

'Our witness picked up on it straight away,' Alex corrected, 'surely our thief would have too.'

'But if it was a kid?' Oldman persisted, 'Maybe that was part of the appeal?'

'It's a high performance vehicle,' Turnbull suggested, 'maybe *that* was the appeal.'

Alex squirmed in her chair as junior changed position. Absentmindedly she rested the paper cup on the top of her bump.

'This Doughty,' she wondered aloud, 'any previous?'

Robinson got to his feet, 'I'll go check,' He replied before turning away.

'Hang on,' Alex called out, copying Doughty's name and address from Robinson's notebook onto her desk pad then tearing off the top sheet before handing it to Oldman. 'I want you to check through the system, see if this guy's got any form,' a thought occurred to her then, reminding her of something Aston had mentioned earlier, about the scam he'd been involved in which led to his spell behind bars. 'Robinson, I want you to go and see Doughty again, find out where he purchased the vehicle, and more important, how he *paid*.'

Chapter 11

Coupland walked through to the back of the house, slid open the patio doors that now led from the kitchen into the garden, a recent edition which brought in more light, enabling them to enjoy the garden on even the coldest of days. A chance to take stock, survey the work in progress from the convenience of their kitchen table. There were other new editions: stone flags and a built in barbeque, a small cast iron table and two chairs, a compost bin in the far right hand corner. He smiled each time it caught his eye, wondered what the hell the lads at the station would think of *that*.

Last year's waste ground had been hacked back, lawn re-seeded, a border dug out in which bulbs had been planted interspersed with established foliage so the garden didn't look too barren. Joe, an ex-serviceman whom Coupland had befriended when he'd fallen on hard times had pitched in, giving the garden a makeover that Ground Force would have been proud of. He'd wanted something Lynn could enjoy during her treatment, to work in or rest in depending on how she felt. Turned out she had a real flair for the garden and the distraction had done her good too.

'Good timing,' a voice called out from behind a pile of stones positioned to form a rockery, a fishpond dismissed as too high maintenance.

'Put the kettle on, love.'

Coupland turned back into the kitchen, lifted the kettle from its stand before placing it under the cold tap. For himself, he retrieved a can of lager from a multipack, removed the ring-pull before taking a swig. Once the kettle had boiled he threw a teabag in a cup, adding hot water and a splash of milk.

He was surprised how much Lynn was enjoying the garden. She seemed to take comfort in organising where things went, as though she relished having something in her life over which she had total control; the flowers that grew in it; the potatoes and carrots that were planned for next year.

Pushing herself up from her knees, Lynn stretched her back, rubbing both hands on a backside numb from sitting awkwardly on the grass. 'Broken the back of the weeding,' she said, nodding to a black bin bag overflowing with clotted earth and dandelions, a trowel lay at an angle beside it. She walked over to the cast iron patio table, lowered herself gingerly onto one of the two chairs either side of it. 'Need to get cushions for these bloody seats,' she grumbled, 'getting too old for this.'

'It's good for the soul, or so I've been told.' Coupland observed. They sat in silence, Coupland desperate to ask how her trip to the hospital had gone, knowing she'd tell him when she was good and ready. It had been agreed that her sister would take her, Lynn refusing point blank that Coupland take off more time than he needed. Better to save his annual leave for if she became ill, she'd insisted, and right now she felt fine, well, as good as the chemotherapy would let her.

Coupland drained his can, returning to the kitchen for reinforcements. Lynn moved onto an herbal infusion she had concocted from a window box of herbs she'd planted earlier in the year. They moved indoors to eat, the autumn evenings no longer providing the clemency of summer, and afterwards he chain-smoked, these being the few cigarettes of the day he really enjoyed. Most smokes were like sex, if he recalled it rightly, the anticipation overshadowing the actual taking part. Yet there were times like this, when the time and mood was right, that he enjoyed it in all its simplicity.

With other thoughts banished from his mind Coupland sat back, enjoying the sensation of the nicotine infusing his lungs. His eyelids began to feel heavy.

'Got a phone call from the Macmillan nurse today.' Lynn began, snapping Coupland's attention back into the present. 'Is there a problem?' he asked, alarmed. Was there something she hadn't told him? A complication?

Lynn shook her head, 'No,' she said carefully, as though she found it necessary to shield him from what was coming next. 'I asked her to ring; I just thought it would be good to have someone to talk to, that's all.'

'You've got me!' Coupland whined. He sounded like Amy whenever they said *No* to her but he didn't care. Lynn was his wife. If she wanted to talk things through she should be able to turn to *him*.

'I know I can talk to you, Kevin.' She said softly, as though his skin had turned to eggshell. 'But sometimes I want to talk about what's going to happen in the future.'

'What *might* happen in the future,' Coupland corrected her.

'See what I mean?'

Since Lynn had got her diagnosis all Coupland was bothered about was the here and now. The future, as far as he was concerned, could take care of itself.

'Anyway,' Lynn continued; her voice more animated now she'd broached it with him. 'She sounded really nice; said she'd pop out to see me, that I could phone her anytime I wanted.'

Unsure whether Lynn was looking for approval or encouragement Coupland got to his feet, deciding a coffee might help him put his thoughts in order. 'Thought getting involved with more medical people would be the last thing you'd want to do.' He attempted.

Lynn nodded. 'It is, but now I've made contact would it do any harm to have a chat and see where it goes?'

Coupland poured himself a coffee while he tried to

think of an answer. He supposed this woman could do no harm, after all they'd already had the stuffing knocked out of them; perhaps they needed outside help to put it back.

'I hadn't realised…' Coupland attempted, unwilling to finish the sentence.

'…That you alone can't solve the world's problems?' Lynn finished for him, lifting the tension.

Smiling, Coupland took a sip of his coffee before pulling a face and placing his mug back on the counter top. 'I forgot the bloody sugar.' He chided himself. He reached for the sugar pot, measured out three heaped spoonfuls, stirring slowly. He was grateful for this small task, this one thing he could do to take away the bitterness.

Chapter 12

Earl's world had spun into freefall. The corners of the room kept twisting out of shape, the floor taking on a life of its own. He'd staggered home after his meeting with Aston, lurched into the bathroom where he'd vomited into the toilet bowl before sliding down onto the cold linoleum floor. He pushed himself up into a sitting position, steadying himself against the side of the bath.

The last few days seemed unreal, as though he was immersed in some sort of nightmare that kept sucking him back under each time he reached the surface. What were the chances? He'd stared into the eyes of the dead girl's best friend, just for a second, but long enough to know that if she saw him again she'd run for her life, that or go running to the police. And now, to top it all, he'd discovered she was going out with his brother.

There was a thumping in his head as though his brain was struggling to keep up with this latest discovery, as though trying to compute his chances of coming out of this intact, and he didn't like the odds it was giving him one little bit. Yet it got worse. It was bad enough to break the law, to commit fucking murder, but it was another thing entirely to get on the wrong side of Pauly. Both of these scenarios had played out over the last 48 hours but the one tiny ray of hope was the thought that Aston would come up trumps, bail him out in some way after making him promise, never, ever, to put a foot wrong again. But after learning of Aston's position in all this he realised with a thud that his brother bailing him out was the last thing that was going to happen. This was a ticking fucking time bomb. Even if he managed to avoid bumping into Abby, sooner or later the photo fit she'd been working on with the police would get splashed across the front page of every paper and go out on the local news, even Crimewatch if he was unlucky enough, and someone who knew him would take one look and the shit would hit the fan.

His stomach churned with unease, not just at what he had done, but what he now had to do. He pulled himself onto his knees; leaning over the bath he took several deep breaths.

'Jesus,' he whispered quietly, his head bowed, hands clamped together as though in prayer. He closed his eyes, tried to think through the consequences of each possible course of action. His eyes snapped open as a plan began to formulate in his mind. Rummaging around in the pocket of his jeans he located his mobile, scrolling through his contact list until he found the right number.

Chapter 13

It was quiet for a weekday morning, the road works along Salford's high street kept to a minimum, workmen leaning against temporary railings, supping from flasks; school run over, the pavement was empty save for the postman balancing parcels, ignoring the junkies sitting on the steps of properties they pretended to live in, arms outstretched offering to relieve him of his burden.

Coupland parked alongside a line of bollards behind a Men at Work sign, showed his warrant card to the foreman, told him he'd be half an hour tops, time it took for his men to smoke through a couple of roll ups and catch up on last night's *I'm A Celebrity*. Pulling his collar up to protect him against the wind he crossed the road to Ego, the scene of Rebecca Louden's murder three days earlier.

Like all night time venues, the club looked out of place during the day, the main entrance deserted beneath a gaudy neon sign. The floral tributes and candles that had lined the nightclub's entrance had been moved by a council official earlier that morning. The only tell-tale sign that a tragedy had taken place was a dark stain on the pavement, hidden from view by a sandwich board declaring discounted membership.

'I give it six months,' Coupland thought sourly as he jabbed at the buzzer with his middle finger. After a couple of minutes the intercom crackled with static followed by a woman's voice saying something indecipherable. Coupland leaned forward, barked the word *Police* before straightening himself up. The intercom buzzed signalling right of entry; he pushed open the door.

The interior smelled of cleaning fluid and pollen. A flower arrangement that had seen better days stood limp on the reception desk. A young woman Coupland recognised as the receptionist who'd been working the night of the shooting leaned against the counter top flicking through a magazine. Make up free and clad in jeans, ear-phones plugged into an MP3 player blaring out a clash of bass and drum.

The girl kept reading as though she was to sit a test at the end of it, pausing only to fiddle with her music player, whether pressing fast forward or hitting replay Coupland couldn't be sure; it was hard to make out any noticeable change in tempo. Eventually she seemed to notice him, jerking her head in the direction of the door behind the counter: 'He's through there.' Whether an observation or an invitation to pass through it was hard to be sure, but Coupland stomped in that direction anyway.

Ashraf Zadawi was seated behind his desk. If he was surprised to see Coupland walking into his office unannounced he didn't show it.

'Welcome, Sergeant!' he boomed, 'Come! Take a seat! Your timing is good, Stacey is just making coffee.' Zadawi got up from his seat and moved towards the office door 'Another cup Stacey!' he bellowed, obviously used to competing with in-ear drum and bass.

They'd been seated no more than five minutes when a rattling tray heralded Stacey's entrance, two chipped mugs balanced precariously on top of it, a sugar bowl placed between them. A dirty spoon had been placed on the tray as an afterthought. Coupland waited while the mugs were placed clumsily on the table. 'How many sugars?' Stacey asked him, intent on playing mother. 'Keep pouring till my spoon stands up on its own.' He informed her, ignoring Zadawi's look of horror.

'Please,' Ashraf began, whilst at the same time

shooing Stacey out, 'let's drink before we talk of the unfortunate business that brings you here.'

As soon as he touched the searing liquid Ashraf's lips pursed as though he'd tasted something foul. 'She's used powdered milk again,' he complained, 'I don't know how many times…'

Coupland grinned, 'S'why I take sugar,' he said authoritatively, 'masks a multitude of sins.'

A couple more sips and Coupland pushed his coffee to one side, mentally putting his questions in order before he began.

'Seems you're a popular man Mr Zadawi.' he began, watching Ashraf's chest puff up with the intended flattery. 'You've put quite a bit of business the way of a couple of local building firms, shop fitters, decorators. Never quibble with the bill, pay your invoices on time, a rarity these days, I'd have thought.'

'I work in the hospitality industry; I see no point in antagonising potential customers, especially local ones. We're the smartest club around here; with any luck what I pay my suppliers will find its way back into my tills one way or another.' He had a point.

'My officers did a little digging, found that before this place opened up you had a bistro in Eccles. What happened to that sir?'

'It wasn't the right venture for me-'

'So what happened?'

'I sold it.'

'And before.'

'Before?' If he needed help jogging his memory Coupland was happy to oblige.

'The women's clothing store.'

Ashraf had the grace to flush, his face and neck darkening as he fumbled with his shirt collar.

'I never saw that as a long term venture, Sergeant, more a short term investment opportunity.'

'And was it?'

'Was it what?' the accent had all but disappeared, replaced by the familiar harsh sounding Salford vowels. Coupland wondered if anything about the man seated in front of him was genuine.

'Did the investment turn out as you'd hoped? Did you make much money?'

Ashraf shrugged helplessly, 'The market changed, how was I to know how fickle high street trade could be?' How indeed.

'Yet you seem to have emerged from a string of failed businesses-' Coupland began, '-I wouldn't quite use that term-' Zadawi interrupted,'from a string of failed businesses relatively unscathed.'

Ashraf spread his hands on the desk in front of him. 'Cat with nine lives..?' he smiled, 'just lucky I guess.'

'So who bankrolls you?' Coupland demanded.

Ashraf shook his head. 'I don't know what you're talking about.'

'Is it so hard?' Coupland asked, beginning to enjoy himself.

Ashraf stared back at him blankly. 'I have absolutely no-'

'Is it so hard to admit you get a hand out from Daddy?' Coupland challenged, 'I mean, I know what it's like to have an overbearing old man,' he continued sympathetically, 'it can get very wearing, but even so...'

'I have accepted help from my father, yes.' Ashraf snapped, defensively, 'I didn't know there was a crime against it.'

'Your grasp of the law is quite correct, Mr Zadawi.' Coupland acknowledged, 'However your familiarity with how the police conduct their enquiries is quite poor. You see, I'm trying to find the reason behind the shooting of a young girl queuing to enter your premises on your opening night.'

'I'm aware of that.' There was a stiffness to Zadawi's demeanour now, his eagerness to please long gone.

'And I asked you whether you might have had any enemies,' Coupland persisted, 'anyone bear you a grudge to the extent they wanted to ruin your business before it got off the ground.'

'I know that!' Impatient now.

'Yet in all that time you failed to inform me that this business of yours is just another of Daddy's little bankrolled exercises, his attempt at placating a favoured child.'

'I still don't see-'

'That during the time we've spent investigating your business acquaintances, we'd have been better checking out those of your father.'

'I'm sorry.'

Coupland sprang to his feet, moved towards Ashraf with purpose: 'Not as sorry as me, Pal.' he spat, leaning over the businessman in as threatening a way as he could muster. 'You've been wasting my time. It wasn't the organ grinder I've been speaking to after all, but the monkey.'

One name and address later, Coupland waved his thanks to the foreman as he climbed back into the Mondeo. He opened the slip of paper in his hand. Zadawi's old man lived on Worsley Road. He'd need to speak to the boss, see if he fancied tagging along to this one. People with money could get arsey, didn't like to speak to anyone below the rank of Inspector.

By the sounds of it Zadawi's old man had serious money.

All the more reason for his enemies to be serious too.

Chapter 14

Omar Zadawi's house was larger than Coupland had expected. Much larger.He knew from the address Ashraf had given them that his father's home would be palatial but it exceeded even his expectations. Situated at the far end of Worsley Road overlooking the golf club on one side and the valley of Irlam over the other the six bedroomed property boasted a tennis court and indoor pool. He was made aware of that fact when the door was opened by a slender woman in her late fifties dressed in a towelling robe, dabbing at short wet hair with a towel.

'Nothing like swimming a mile to keep the metabolism going.' She said breathlessly as though she'd had to walk up a flight of steep stairs. Coupland could only imagine. She waved away his warrant card, standing aside to let both detectives enter the large entrance hall, 'blind as a bat without my glasses, love,' she explained, 'you could be showing me your Costa loyalty card for all I know.' Petite, with grey hair that stood in spikey tufts from the towel drying, she had intense brown eyes and cheekbones that hinted at a career in front of the camera in her youth. Coupland made the introductions, explaining that they wanted to speak to Omar.

'I take it you're his wife?' He said hesitantly, it was easy enough these days to get that bit wrong from the outset.

'I am, for my sins.' The woman replied. If she was in the least bit concerned at two detectives arriving on her doorstep she kept it well hidden.

'I'm Sofia,' she said warmly, 'Omar's much better half.' There was an awkward silence while the three of them stared at each other then looked away, Coupland tried another tack. 'Is he in then, love?' he prompted, 'Only we need to be getting on.'

Sofia had been staring at Mallender as though she was trying to place him; she jumped guiltily, shaking her head. 'He's at the office,' she informed them, 'but I can give him a call. Is it anything urgent?' Coupland shook his head. 'Just routine,' he paused, 'following the shooting outside your son's nightclub last Friday.'

A flash of recognition crossed Sophie's face. That's where I knew you from,' she said, looking at Mallender once more, 'the press conference on the tea-time news.' She shook her head slowly, as though checking it still worked. 'A terrible, terrible business,' she whispered and Coupland wondered for a moment if she was referring to the shooting or Ashraf's latest venture.

'You were standing in the background,' she said to Mallender as though accusing him of not pulling his weight, 'there was a senior officer, in uniform, who spoke to the press.' Mallender ignored Coupland's smirk. 'Above my pay grade.' He said as politely as he could, 'I only get the limelight when it all goes wrong.'

His comment seemed to pacify her, as though she was familiar with a world where blame rolled downhill.

The room reminded Coupland of a First Division footballer's home, not that he'd ever been inside one but from what he'd seen on TV. Textured walls in cream from floor to ceiling, leopard skin cushions artfully scattered on oversized leather sofas, a smoked glass coffee table nestled ostentatiously between them.

It was as far removed from the home he'd gown up in as you could get, but he knew enough to know wealth didn't equal happy.

'Nice place you've got here.' he commented.

'Thank you.' Sofia acknowledged with a bow of her head. 'Though not down to me I'm afraid, got interior designers in the moment we picked up the keys.'

Coupland glanced round at the ornate furniture and gilt mirrors, wondering who in their right mind had a white leather sofa and cream carpets? It was a glamorous home, for a glamorous woman, not a woman that had to work hard for a living, nor spend her time keeping the place clean. Sofia probably had people to do that, hard up women like Abby's mother, only ever destined to play the put-upon role, he thought sadly.

'Please excuse me while I get changed.' Sofia said, 'make yourself at home.' She gestured to the oversized settees before retreating. Coupland noticed her slip a mobile phone from the pocket of her bathrobe, punch a single key before speaking quietly into the mouthpiece.

Left alone in the room the detectives moved in opposite directions, getting the lie of the place. Patio doors led to a terrace overlooking landscaped lawns then further still onto the valley of Irlam. A uniformed man sat atop a ride-on mower, and Coupland remembered seeing a transit van parked along the side of the house, Greenfingers, or Greenworks, he couldn't be sure.

The tap of heels along the tiled floor of the hallway signified Sofia's return.

'My husband's on his way,' she informed them smiling, 'Can I get you both a drink?' She'd changed into a simple belted catsuit, low heeled but expensive looking pumps and a smidgeon of make-up. 'Don't need to make so much of an effort when I'm working from home,' she added.

Coupland shook his head at the offer of a drink, 'We'll not be long.' He said simply, although that rather depended on how long her husband took to return from his office.

'He's overseeing the refurbishment of our newest venture,' Sofia informed them, 'a small restaurant just down the road from here. Handy for the United players if they don't want to travel into the city centre.' Coupland made a show of looking at his watch. 'It's walking distance,' she reassured him, 'but my husband's hands are welded to the steering wheel of his car so he'll drive himself over – he'll not keep you.' As if on cue a man resembling an older version of Ashraf strode into the room halting abruptly in the middle of it as though staking claim to his castle. As Coupland walked towards Omar Zadawi to introduce himself the man kept both hands clasped behind his back. A curt nod was all that passed in response to his outstretched hand. The man was older than Coupland had expected, but then beneath all that hair gel Ashraf was no spring chicken. Omar's hair was long and thin; strands of grey appeared around his crown. His hooded eyes had grown an extra layer of skin, making him look reptilian each time he blinked.

'Through here.' Zadawi instructed them, leading the way through a series of reception rooms until they found themselves in what Coupland would have described as a library - given the antique style book shelves that surrounded the room - only there wasn't a book in sight. Instead each shelf contained what looked like entire volumes of glossy magazines – Top Gear, Homes and Garden, each issue appeared to be in perfection condition, no torn pages or well-thumbed editions. It resembled an upmarket newsagents, Coupland thought unkindly.

They were sitting on four club-style chairs placed around a small wooden table. A bowl of what looked like sugared almonds at it centre.

Coupland cleared his throat, pulled his notepad from his pocket: 'I don't want to take up any more of your time than is necessary,' he began, 'but we're here to ask you about your son, Ashraf.' There was a twitch in the older man's eye, an involuntary response perhaps, to the black sheep of the family, Coupland wondered.

'What of him?' Omar challenged, refusing to make it easy.

'We've been questioning him in relation to the

shooting outside his nightclub last Friday evening,' Mallender took over, 'It strikes me now that we've been talking to the wrong person.'

A smile flitted across Omar's face as he studied Mallender for a moment or two, Coupland already dismissed as not worthy of his interest.

'You have children, Chief Inspector?' The elder man asked.

Coupland watched as Mallender shook his head, though not before a look of disappointment flitted across his face. Omar shrugged his shoulders slowly, as though discussing the inevitable.

'Parenthood is quite simply the triumph of hope over experience,' he explained, adding, 'yet despite my instincts *and* experience telling me otherwise I continue to bankroll my son.'

'He was an easily led boy,' Omar continues, 'different from his brothers; he found it hard to concentrate, to stay focussed on any one thing.' Omar shrugged, 'if we helped him more-'

'-Which we did!' Sofia had joined them, carrying a whisky tumbler half filled with ice. She placed the glass in front of Omar before taking the one remaining seat. Omar swatted her words away as though he'd heard them too many times before, as though he'd never admit the truth of it. 'If we helped him more it was because he needed our help more.' Omar added simply.

Sofia picked up the story, 'He got in with a wrong crowd,' she began, blushing slightly, 'I know most parents must use this excuse but it's true. We started making allowances, tried not to be as critical, but that never really solves anything does it?' She looked over at Coupland, a kindred spirit perhaps, more likely to see things in shades of grey rather than black or white.

'Look,' Omar said impatiently, 'he's stupid, not bad. There were minor incidents: vandalism, property damage, our lawyers persuaded his victims to settle out of court. I was always very generous.' As though that made his actions sound better than they were.

'So you bought him a clean slate.' Coupland put it succinctly, ignoring Omar's wince.

'You would do the same,' Sofia reproached, 'if you were able to.' There would always be winners and losers in this world, Coupland understood that, it was just that sometimes, like now, it rankled.

'Not the sharpest tack is he?' Coupland added, enjoying himself. Truth was all that separated Ashraf from the toe rags he'd lifted over the years was the ability of his parents to keep him out of the gutter, yet even so by the look of it he hadn't progressed far. Granted, his clothes were better quality and his lifestyle was 'desirable', but he didn't exactly have a track record of turning these ready-made businesses his father bought for him into a success.

Omar glared at Coupland before averting his gaze, as though deciding the sergeant was too rough and ready to take seriously. That his views didn't matter, in the grand scheme of things. Mallender leaned forward in his chair in a bid to get the two men to cease their pissing contest and return to the matter in hand. A tactful approach: 'Were the businesses going concerns when you purchased them for your son?'

Omar nodded.

'And he ran them for how long?'

A shrug. 'Maybe six months.'

'And then?'

'Then they become a rescue mission.'

'Why?'

'Because he cuts corners, sources cheap products, brings in cowboy tradesmen. Customers are more savvy than they used to be, they know their rights.'

'So what do you do?'

Omar sighed, 'I throw good money after bad,' he said bitterly, 'trying to put things right, compensating angry suppliers, placating unhappy customers; then I sell the business onto people who know what they're doing.'

'Why bother?' Mallender persisted, 'Why not turn the business around by putting in a good manager?' Mallender's own father was on the ball but he knew where his weaknesses lay – he liked a drink and had no time for figures. So he'd employed the best barmen in town and had the senior partner from a city accountancy firm on a retainer – he'd never looked back. There were other success factors he was sure of it – John Gibson was a man who negotiated with rivals once he'd strapped them to a chair – or rather had someone do it for him. One look at Omar and it was obvious he was another man who didn't hear the word no that often in his life.

'Ashraf was always a fidgeter at school,' Sofia explained with the air of a mother used to making excuses for her son, 'and even now he gets bored very easily. Six months into a new venture and the novelty's worn off – he's itching to move on.'

Coupland wondered what happened to the people who were caught up in this family's homage to their feckless son – employees who lost their jobs once he ran each business into the ground. He looked over to Mallender, hoped the inspector had picked up on it too.

'Can you give us a list of all the employees who've worked for your son, Mr Zadawi?' Mallender asked on cue.

Omar shrugged. 'I can.' Said Sofia, 'I tend to look after that side of things.'

'Will there be anything else gentlemen?' Omar asked, politely dismissing them.

Coupland was the first to get to his feet. He held Omar's gaze as he leaned over the man, holding his hand out steady until the Turk had no option this time other than to shake it.

'Oh, I'm sure there will be, Sir,' he said politely, 'you can count on that.'

Chapter 15

'There's another fucking witness!' Earl whispered into the receiver.

'How d'you know?'

'Just trust me, OK?'

Like Pauly would ever do that again.

Earl's breath caught in his throat. He was doing the unthinkable, but what other option did he have? He'd never met Aston's girlfriend but that didn't make it any easier. She was probably OK, Earl reasoned. They'd probably have got on under normal circumstances, like if he hadn't killed her best fucking friend. But he was scared. Scared of the possibility that one day she'd remember something, some detail however small that she'd mention to Aston that would set his alarm bells ringing. She was just too big a risk.

He faced an impossible choice: a life sentence or a lifetime looking over his shoulder should he drop Pauly in it in any way, and of the two he wasn't sure which fate terrified him the most.

Right now he despised himself, couldn't imagine sinking any fucking lower. But like in those X-box games he played, or the war films he watched when nothing else was on TV, there were times when civilians got caught up in the crossfire, wiped out for being in the wrong place at the worst possible time. Collateral damage.

He might be scared of being caught by the police, but he was sure as hell more scared of Pauly.

It was Kester who'd noticed the shopkeeper smoking on the pavement. It had been their second time round the block; Pauly was talking into Earl's ear, pumping him up, telling him he was his main man. Kester had seen the guy clocking the car, turning his head as they passed by to get a better look. 'Fucksake!' He yelled at Earl, 'You better get it right this time.' Pauly had shifted his gaze to the shopkeeper, studied him briefly before turning his attention to Kester. 'No matter.' He'd said. His face was impassive but his words cold as ice.

Now there was a second witness. Another inconvenience that Pauly had to deal with. Earl could hear the irritation in the gangster's voice.

'Come to the lock-up.' Pauly barked. 'I'll text you when.' His anger made Earl feel guilty, as though he was in some way to blame that two people had got a look at them.

He wondered if he was being set up, that already Pauly was planning what would happen to him. He was a weak link in the chain, a weak link that could see Pauly and his cronies get sent to prison if he, and the shopkeeper, and Abby, couldn't keep their mouths shut.

Chapter 16

It was closing time when Robinson arrived at the Pawnbrokers on Pendlebury Road. Even so the line of people waiting to be served surprised him. It was a double fronted premises split into two – one half being a traditional pawnbroking shop that lent money on pretty much anything as long as it could be carried over the threshold, the other half was a franchise of one of those cash for gold places that seemed to have sprouted up everywhere. The punters waiting their turn on this side of the room had a shifty look about them, as though it was someone else's jewellery they were flogging rather than their own.

'I'll be with you in a minute,' Doughty said to Robinson as he began the process of locking up. Turning the 'Open' sign to 'Closed', he put the door on the latch before holding down a switch behind the counter which lowered a metal shutter over the window, keeping an eye on his assistant as she weighed the gold pushed under the safety glass to her then told the punters how much they'd be paid for it. Doughty waited by the door, opening it to let each person out, joking with each of them like Santa in a toy store. Once the last straggler had left he led Robinson through to the back office.

The dimly lit room consisted of a desk and a chair, a small flat screen television fixed onto a far wall, a filing cabinet and another chair, currently occupied by a pasty-faced man with a shaved head, DIY tattoos on the back of each knuckle. Alarmed, the man sprang to his feet, the instinct to bolt obviously never leaving him. 'I couldn't see her outside, Dale,' Doughty reassured him, holding his smile in check, 'but you're better leaving through the back door just in case.'

It was clear this was a regular occurrence, without need for directions Dale moved towards the neighbouring room, pausing before pushing down the door release bar.

'What about my money?' he asked without a shred of embarrassment.

Doughty reached into his pockets and found three ten-pound notes which he handed over. 'Look, I'll give you this in good faith,' he said magnanimously, 'there's not much call for old PlayStations now but seeing as it's you...Now bugger off home and make sure you feed them kids.' Dale nodded, pocketing the money gratefully before scarpering. Robinson shook his head. How many men like Dale thought selling their kids toys was the only route out of the rut they were living in – and he knew damn well the money Doughty had given to Dale wouldn't be going into the tills of a supermarket any time soon.

Doughty grinned at Robinson like he'd done a good thing.

Robinson stared right back.

'Right then, officer,' Doughty said lightly, 'What can I do for you?'

Robinson moved to the seat Dale had vacated, lowered himself into it without waiting to be asked. 'I'd have thought,' he began, 'that having had your car stolen, you'd have been keen to find out if we'd caught the little buggers.'

Doughty, who'd been leaning against his desk, lifted a buttock as though his backside had gone numb, either that or he was quietly passing wind. 'Well yeah,' all flustered now, 'of course I'd want to know, but it's not like it'll be up there on your list of priorities, like you'd be pulling out all the stops on my account,' he paused, making eye contact with Doughty then glancing away again, 'Don't tell me you've got 'em?'

Robinson smiled his best wind up smile and leaned back in his chair. 'Care to explain why your face tells me that's the *last* thing you'd like to happen?'

Chapter 17

Alex licked the icing from her fingers, reminding herself that there were perks to being pregnant after all; it seemed to bring out the nurturing gene in the officers around her. They brought her drinks and sweets like pagan offerings which she accepted gratefully, no point in cutting your nose off to spite your face. Todd Oldman entered the CID room making a beeline for her desk. He seemed surprised to see her sitting there.

'I've not gone on leave yet,' she scolded him, motioning with her hand for him to pull a chair over from one of the other desks. It was late and the room was deserted bar the two of them. Alex was staying late, waiting to see how Robinson had got on at the Pawnbrokers with James Doughty. She was tired and hungry, but the sugar lift she'd just had would keep her going.

Her filing had all but disappeared, she noted appreciatively, although there were signs that Oldman was setting up his stall ready for her departure. He'd begun treating her desk like his own, eating at it, drinking at it, she shuddered to think what else he might be doing to mark his territory. She tried to reign in her irritation every time she found herself clearing empty Coke cans away that he'd left behind but she wasn't his bloody mother.

He wasn't so bad, she reminded herself, he was just finding his feet. She'd had worse stuff left on her desk over the years: Porno Valentines cards, her desk tidy filled with pens showing naked women if you turned them upside down. Stuff of adolescence, a period her colleagues seemed permanently stuck in. None of it was personal, she was partial herself to telling bloke jokes and discussing the merits of Gerard Butler over Max Beesley to anyone who'd listen, it was part of the banter that kept their head above ground when the cases they worked on threatened to drag them under. There were times when a case was so harrowing it really did matter who was voted off Big Brother, who they thought was going to be in the X-Factor final. They were distractions, coping mechanisms. A way of keeping sane when the world around them clearly wasn't.

All she had to do to keep Oldman out of her hair for the next few days was to keep him busy. A couple of weeks and he'd no longer be her problem; she'd have her hands full with a more demanding little person. Still, somewhere deep inside it rankled that she was being replaced by a much younger model at a time when she felt clumsy and vulnerable – what if he settled in so well no one missed her at all?

'Ma'am?'

Oldman was asking her something but she hadn't been listening.

'I've prepared the report on James Doughty like you asked; I can run through it with you now if you have time?' Alex looked at her watch, hadn't realised it was way past the end of his shift.

She smiled appreciatively while shooing him away. 'You've done well on your first day kiddo, you're allowed to have a life, you know,' she paused as though giving her words some thought, 'for a while anyway.'

He didn't move, instead he swept his gaze over her desk as though looking for something. Whatever it was hadn't been left *there*, she thought irritably, she'd have noticed.

'Lost something?' She asked him.

'Er, you haven't seen an ice -' he stopped abruptly, his eyes locked onto the tell-tale wrapper in her wastepaper basket. 'Nothing,' he mumbled, backing away, 'I'll see you tomorrow.' He turned so quickly he almost collided with Robinson.

Alex's face flushed scarlet. 'I'll buy you one back.' She called out but he'd gone.

'You alright, Ma'am?' Robinson asked.

'Oh,' Alex squirmed, 'just wondering precisely when I morphed into Coupland. Anyway,' she said, brightening up, 'I've been waiting to hear how you got on.'

Robinson ran through his visit to the pawnbrokers.

'Doughty's got a mate in the car business.' He began, 'Reckoned he could get him a decent car no more than cost.' Robinson looked at Alex, shrugging his shoulders as he did so. 'Nothing wrong in that I'll grant you. So he hands over his dosh – cash only, of course – gets the Subaru in return.'

'And ?'

'Some time later this mate phones him suggesting he might want to trade up, got a cracking coupla' motors come in, would suit him down to the ground.'

"Do you think I'm made o' money?" Our fella moans, "The missus will have my bollocks for earplugs. I'll stick with this one, thanks."'

'Only it never works like that does it?' Alex prompted, wishing not unkindly he'd get to the point. Her feet were sore and she wanted to check on Ben's homework while her brain cells were still working.

'"What are mates for?" his pal says, "I'll shift your old one faster than you can say 'Where do I sign?' and we're all happy as Larry."'

Alex pricked up her ears, sighing inwardly at the increased volume of paperwork – this case was expanding faster than her dress size.

'So Doughty's mate arranged for the car to be stolen?' she clarified, 'So Doughty could claim on the insurance and buy this other motor.'

Turnbull nodded.

'Well, it's not like he's averse to breaking the law,' Alex informed him, skim-reading the report Oldman left on her desk. 'Sent to a young offenders' institute in his teens following two counts of car theft.'

'So the guy who lifted the motor – he's in on the scam, right? Taking motors to order.'

Robinson nodded again. 'Gets a fee for his expenses, so to speak.' It was Alex's turn to nod. 'Only he doesn't stop there, does he?' Alex spoke slowly as she unravelled the thread, 'There's plenty of call for knocked-off motors, especially if they're to be used as a getaway vehicle, why pass up the chance to hand Doughty's Subaru to a grateful new – albeit temporary – owner. All for an additional fee of course.'

Alex pushed herself to her feet. 'I'd better take this through to the boss.' She sighed inwardly, by the time she got home Ben's history project would be a cut and paste job from the Internet.

'What's the name of the garage?'

Robinson pushed his notepad across the desk for her to copy down the name and address of the owner. She pushed it back to him without bothering to write it down.

'I already have it.' She informed him, thinking of a particular conversation she'd had earlier in the day.

Mallender was pre-occupied. Even though Coupland was following up employees who'd lost their jobs whilst working for Ashraf Zadawi he knew it was a long shot. Disgruntled staff made nuisance calls or stalked the premises to vent their anger; they seldom resorted to shooting someone, a complete stranger at that. It didn't make sense. Mallender felt as though he was searching in a haystack for the world's tiniest needle; the team were doing as he asked, more even, yet none of their actions had amounted to finding a real lead. Meanwhile Superintendent Curtis was waiting upstairs for an update, one that at this rate would involve him explaining why he hadn't found the killer yet.

It occurred to him that he spent most of his life disappointing someone – from his heartbroken mother to the families of victims, often trampling on their loved ones' memories to get a result. He tried to think of the last time someone was pleased to see him.

Alex Moreton stepped into his line of vision with a huge smile which startled him. 'Alex,' he said briskly, his eyes dropping to her stomach, 'I'm needed upstairs in a minute, can it keep?'

'You'll want to hear this, Sir.' She replied looking pleased with herself and Mallender felt the first stirrings of anticipation build inside him. Could this be the break he was looking for? 'In that case you can stay,' he said smiling, pointing to the chair in front of his desk. 'take the weight off your feet,' he added before flinching, 'or am I not supposed to say that?'

'It's fine.' Alex grinned, sinking into the seat gratefully. She told him about Doughty's involvement in the theft of his own car, that the garage owner who initiated the theft was the same individual Aston Baptiste - the boyfriend of their key witness - had worked for when he was sent down for cloning cars several years earlier.

'Billy Peters?' Mallender said aloud, 'I remember hearing about the size of the surveillance operation that brought that ring down,' he informed Alex, 'Overtime alone nearly crippled the Division.'

Alex nodded.

'How come Billy wasn't picked up alongside Aston at the time?' she asked.

Mallender pulled a face like he'd tasted something bitter, 'Teflon coated I heard,' he said, 'he claimed this lad - Aston Baptiste - was working independently and since no one could uncover any evidence to the contrary, they had to let Billy Peters go.'

'Like it was feasible for a sixteen year old to have the resources and contacts to bring stolen cars back to the garage, duplicate their ID numbers onto identical vehicles with their boss none the wiser.' Alex sneered.

'Pretty much sums it up.' Mallender confirmed.

Alex considered this.

'Billy Peters is still lifting cars right under our nose,' she observed, 'must be starting to feel he's untouchable. Why don't we pay him a visit, rattle him a little, keep an eye on him for 24 hours to see who he goes running to.'

Mallender agreed. 'You need to pass this on, Alex,' he said tentatively, hoping to avoid a confrontation. 'You're on desk duty, remember.'

'I know, I know.' She acknowledged, relieved at the prospect of not spending another day on her feet.

'Can you assign it first thing?' Mallender asked, glancing at his watch, relieved he had some positive news to relay to Curtis. They still didn't know who the shooter was, but James Doughty had unwittingly provided them with a precious link. 'Coupland can follow this up, Robinson can be his wing man, take turns with surveillance.'

'Actually,' Alex paused, pulling herself to her feet just as a Braxton Hicks contraction caused her to suck in her breath. She waved away Mallender's look of alarm. 'Might be worth letting my mini-me give Coupland a hand.' She said, thinking of Todd Oldman's eager face, his schoolboy's interest in cars.

Mallender looked at her quizzically.

'Mini-me?' He asked, trying not to look at her stomach which was eye-level now she was standing.

'I suspected as much,' she said wryly, returning to her seat while she updated him on Todd Oldman's arrival.

Mallender took the short walk to Superintendent

Curtis' office mentally working his way through the possible scams going on in Billy Peters' garage. Why would a car salesman be willing to sell cars off at cost? *We may be in a recession but he's still got a living to make,* Mallender muttered, *unless he's a sodding charity.* Of course if he suspected money laundering he'd be obliged to hand it over to the National Crime Agency but right now his prime interest was finding out who Peters had paid to steal Doughty's car – and more importantly who it was passed onto after that.

He knocked twice on the Super's door before entering. Ignoring the hostile look that greeted him for not waiting for right of entry he spoke at a point just above Curtis' head. 'Thought you might want to hear this straight away, Sir.' He began.

By the time Alex returned home all evidence of homework had been tidied away. Ben acknowledged her smugly; he'd completed his work without her help and was now playing fantasy football on the X-Box. He looked over from his position on the sitting room floor and grinned, the way children do when they've been granted access to a bone of contention.

Seeing the serious look on Alex's face Ben lowered his eyes. 'Dad said it was OK.' he offered up in mitigation before she'd even opened her mouth. Since when had she become the resident Killjoy? She hurried over to plant a kiss on the top of his head, 'It's OK sweetie,' she reassured him just as Carl called through that dinner would be ready in half an hour. 'Right,' she said, dumping her bag on the sofa and lowering herself onto the footstool so she could remove her shoes with ease. 'Pass me the other controller, Ben. Prepare to be amazed!'

After dinner Alex found herself caught up in the usual routine of bath time and bed. It was her turn to read to Ben, he had a book on dinosaurs he was particularly fond of and she'd mastered all the names, had a knowledge of leaf eaters and meat eaters that would put David Attenborough to shame. Eventually as his eyelids began to droop, she returned the book to its place on his bedside table in case he woke up in the night and wondered where it had got to. She nuzzled the top of his head, breathing in his little boy smell.

Carl was in the kitchen designing a stencil of the planets he wanted to paint in the baby's room. She leaned over his shoulder as he sat at the table. 'Not bad.' She observed a little grudgingly, she didn't have a creative bone in her body. 'Is that Pluto?'

'That's not even a planet anymore.' He corrected. 'It was relegated.' He pointed to a book on the Solar System he'd borrowed from the library, he'd propped it open so that its centre pages fell open to display a range of rocks around the sun with names she could barely pronounce. It wasn't the solar system she remembered from school, had the earth moved into another galaxy when nobody was looking? 'It's life, Carl,' she conceded, 'but not as I remember it.'

She put a pan of milk on the stove, spooned generous heaps of powdered chocolate into two mugs. It was this time of night, when Ben was no longer around to distract her, that she found it hard to prevent parts of the day, conversations that she'd had, seep back into her mind. She found herself raking over the conversation she'd had with Aston, a man trying hard to create a better future for himself following the mistakes of his past.

Aston had learned the hard way that possibilities were the first casualty of prison life. Even men who served a few months or a couple of years soon worked out that the options in their lives had diminished along with their privacy. Before, they might have hoped for good jobs, now they could only expect labouring or the dole.

'But I was lucky,' Aston had insisted, 'I got a placement in a decent garage while I was on parole, they gave me a chance to prove myself, decided to keep me on.' He was so determined to turn his life around. And yet.

Alex sighed. She was too loyal to the job to say it out loud but she was glad she was leaving at the end of next week. She was tired, but it wasn't just a physical state, she felt bogged down by the eagerness of certain folk to be cruel to their fellow men. Keen to take the profit but none of the balls to take the blame. She wanted time out from that, to believe in fairy-tales and dinosaurs and learn about planets she'd never even heard of.

She was brought back to the present by the sound of milk bubbling over the side of the pan, forming brown stains around the gas ring, reminding her of dried blood.

Chapter 18

Tuesday morning in the Incident Room. Four days after the fatal shooting outside Ego nightclub.

'We've uncovered a new development.' Alex began, 'Which may start to open this whole investigation up.' She described to the assembled team the scam James Doughty had been trying to pull regarding his stolen car, and Billy Peters' involvement.

'Seems he's up to his old tricks again,' she added, 'But he's slippery, he sees us coming and manages to wriggle away every time. Kevin, can you go and have a man to man chat with him, and if that doesn't work keep an eye on him for 24 hours, see if he can lead us to the next piece of the jigsaw.'

Coupland nodded, turning to give Robinson the thumbs up. Robinson had found the lead; it made sense to buddy up with him.

'Thought kiddo could go with you.' Alex added quickly, glancing at Oldman in time to see his face light up. 'Just…' she paused long enough to glare in Coupland's direction, 'just be bloody gentle with him, alright?'

'Any clues from the car itself?' Robinson asked. The vehicle had been found torched behind a row of garages on the Tattersall estate two nights before. 'Forensics couldn't find anything.' Alex replied, 'This person knew what they were doing.' She was referring to the even way the petrol had to have been distributed around the vehicle to destroy any tell-tale DNA. This was looking more and more like a professional ring.

Coupland read out his ballistics report, assigning Turnbull and Robinson the task of tracking down the gun the bullet came from. He smiled at Oldman amiably. He enjoyed the banter that came with working with a familiar face, the insider knowledge that meant they could communicate in shorthand, but the prospect of imparting his wisdom onto a new kid on the block was appealing. No eye-rolling because they'd heard it all before, no back chat because they knew better, what wasn't there to like?

'Not a patch on you, Alex.' Coupland quipped when he caught her looking wistfully after Oldman who had dressed casually in a leather jacket and black jeans, more Gaultier today than Hugo Boss. She smiled in surprise at Coupland's kindness only for the smile to freeze when he quipped: 'Doesn't have your legs for a start.'

'You will be easy on him won't you?' she blurted, resenting the fact it made her sound like a clucky hen. 'He's polite, articulate, doesn't feel the need to scratch his genitals in public, please bring him back the way you found him.'

Coupland chuckled, searching Alex's face for that tell-tale trace of humour that told him she was joking. She stared right back.

In the drive over to Billy Peters' garage on the other side of Salford Coupland alternately quizzed Oldman on his background and interests while filling him in on his own domestic set up.

'Got a daughter not much younger than you.' He informed him. 'She's our only one but a handful all the same.'

Oldman laughed at the look on Coupland's face as he said this. 'There's five of us.' He said, 'I'm the oldest, I've a sister in uni, the rest are in senior school, primary and nursery.' He saw the question flit across Coupland's face unasked. 'No,' he smiled, 'we're not a religious family and yes, we do have a television, my parents just can't seem to get enough of dirty nappies.'

'Jesus,' Coupland observed, 'must be bloody chaos in your house.'

'I wouldn't know, would I?' Oldman reasoned, 'I've no idea what normal's like.'

As Coupland slung his Mondeo onto the kerb beside Billy Peter's garage, an oversized Doberman came bounding out of a side door.

'You get some warm welcomes in this job.' Coupland muttered.

The garage comprised of a car lot out front containing half a dozen nearly new cars and a workshop behind where not a soul could be seen. The interior of the garage was lit up by an array of lamps in differing sizes. Set into railway arches the radio was turned up loud to mask the rumble of overhead freight trains. They wandered into the garage's interior to the strains of Ellie Goulding, picked the best vantage point to wait for Peters to emerge.

A man dressed in clean overalls appeared in the doorway behind them. 'Can I help you, gents?' he asked, friendly enough.

'Billy Peters?' Coupland called out, and he could tell the way the man's face shut down he was right first time. 'Show the nice man your warrant card.' He instructed Oldman though more for effect, as the rookie's ID hung round his neck on a chain like a council official. Coupland rummaged in his pocket for his own card, held it up for a nano-second. Small talk out of the way, he got to the point: 'Hear you're doing your bit for the environment Billy.' He said evenly.

Billy Peters was a hefty, muscular man, the kind that caused damage if you got on the wrong side of him. Coupland held his ground. 'What d'you mean?' Billy challenged, his affable salesman demeanour replaced by a scowl. 'I mean, Billy,' Coupland explained patiently, moving into the other man's space, 'that a car you sold recently has just been stolen.'

Peters moved his shoulders in a *What the fuck* shrug. 'And that has something to do with me because..?'

'Because you'd virtually sold the owner another car before his old one had rolled off the drive.'

'Must be psychic or something.' Peters said flippantly.

'You'll be able to tell me what your next cell mate looks like then,' Coupland volleyed, 'When we nail you for theft. All it would take is for the CPS to link you to the cloning syndicate that you walked away from five years ago and you'd be doing serious time.'

Peters picked dirt from beneath his nails. His hands were wide, knuckles misshapen, the skin on his fingers were chapped. There was a homemade tattoo of a swallow on the back of his right hand.

'Are we done yet?' he asked, 'or do I need to call my solicitor?'

'Help me out Billy,' Coupland soothed, 'All I need to know is who nicks the bloody cars. Otherwise you'll have me wondering why you want to protect them.'

Peters shrugged, but Coupland could tell he had rattled him. He pulled a photo of Doughty's Subaru out of his pocket. 'All I'm bothered about is this car. Who did you get to steal it?' Peters' face was impassive as he walked over to what looked like an oversized cubby hole that was being used as a combined office come kitchen; a young man slouched on a PVC swivel chair, his fingers rattling across a lime green smartphone.

'Dale!' He called out. 'Have you got a minute?'

Chapter 19

Osman's kebab shop had a dining area that resembled a typical interview room at Salford Crescent station: Pokey. Functional. Not entirely clean. No one ever ate in there; the whole point of a kebab was that the pissed or those working towards it could eat while on the move.

Today was a first. Coupland took a seat politely, not wanting to embarrass Oldman by telling him the tops probably hadn't been wiped down since being installed; Alex's words about being kind to the boy rang in his ears. Stifling a smile as the young DC leafed through the sticky menu Coupland raised an eyebrow at Osman's brother. 'Usual Kamal,' he called out, 'all the trimmings, mate.' The Turk nodded and set about the rotisseried lamb like a serial killer practising his craft.

'Osman not around?'

'Cash and Carry followed by the bloody bookies going by the length of time he's been away.'

Coupland nodded his approval.

'So you're a regular then.' Oldman observed, scanning the menu, 'Only you seemed keen to bring us here.' Coupland nodded. 'The owner – not the guy behind the counter now but his brother – he saw the car involved in the shooting. I like to call in when I can, check he's not lost his bottle, being a witness and all.' He didn't want to add that he'd have called in anyway, his blood sugar demanded it at least a couple of times a week. Oldman nodded. 'So did he get a good look at the shooter?'

Coupland shook his head. 'Only enough to confirm he was black, wore street colours too.'

'Which?'

'Red and Green.'

Oldman nodded his head like the colour scarves the gang members wore made some statement about their psyche, that of all the gangs in the vicinity those that wore red and green were predetermined to become killers. Coupland swept his eyes over the rookie as he struggled through the menu. He reminded him of a young Mallender, far more upmarket than the rest of the officers at the station. Like the DCI this kid was a breed apart. The only scarf he'd ever worn was the black and gold of Bridgewater, the private school in Worsley Mallender had attended as a child. Only *he'd* boarded. Always weird that, Coupland thought. To board at school in a town where your family lived. Didn't add up. He'd hinted as much when Mallender had told him but the DCI had frozen him out. The boss didn't make small talk; reminiscing about his childhood whether it was good or crap was never going to happen. The snippets of information he had gleaned were when Mallender let his guard down while Coupland ferried him around and always seemed to be followed by regret. Coupland shrugged, nodded at Kamal as he brought over his kebab and uttered the immortal three words: *On the house.*

'If you value your arsehole,' Coupland warned Oldman, chuckling, 'Stay away from the chillies.' He almost felt sorry for him, having to spend the afternoon with him couped up in the car. Kamal flicked a glance at Oldman who dropped his eyes and muttered 'Still looking.' There was a gentleness about him that hinted at growing up in a home where voices were never raised in anger. Placid. Polite to the point of painful. Coupland felt like the ghost of Policing Past as he stared at the future of the modern service, where scrotes were caught through DNA and technology rather than cunning and brute force. All very well until you're backed up some alley with a balloon head with HATE inked across his forehead,

Coupland mused. He sighed, the truth of it dawning on him.

'You're a bloody vegetarian aren't you?'

Oldman swallowed the last of the cheese and tomato toastie they'd picked up from a sandwich shop on the way back to Coupland's car. Coupland stifled a smile as the rookie folded the paper bag it had come in into half, then half again before placing it in his pocket. 'Like saving the planet do you kid?' he asked good-naturedly as he unlocked the car and lowered himself into the driver's seat.

'I like to do my bit,' Oldman agreed, declining the offer of a cigarette reminding Coupland once more that he didn't smoke.

'You just haven't started yet, kid.' Coupland joked, like there was a difference.

'So what did you make of our Dale then?' He asked Oldman, referring to Billy Peters' mechanic who'd owned up to stealing Doughty's Subaru on the night of the shooting.

'You think he'd come up with something better than he sold it to a bloke in a pub!'

'We know he's done time for Twoc'ing in his teens,' Coupland added, 'once you've been inside you attract other cons like a magnet, chances are it'll be someone already known to us so it won't be that hard to track them down.'

Oldman leaned away from Coupland's exhaled smoke, wafting clouds of it out of his passenger window: 'I don't see why we can't just bring him in, interrogate him until he gives up the information we need.'

'So that's how it works, eh?' Coupland laughed, though not unkindly. This over-keen fella reminded him of himself twenty years back, desperate to make the world a better place in his first week.

'Things have changed over the years, son.'

Coupland reminded him. 'We're a service now, not a force, and that impacts on the way we go about things,' he explained patiently, trying hard to conceal the fact he didn't believe a word of it. Alex'd never forgive him if he corrupted the kid in one fell swoop. Anyway, Oldman was part of the incoming generation; it *was* going to be harder for them, always on the back foot, minding their P's and Q's while the criminals ran rings round them.

'We gather evidence, we build a case, we don't rush in gung-ho anymore,' he added, 'Joe Public's too well aware of his rights.' Jesus, thought Coupland, if Alex could hear me now.

'So what do we do?' Oldman asked impatiently and Coupland would have been lying if he didn't admit it felt great to have someone hanging onto his every word. Experience told him it wouldn't last long, that this kid was one more in the steady stream that would overtake him over the next couple of years. He accepted it now, in the same way some people have to accept a harelip or a clubfoot.

'Tonight we keep our eye on Billy Peters. He's the gaffer; he knows damn well what goes on under his roof.'

'And Dale?'

'We put Dale's details through CRIMMINT,' he explained to Oldman, 'see where that takes us. In the meantime we set up stall near the garage and see who Billy heads off to when he knocks off for the night.'

'But it was Dale who took the motor,' Oldman persisted, 'he's the one who passed it onto the killers.'

Coupland nodded. 'Under orders.' He added, as if making a point. 'Look,' he placated, 'we don't find what we're looking for with Billy then we go after Dale. Let's just see who his boss leads us to first.'

'We already know he has a record,' Coupland pulled a face as if to convey that went without saying about men like Billy, 'so we track down his associates. These guys don't work alone – they need a network.

Whether it's a look-out or a mate that's connected, they don't work in isolation.' He caught a look flicker in Oldman's eyes.

'The same goes for us, Tonto,' he emphasised, 'We do everything by the book so that when we catch this shooter – and we will – he'll go away for a long time.' He stared at Oldman to make his point, 'Okay?'

Oldman didn't even blink. 'Who's Tonto?'

It was still light by clocking off time. Coupland and Oldman, parked some distance from the lock up, watched Billy secure the yard before heading towards a Hyundai parked out front. He handed Dale a wad of notes before telling him to keep his head down, not cause him any more fuckin' bother. Dale, seemingly oblivious to Peters' rebuke, headed in the opposite direction.

Coupland waited while Billy's Hyundai pulled out onto the main road before starting the Mondeo's ignition.

'Are you sure we can't follow Dale?' Oldman attempted, like a kid hell bent on getting his own way.

'Billy's our target.' Coupland reminded him. 'I don't wanna lose the bugger before we've even started.'

Coupland pulled into the flow of traffic two cars behind Billy's car, staying close to the rear of the vehicle in front in case the traffic lights at the junction ahead went against him. As they entered the dual carriageway that headed into town Coupland moved into the outside lane slipping behind Billy when he signalled he was taking the next exit onto Pendlebury Road.

'Any idea where he's going?'

Coupland shrugged. 'I think we're about to find out.' He replied, pulling sharply into a parking bay behind Billy outside a row of mid rent shops selling cheap women's clothes and off-cuts of carpet. Billy climbed out of his car and walked purposefully towards a pawnbrokers at the end of the row.

Chapter 20

James Doughty was busy counting notes at his desk when a text arrived on his phone telling him his mate was waiting to be let in. He moved the cash into a drawer before going through to the front of the shop, peering through the glass to be certain it was Billy before drawing back the lock.

'Hello Jim.'

Doughty nodded, locking the door behind Billy and signalling for him to go through to the back room. He followed Billy through, returning to his seat he pulled out the cash from his desk drawer and continued to count it. 'Just give me a minute,' he said, his fingers moving swiftly through the notes. He recorded his takings on a piece of paper, put the paper and cash in his pocket.

Ignoring the empty seat opposite Doughty, Billy Peters perched on the edge of his desk, all the more easy to intimidate him like he used to when they were at school. Doughty wasn't really a mate, more a gopher, someone he could rely on to turn a blind eye, give him an alibi when needed. Usually anyway.

Billy studied his friend. 'Seems you've been speaking to the cops, Jim.'

'You have to report a car theft, Billy,' he began, 'It's how you claim on the insurance.'

'I know it's how you claim on the insurance, you fucktard,' Billy said menacingly, like they were in short trousers once more. His face was a savage twist; his breath came in noisy little bursts.

Doughty was having none of it, Billy playing the

hard man was a sure sign he was trying to cover his tracks. 'Fucktard?' he spat, 'My car was used in that shooting! What the hell have you got us mixed up in?'

'Nothing!' It was Billy's turn to be on the backfoot. 'Nothing for *you* to worry about anyway.'

'What's that supposed to mean?' Doughty looked at his friend in alarm, 'Don't tell me you knew what the car was going to be used for…'

Billy was looking decidedly shifty.

'Better you don't ask me any more questions then,' he said harshly, ''Cos I've a feelin' you won't like the answers.'

Coupland was fantasizing about a cold beer when Oldman's elbow brought his attention back to Billy Peters in time to see him leave the pawnbrokers with a man he took to be the proprietor given the painstaking way he locked up behind them.

'Reckon that's the guy who's Subaru was stolen?' Oldman asked. Coupland nodded, 'Well, if it isn't, it's a coincidence, and I stopped believing in them round about the time I caught my mother checking under my pillow to see if the Tooth Fairy had been.'

The men crossed over the road to a pub built on land where a monthly meat market used to be held, aptly named The Butchers.

'Now what do we do?' asked Oldman.

Coupland was tempted to say let's call in for a couple but he didn't have the full measure of Oldman yet, besides, he was a kid, likely as not to get carried away by the whiff of the barmaid's apron. Not that Ursula, the five foot ten shaven-headed bar manageress would thank Coupland for that analogy. She'd been known to drink many an off duty cop under the table during her regular lock-ins. Jesus, thought Coupland, please God let this be the night she sticks to legal licensing hours, it would be too cruel to mention if he had to sit outside here all night.

'We sit tight.' he said evenly.

Chapter 21

A boy in a beanie hat played an old guitar badly and sang 'Happy,' in a dull monotone. Beside him on the pavement a blanket displayed a collection of euros and dimes, the odd twenty pence piece scattered among them. A few drops of rain were breaking through from the clouds overhead causing passers-by to hasten their steps. Pulling her good coat around her Abby walked along the pavement wishing she'd let Aston accompany her after all. She could be too stubborn for her own good sometimes, but she was used to being the responsible one; found it hard to let people put themselves out for her. Aston had been shocked when she'd told him she was returning to work but what other option did she have? She couldn't stay hidden away in her room forever. 'Let me borrow a car from work, I'll take you in,' he'd offered, but she'd turned him down flat, 'This is something I've got to do on my own,' she'd said foolishly.

One bus journey later and already Abby was having second thoughts. Every time a car stopped at the traffic lights she found herself staring at the passengers, wondering whether one of them was going to pull a gun on her. She tried to rid herself of morbid thoughts by being rational, asking herself what were the chances of lightning striking twice. The truth was she'd never known the answer to that, so instead of feeling reassured she felt on edge.

A Mondeo slowed to a halt as she used the pedestrian crossing, she caught the eye of the driver. His face was familiar but it was only as he waved at her to wait while he pulled in sharply on a set of double yellow lines that she realised he was the detective investigating Becca's murder. Abby walked towards the car, secretly pleased to see someone she knew, however vaguely.

'Hey,' she smiled as Coupland climbed out of his car, leaning against the driver's door with his hands in his pockets.

'Think it needs a bit of a clean,' she commented, taking in the dirty bodywork, mud spattered wheels and cluttered interior. 'What's the point?' he quipped, 'It'll only get filthy again.'

Abby's face turned serious. 'I'm going back to work today.'

'You sure you're ready?' Coupland asked, alarmed. They'd made no inroads on the killer; he wasn't entirely comfortable with her leaving the safety of her home. She rolled her eyes like he was the thousandth person to have said that to her today and it wouldn't make any difference now.

'Is there a prescribed time for these things?' she asked him, raising her hands helplessly, 'a statute of limitations I can refer to: "return to work after three weeks," "erase best friend from memory after six months"?' Coupland shook his head; he hadn't meant that at all.

'You've suffered a huge shock,' he began to explain, 'and that takes time to work its way out of the system. Just don't expect too much.'

'I'll be all right because I have to be,' She said firmly, 'too many people rely on me being strong. Weakness is a privilege, a luxury I can't afford.'

'At least let me see you into your office safely,' he insisted.

Abby smiled though it didn't fool him. 'I'll be fine,' she said, shaking her head, 'I'll get on with my job,' she said lightly, 'so you can focus on yours.'

Coupland stayed by his car watching Abby walk up

the street. Her body language had given lie to her words; there was no lift in her step. She moved cautiously, like she was working her way across quicksand.

Abby stopped a couple of yards from her office and leaned her head against a lamppost. She didn't really want to go back to work, she wanted to stay in the flat and cry. That's all she felt good for, sobbing for her lost friend, for the future Becca had been deprived of, for the future they would have shared. But what good would it do? In the grand scheme of things what use would she be to her mother and brothers if she gave in to her sorrow?

Well-meaning friends called round with self-help books ranging from dealing with survivor guilt to overcoming grief. Abby had only flicked through a couple of them but she got the gist: There was nothing she could have done to prevent the killer from taking Rebecca's life, but she must do everything in her power to stop him taking hers too.

Chapter 22

When Alex called Aston on his mobile asking if they could meet again, she wasn't sure how he'd react. Instead of a surly reply he'd been quite amenable, agreeing to meet in the community centre once more saving Alex the hike of the stairwell and him the trip across town in his lunch hour. He'd arrived there first, had already dragged a plastic chair into the back room for her.

'So what's your current boss like?' she asked him, straight to the point.

'Um,' Aston shrugged, 'OK I s'pose.'

Alex nodded her encouragement. 'He's legit though,' she persisted. 'He's not had you involved in anything untoward?'

Aston shook his head. 'He's cool,' he reassured her, 'for a boss. You think I'm gonna make the same mistakes I made when I was a kid?' His brow furrowed as he tried to work out whether she was trying to trip him up.

Alex paused, weighing up her words before she said them. 'I know you've learned the hard way,' she began, 'but it's hard when you first get out, right? Must be tempting to go back to old friends, revert to old ways.'

Aston tutted as though she was slow catching on. He'd already told her about the main players on the street; didn't that prove he'd moved away from all that, that he didn't see the old crew in the same light anymore? 'That's why I had to give Pauly and them a wide berth.' He said, animated now. 'They don't care about you, just what you can do for them. Only it took me going inside to realise that.' He paused, as though weighing up whether to tell her the rest of it. 'He has mates inside, you know, mates that can get you anything you want. A mobile, skunk, coke. If you're one of Pauly's boys you get looked after.'

Alex hadn't realised this Pauly's reach was so long.

'And did you let them look after you?'

Aston shook his head. 'No!' he persisted, 'That's my point. From the moment I went inside I knew I'd made a big mistake but I learned from it. I wasn't gonna let them drag me down even further. I knew that turning down what he was offering would set me apart. Pauly don't like that, he likes to give you stuff, just so you owe him. Only you can be sure that what he wants in return will cost you more.'

'So your old boss, Billy Peters, he never got in touch?'

'That's not how it works. If you live on Pauly's manor, or even run a business on his manor, you don't do anything without his say-so first. It was Pauly who got me the job at Billy's in the first place, Pauly who put the dodgy work his way. He controls it all. He has spies, little kids who don't know any better, gives 'em mobile phones, tells 'em to let him know if anyone trespasses on his patch.'

Aston stalled, as though he'd forgotten his lines, looked about the room helplessly. 'When I got out of jail Pauly sent for me, told me he heard I'd been uncooperative inside, but no matter, he could afford to let me go. He told me he had a new soldier now, one he'd been grooming during my time inside – my kid brother Earl. I knew then that he'd won, that he might not have me to run his dirty errands any more but he'd gained my silence, I'm hardly going to interfere, do anything to rumble his activities if it means shopping my own brother am I?'

'No.' Alex replied sympathetically.

'So the point I'm making is that Billy approaching

me direct when I got out of prison would have been a sign of disrespect, Pauly would have cut him adrift. As it was, Pauly had fixed him up with another lackey as soon as I was sent down.'

'Who?'

'Dale Brown. He's been with Billy ever since. Brother of a woman Pauly was knocking off at one time. He'd run up gambling debts all over town and that's what Pauly thrives on – a weakness that gives him power – whether an addiction to the horses, drugs, whatever, it doesn't matter but once he discovers it he's got you.'

'Besides,' he added, 'Dale's got a better temperament than me, won't ask too many questions.'

'We think Dale stole the motor used in Becca's shooting.' Alex said as softly as she could.

'*What?*' Aston's mouth twisted out of shape as he tried to spit out more words. Questions she wouldn't be able to answer. He'd been slouching on a moulded plastic chair, now he jumped to his feet, stood ramrod straight like a squaddie. An angry squaddie ready to charge into battle. Alex raised a hand. 'We've no reason to suspect he had any involvement with the shooting,' She added quickly, 'nor that he knew the intended purpose for the car after he passed it on – you said yourself, he doesn't ask any questions. Look,' she added, 'I need to trust you to let us handle this. I'm putting a hell of a lot of faith in you by telling you this much – was I wrong to do that?'

'You can't expect me to do nothing!' he demanded.

'I expect you to let us get on with our jobs.'

'So why bother telling me?'

Alex had asked herself that question. There was a part of her, she hated to admit it, that had needed to test Aston's reaction, final proof he no longer ran with his old crowd. The problem now was what he was going to do with the information she'd given him.

'I came to ask you who you thought Dale could

have passed the stolen vehicle onto as he's remaining tight-lipped, or at least who could've helped take it off his hands.' She paused, 'but I've already got my answer to that, haven't I?'

Aston looked at his watch; he was due to meet Abby from the bus. His attention was shot. His mind working its way through a roll call of Pauly's associates, trying to work out who'd be dumb enough, or crazy enough, to kill someone to order.'Just one more thing,' Alex asked, 'why would a man like Billy Peters be happy to sell cars at cost?'

Aston shrugged. 'I ain't no accountant,' he said simply, 'maybe there's a tax dodge?'

Junior's attack of the hiccups caught Alex unawares. Absentmindedly she patted her stomach.

'When's the baby due?' Aston asked her.

'Next month.'

He smiled self-consciously. 'I remember when my sister was born I could hold her in the crook of my arm, she was so tiny!' He stopped abruptly, as though realising he'd steered off topic with a cop of all people. 'Next thing I know I'm banged up for two years and when I come home she takes one look at me and starts crying like I'm an intruder. I knew there and then I didn't ever want that to happen again.'

Alex pushed herself to her feet and picked up her bag. After retrieving her car keys from the debris at the bottom of it she paused to lay a hand on Aston's shoulder.

'We'll get whoever did this,' she said brightly, 'and then who knows, maybe you and that girlfriend of yours can think about having one of your own.'

During the short drive back to the station Alex's mind travelled back to Ben's birth, the look on her mother's face when she'd confessed she didn't want to go to the hospital alone after all. Carl had been gone eight months, volunteering in Africa, wouldn't know he was a father for another two years. The midwives kept telling her the labour had been quick for a first child though it hadn't seemed like it to her. She'd spent so much of her time proving herself – at police training college, as a probationer – that it'd seemed perfectly natural to hold off going to the hospital for as long as she could bear, ignoring each wave of pain that engulfed her just to prove she could. By the time her father had driven them to hospital she'd been close to collapse, not that she'd wanted to admit it. The last thing she remembered in the final hours before Ben was born was her screaming at a midwife: *Give me drugs, lots of them,* and her mother telling her to get a grip.

This birth would be different. For one thing Carl would be with her. Ben was to stay with Carl's parents and her mum and dad would drive over once the baby was born.

She wondered whether Carl knew quite what he was letting himself in for, her too for that matter. Did she really want him lapsing into the stand-up routine he resorted to whenever he felt out of his depth? Or wearing his comedy teeth when she was least expecting it? She'd planned on them going to a couple of ante-natal sessions at the hospital but her shifts had always clashed and in some subliminal way she'd been in no hurry to remind herself of what was to come. She'd dug out a couple of pregnancy books to show Ben, keep him involved along the way, maybe it was worth showing them to Carl too, so he could see what he was letting himself in for.

The CID room was quiet. Several DCs were following up the leads from Alex's first meeting with Aston Baptiste. She looked around for Oldman, she was getting used to seeing him about the place even though he signalled her temporary demise. Coupland was sitting at his computer, typing two-finger style and cursing under his breath.

'Where's kiddo?' she asked. She wondered how the pair of them had got on, hoped Oldman wouldn't return reeking of fags and swearing like a trooper, she didn't want to be responsible for sending him home to his mother like that.

Coupland nodded at the clock on the wall by Mallender's office. It was 6pm.

'Home time. Early parole for good behaviour.' He said. 'Told him to grab a coupl'a hour's sleep, though if I'd have thought on I could've got him to type this lot up first.' Coupland's clothing was dishevelled after a night sitting in a car, his face unshaven. He emitted a body odour sour enough to force Alex to move downwind of him before drawing another breath.

'How did you get on?'

'Me and Kiddo or us and Billy Peters?'

Alex shrugged. 'Both, I guess.'

'The kid's fine,' Coupland informed her. 'Got a good head on his shoulders. Hungry for action, needs reigning in a little but didn't we all at his age?'

'I was never his age.' Alex observed dryly.

'I know the feeling,' Coupland shot back, 'was I ever his shape?'

She let her eyes drop down deliberately to his paunch. 'Only in your head, Kevin.'

'I'll have you know I've worked hard to get this figure,' he retaliated, 'that amount of beer and food doesn't come cheap.'

'You're not wrong,' Alex agreed, 'no one can say you don't give your stomach the attention it deserves.'

Coupland smiled, 'It's a pleasure.' He pressed the print button on his PC before heading over to the shared printer. Alex rummaged in her bag for some change. 'Getting a cuppa, want one?' she asked before heading down the corridor to the vending machine. Coupland grunted a yes. Alex pushed the button for hot chocolate at the same time eyeing up a Crunchie in the neighbouring machine. *What the hell,* she thought defensively as she entered the correct money before pocketing the bar, *I'm worth it.*

'Slippery bastard, Peters.' Coupland began when she returned to the CID room. 'Claimed his lackey sold Doughty's stolen Subaru on of his own accord. You should have seen the kid, Alex. He didn't know what day of the bloody week it was. If I'd told him I was Santa come early he'd o' believed it.'

He held out the report he'd prepared for Mallender, gulping his coffee while Alex skimmed through it, ignoring the finger smudges and typos. Billy Peters' speciality was car crime in all its varieties; his skill was in recruiting young men desperate enough to carry out his dirty work. 'Funny how for a man who spent his youth behind bars,' Coupland began, 'and claims he's now gone straight he employs kids who've all gone on to be convicted of motor offences. What are the chances, eh?'

'What's the opposite of rehabilitation?' Alex observed, 'If there's a word for it, that's what this guy is doing.'

'Meaningless bloody word anyway,' grumbled Coupland, warming to his favourite theme, 'it exists only in the mind of the middle classes, helps them sleep better at night if they don't think we're all fucked…'

'So we're interested in Peters, not the kid?' Alex interrupted; keen to bring him back on track. This would at least concur with the information Aston had given her. Coupland sat and thought for a moment, picturing the lock-up and all its contents, Billy Peters in an overall yet not a spot of dirt on him.

'I know this sounds stupid, but the garage is all wrong… There's no real work being done in there. Something felt odd when I was there – and Kiddo felt it too - but I couldn't put my finger on what it was. Come to think of it the phone never rang while we were there, no one checking when their car would be ready…' no coffee mugs or food wrappers in sight either, nothing that gave the impression that either Billy Peters or Dale spent large amounts of time there. 'I don't dispute Peters buys and sells cars Alex,' Coupland concluded, 'but that's not how he makes his money.'

'He made a beeline straight to the pawnbroker's place - met with the owner after he locked up last night.' Coupland ran through the previous evening's events. 'Didn't stay long though. Him and Doughty both came out, went across the road for several pints, given the time they finally emerged.' Coupland failed to keep the longing from his voice. 'They came out on their own, had a smoke while they waited for a cab.'

'And then?'

'Doughty was dropped off at the entrance to the housing development at Ellenbrook – he's got a flat there – while Peters was dropped at a semi in Swinton, last we saw of him till he left for work the next morning.

'So he's big pals with Doughty, but then we already knew that.'

Coupland nodded. 'Dale was already at the garage when Peters arrived, slouched against the lock-up door like he was waiting to be told what to do next. The business is a front.'

'Laundering, then.'

Coupland nodded. 'But I'd go one step further and say Peters isn't the brains behind it.'

'What makes you say that?'

'He's low rent, likes to act the big man but he and Dale are window dressing. We just need to work out who's behind them…' Alex waddled to her desk, rubbing her bump as she did so. Pulling the report she'd written up on Pauly out of a file she was about to take to Mallender she brought it over to Coupland.

'You've shown me yours,' she said suggestively, 'the least I can do is show you mine.'

Chapter 23

Mallender read the files Alex and Coupland had compiled on Pauly and Billy Peters. 'Paul Constantine, 38. Been up on charges of attempted murder, kneecapping and dealing. Accused of murdering a rival dealer, Declan O'Leary outside his home in Whalley Range. At the time, O'Leary, 31, was serving an 11 year sentence for heroin dealing and was home on a three day leave from prison.'

'Nice.'

'I remember that.' Said Coupland, 'Back in 2010. Case fell apart when all the witnesses started contradicting each other. Bastard walked out of court laughing.'

'He used to work for Declan O'Leary senior, who'd befriended him after a firearms conviction. The old man took him on as a debt collector, or 'enforcer' as they're known in the trade. Only he saw the benefit of being the organ grinder and took over O'Leary's patch when he retired following his son's murder. He's a canny bastard,' Coupland added, 'he was acquitted of possessing crack cocaine after convincing a jury he was taking it to improve his skin.' Coupland shook his head as though he still couldn't believe it. 'How he got away with that I'll never know.'

Mallender pushed back his chair, pausing as though struck by a thought. 'There's no way round it now,' he said reluctantly. 'I'm going to have to take this upstairs, get a steer on how we're to proceed.'

'National Crime Agency?'

'Maybe.' Mallender replied regretfully, wondering what the hell Abby had got herself caught up in.

'If we show willing, reassure the powers that be that we're capable of playing ball, maybe they'll let us stay up a bit longer.'

Coupland's face told him he didn't believe a word of it. 'It's the best I can come up with,' Mallender shrugged. 'Though I can't be certain Curtis will feel the same.'

Curtis held eye contact with Mallender the entire duration of his phone call. Mallender stared right back.

'The Drug Squad are about to put Constantine under surveillance,' Curtis informed him when he replaced the receiver, 'want us to back off a bit, don't want to make him start looking over his shoulder. He's netting nearly £20,000 a week supplying virtually all the drugs in Salford.' There were thousands of injecting drug addicts in the town, this was a lucrative business.

'Seems the shooting was about protection after all,' Curtis observed, 'sending a warning out to rival suppliers, only it went badly wrong.'

Mallender shook his head. 'If we were looking at Paul Constantine on his own then I'd agree, but in conjunction with Billy Peters?' This guy's laundering money equivalent to the tune of one or two second hand sports cars a week. If we pull in his books I bet you'll find very few receipts.'

His thoughts jumbled around his head like patterns in a kaleidoscope.

'Maybe the shooting was intended as a warning all along.

'A warning for what?'

Mallender paused, 'I'm not sure, maybe Ashraf Zadawi owes money after all, money he's too frightened to tell his father about?'

'So what do you propose to do next?'

'Get a Production Notice issued for the garage accounts. Have a Forensic Accountant take a look through, see how well Billy's managed to cover his tracks. In the meantime, we'll give this Paul Constantine a wide berth.'

Curtis nodded, satisfied.

'But if his name continues to crop up,' Mallender warned, 'we'll have to bring him in for questioning.'

Curtis' mouth straightened into a thin line.

'Try not to push too many buttons, eh, Stuart?' Curtis asked, his features returning to their politician's grimace. The rare use of his first name wasn't lost on Mallender, the inference that this was a friendly warning.

'Message understood, Sir,' he responded, trying but failing miserably to return the smile.

Chapter 24

There was a point in the day when Abby thought someone was watching her. When she'd slipped out for a sandwich at lunch, she'd felt a presence, yet each time she looked around there wasn't anyone there. She spent several minutes window-shopping, certain that each time she looked at a store's display someone was standing behind her in the window's reflection. She stifled a shudder, pulling her coat around her. *Don't be stupid,* she scolded herself, *you're looking for trouble where there isn't any.*

Angela had been signed off on indefinite leave and the work was piling up. One of the senior partners had taken on the role of delegating tasks but he wasn't as familiar with what was a realistic work load for each junior staff member and spent a lot of his time asking what Abby thought were quite basic questions. He seemed interested in the smallest detail, was keen to know what each member of the office staff was responsible for and how each piece of work was signed off. This impeded how quickly they could handle enquiries and the other assistants warned Abby it was rare these days to get away on time.

No skin off my nose, Abby thought sadly, not like I'll be going out any time soon. She remembered her last day at work with clarity, counting down the hours until she was due to meet Becca, the night stretching before them with endless possibilities. Abby had half hoped Becca would meet someone that night, give her more of an incentive to return home at the weekends.

Not that it mattered now.

Mike Rogers returned to the office just before five

causing Abby's heart to sink. She might not be that bothered about staying on after work – but Mr Rogers was a stickler for detail and she didn't know if she was up to trawling through individual accounts to find the entries he'd been looking for earlier that day.

'Abby,' he called out to her as he walked by the main office before she'd had time to log out of her computer, 'would you mind coming up to the boardroom please?'

She noticed that he didn't have the files with him that he'd asked her to pull out for him before he'd left for his appointment. Client files weren't allowed to be kept off the premises overnight, so she assumed they must be in his car, either that or he was making the most of Angela's absence – she'd made the rule and insisted it was adhered to – as office manager the partners' bowed to the systems she put in place.

'Pointless having a dog and barking yourself,' she'd overheard Mike Rogers sneer to John Black on several occasions, which she hadn't thought was very nice, all things considered. Angela worked so hard for the firm, was often the last person to leave at night; the least she deserved was their respect. Abby pushed open the door leading to the grand oak panelled room to find both partners seated at one end of the vast polished desk. What on earth could they want with her that they couldn't have discussed downstairs in the main office?

Mike Rogers cleared his throat. 'We seem to have a problem.'

Abby rushed to the bus stop trying to make sense of the endless stream of questioning the partners had subjected her to. It was strange that they didn't speak to Angela, the one person who could put their minds at rest straight away. She looked at her watch, sighing; the inquisition had made her miss her usual bus, the later ones, caught up in the rush hour, weren't as reliable. She texted Aston to tell him she would be later than planned before ringing home to leave a message that her mother would hear from her room. The child-minder would be dropping the twins off any time now but they'd be happy to slump in front of the TV until Abby got home – Marion's presence would keep them out of mischief so there was no need for her to worry – just yet.

Finally a bus trundled into sight. About bloody time, Abby muttered to no one in particular as she swiped her pass over the ticket scanner before moving along the now full aisle pressing herself against the luggage rack. The vibration coming from her coat pocket told her someone was trying to reach her. She pulled out her mobile, glancing briefly at the caller display which told her the number was withheld. Placing her free hand over her other ear to block out background noise from the passengers beside her she hit the green button before lifting the phone to her ear.

'I know where you live, bitch.' A voice said before the line went dead.

Chapter 25

Coupland had powered down his computer and was starting to think about making tracks when the shrill ring of his desk phone startled him. He paused, sensing a shift in the room as though the earth's plates had moved just a little too fast. He swiped a hand across his brow as he spoke into the mouthpiece. Seconds later he grabbed his car keys before making his way unsteadily to his car.

Abby Marlowe's flat was ablaze.

He pushed his way through the crowd that had gathered around the entrance to Byron House, cursing under his breath. The usual ghouls and rubberneckers had come out, attracted by the flashing blue lights; several officers were working their way through the crowd dispersing anyone who didn't have a reason to be there.

On Coupland's instruction Abby had been collected from the bus stop where she'd arranged to meet Aston and was now under police escort in the relatives' room in A&E. An ambulance was preparing to take the twins to Hope Hospital suffering from second degree burns and smoke inhalation; Paramedics were still working on Abby's mother at the scene. 'Will she survive?' Coupland asked the paramedic waiting on standby. He looked at his colleague who merely shrugged; these were the hardest to call, where there were underlying health conditions which made matters worse.

Coupland had organised uniformed officers to collect names of the tower block's residents and arrange transfer to the local community centre, which would provide emergency shelter for the evening. Alex was on her way over, would work through the list getting everyone to account for their actions. 'Be surprised if you get any witnesses coming forward,' Coupland said out of earshot to Mallender as they stood by a squad car surveying the scene. Fire-fighters had managed to contain the fire within Abby's flat, had doused the flames and the Fire Investigation Officer was now conducting an initial inspection to determine the cause of the fire.

Mallender turned his attention to Coupland but said nothing. 'I mean,' Coupland continued, 'hell of a coincidence that a fire breaks out at the home of the chief witness to a shooting.

'Jesus,' Mallender muttered, shoving both hands deep into pockets in an attempt to protect him from the dropping temperature, whether the chill came from around him or within he couldn't be sure. 'They fire-bomb a house with kids in to send a *message* to their sister?' Coupland turned, fixed Mallender with an adrenaline-charged stare: 'We have ten year old boys who abduct a toddler leaving him for dead on a railway line. Men who fuck then murder their own children, mothers who drown their babies through fear. Should we be shocked that someone is trying to silence our witness by trying to cremate four year old twins?'

Mallender said nothing; he shook his head as though trying to make sense of what he was seeing.

'Whoever did this means business,' Coupland said to him, 'and if this *is* a warning I'm not sure who scares me most - the sender - or the messenger.

Chapter 26

Coupland moved through the A&E corridor like the Hounds of Hell were snapping at his heels. Ignoring the receptionist he collared a male nurse who'd tended to a friend of his a couple of months before. He could tell by the look on the man's face he remembered him, though not too fondly.

'Two boys in the tower block fire.' He barked, staring at the medic as though he was somehow complicit in their injuries.

'This way.' The nurse instructed, placing the face to the cop with the attitude that he'd got on the wrong side of once before. He led Coupland through a set of double doors, into a room packed with doctors standing around two small figures in neighbouring beds. Nursing staff filled in charts while a medical student took blood from the boys while they lay sedated attached to machinery helping them breathe. Coupland remained rooted to the spot, aware of the questioning glances several of the medical team sent in his direction but still he said nothing. His throat felt as though it had doubled in size. He felt a tap on his arm, turned to see the nurse who'd brought him through motioning for him to leave.

'They've had a lucky escape.' The nurse commented in an attempt at conversation. Coupland baulked at the word lucky but said nothing. He was sure as hell Abby wasn't feeling lucky at all at this moment. 'Their mother's on the way in,' He said bleakly, 'look after her, please,' as though his words would spur the nurse on to do the impossible. 'Their sister – is she in the relative's room?' Coupland asked. The nurse nodded, backing away. Coupland retraced his steps back through the double doors until he found the room he was looking for.

Abby sat dazed in the hospital relatives' room wondering if she was locked in some virtual nightmare that kept propelling her back to A&E. Aston had gone in search of a hot sweet tea for her when DS Coupland appeared in the doorway.

'Can I see them yet?' She asked.

'Soon.' Coupland said, pulling out his notebook and taking a chair beside Abby. 'I need to ask you a few questions first.' he began, mindful not to use the word *again*.

'Jesus! Don't you lot ever give up?' Aston snarled as he returned with Abby's tea and a bottle of orange for himself. 'She was at work. She wasn't even in the flat when the fire broke out. How the hell can you have any questions for her?' He had a point, which Coupland acknowledged with a nod, keeping the notebook on his lap anyway.

'Actually,' Abby began, as she was stuck by a notion that the conversation she'd had with her bosses that evening might be worth mentioning. 'There may well be something...'

By 8.30am the next morning Coupland had read the Fire Investigation Officer's initial report on the arson attack on Abby's home. He'd requested a faxed copy the night before and the FIO had been as good as his word. Coupland had asked the team to assemble at 9am, which gave him a couple of minutes to brief Mallender who had been summoned to the Super's office as a further press conference had been arranged for later in the morning. Mallender's presence would not be required.

At 9.00am Coupland was briefing the team:

'The fire was started with lighter fluid, the type sold in your average newsagents or tobacconist's store.

Uniformed officers have been tasked with combing the area including refuse bins and council waste bins to see if we can locate the original canister.'

'As of now annual leave has been cancelled we will need to push on through the weekend to make sure we gather as much evidence as we can find before it gets damaged or destroyed.'

'But the Tattersall Estate has nearly three hundred homes.' Robinson objected, 'It'll be like looking for a needle in a haystack.'

'Whoever did this,' Coupland said evenly, 'would have seen the light was on inside the flat, they may have even waited in the car park, watching as Abby's brothers, Finlay and Jordan were brought home by a neighbour.' He paused, 'And it was then, only then, once they saw the kiddies reunited with their invalid mother did they stand in front of the flat door and squirt highly flammable liquid through the letterbox before striking a match.' He placed his arms on a desk to steady himself. 'If you can tell me of a quicker way to find who did this then please, the floor is yours.'

Robinson was the first to his feet. 'I'll organise the teams.' He said, before quietly leaving the room.

'What about the threatening phone call?' Alex asked, referring to the call Abby had taken on her mobile moments before the fire broke out at her home.

'Came from a Pay As You Go,' Coupland responded. 'She didn't recognise the voice; all she could say is that it was male.'

'There's one thing,' He began, unsure whether he was muddying already cloudy water. 'Bearing in mind this was Abby's first day back at work, seems that she'd been grilled by her bosses about so called irregularities in some of the client accounts. Said she kept telling them they'd be better taking it up with the office manager but they seemed intent on hearing her side of things. The office manager is Angela Louden, the mother of our shooting victim.' He acknowledged the raised eyebrows in response to that comment, 'Now I'm not sure there's any relevance to the arson attack,' he conceded, 'but we need to make a couple of enquiries.'

'I can do that.' Alex offered.

Coupland nodded his agreement.

Chapter 27

The only good thing about the temporary accommodation they'd been moved to was the fact that it was temporary. Or so the council assured them, Abby thought bitterly. Her experience of what the housing department promised and what it delivered was already poles apart. She and her family had been moved to Byron House because the block of flats she'd grown up in had been demolished. Aware of Marion's condition the housing officer had softened the blow by finding them a second floor flat with a promise that as soon as one on the ground floor became available they'd be a priority. That had been a year ago.

Following the arson attack the emergency housing team had secured two rooms for them in a local hostel, the boys shared with Abby as Marion needed space for her carers to dress her and give her physio once her broken leg had healed. Abby sighed as she looked around her dismal room taking in the cigarette burned carpet and manky curtains; they sure as hell must be a priority now.

She'd had to reduce her hours at work; the twins had lost their place with the child-minder so she had to take them to school and pick them up herself. With fewer hours to do her job the work was piling up and she could feel herself falling further and further behind. Angela had been signed off on long term sick but instead of arranging for one of the more experienced clerks to act up the partners were intent on doing her work themselves, checking every detail as they did so. It was as if they didn't trust the staff to do anything on their own any more.

Every day she went into the office there seemed to be a new face checking through files she'd worked on before entering something into a laptop. Strangers traipsed in and out of the boardroom.

This morning she was late – the bus had broken down and by the time another one came for the passengers to transfer onto, it had already gone 10am. No sooner had she taken off her coat than Mr Rogers appeared in the office doorway summoning her into one of the meeting rooms.

A small bespectacled man was already waiting in there. Unfriendly, officious, he had the kind of face that looked like it hurt when he smiled. 'I'd like to introduce you to Fergus McClintock,' Mr Rogers began, waiting while they shook hands before pulling out a chair for her then returning to his own beside the serious faced visitor. She hadn't caught everything Mr Rogers said, though she heard the word forensic but that couldn't be right because that involved dead people didn't it? Mr Black was there too, but he didn't smile either, nodding gruffly at Abby instead.

They all had notepads open in front of them, the large ring-binder size, and they stared at her expectantly like she was about to give a lecture.

'I'm sorry I was late,' she said feebly, 'I don't blame you if you want to sack me...' Mr Rogers glanced at the other men before lifting his hand to stop her mid-sentence. 'That's not why we've asked you in here, Abby,' he began, 'We will be talking to the other members of staff but we wanted to speak to you first, given your relationship with Angela.'

Abby looked at the men uncertainly: 'OK...'

With a nod to the incoming season the day had started out cool; Coupland turned up the Mondeo's car heater, hugging onto a takeaway coffee as he explained the procedure to Todd. They were parked out of sight of

Billy Peters' garage, two police vans behind them waiting for the signal.

'As we serve the Production Notice to Billy the officers behind us will search his premises and remove any ledgers, computers, receipts - in fact anything remotely suspicious - for examination by fraud officers. These guys are good; they'll go through his books with a fine tooth comb, if there's anything shady they'll find it.'

Kiddo nodded, turning to look through the car's rear window. 'What's the second van for?'

Coupland laughed. 'If it all goes tits up.'

As it was Peters took the raid in his stride. He'd been caught up in enough of them to know the simplest way to come out intact was to act numb and look bored. He stood by the garage entrance feigning disinterest in the officers carrying his desktop and hard drive into the back of a van. 'Don't forget his job book and MOT records,' Coupland called out to one of the men, enjoying himself.

It was Dale who seemed more rattled by what was going on around him. He paced up and down in the car lot out front, chain smoking roll ups to keep warm. Dale had the most to lose, Todd reminded himself, he was the one who'd passed the stolen Subaru onto Rebecca's killers after all.

It had been obvious from their previous visit to the garage that Dale had something to hide. He seemed to propel his body forward in shifty little movements, his eyes all over the place, from Billy's face to Oldman's chest to Coupland's shoes. At least he hadn't the brass neck to front it out with them, his stuttered answers and increasing perspiration telling them loud and clear they'd found the next link in the chain.

Oldman had started to get a funny feeling in his stomach, an excitement he felt hard to contain. 'Let's follow him instead of Billy Peters, Sarge,' he'd pleaded after returning to Coupland's car to begin their surveillance, 'We could be nailing the shooter by the end of our shift.'

Coupland had smiled like an indulgent uncle. 'We have to report back to base,' he responded, 'get the intelligence on Dale and his known associates before we take any further action.' He'd put a restraining arm on Oldman's shoulder, 'We need to know who we're dealing with.' He explained.

Oldman had agreed, but deep down couldn't see the harm in giving things a gentle nudge. He and Coupland had already built up a profile of Dale and his haunts:

A junkie who'd progressed to dealing even though that was a recipe for disaster. He'd ended up injecting more than he'd sold; left himself with debts he had no chance of repaying. The opportunity to earn a bit of extra cash would have been irresistible.

Of course Dale hadn't said a word; it was his reaction to their questions that gave him away. His unsteady voice and shifty gaze, what else did they need to bring him in? Todd sighed. That was the problem working with guys close to retirement, they could smell their pension, didn't want to do anything to risk it. Oldman moved around the workshop trying to keep out of everyone's way as shelves and worktops were searched. In the tiny makeshift office desk drawers were being upturned and memory sticks logged and placed into evidence bags. 'Mind out son,' a WPC said as she moved in front of Oldman to check beneath some shelving, 'the grown-ups are working.' Oldman grunted an apology as he backed out of the room. It was as he was leaving he saw the lime green rectangle poking out of the pocket of a jacket hung over the cupboard door. Dale's smartphone. It was like fate intervening. Todd glanced about guiltily. The officers around him were too focussed on the job in hand to pay him any notice; a quick check in Coupland's direction told him the coast was clear.

He lifted Dale's phone and slipped it into his pocket.

Coupland was in a celebratory mood during the drive back to the station. 'You could tell he was seething,' he gloated, 'we've confiscated evidence that'll prove his involvement in money laundering at the very least, on top of that we should get a better handle on who his associates are; we might finally be able to nail that slippery bastard to the mast.'

'And Dale? What about him?'

'He's a foot soldier,' Coupland shrugged, 'nothing more; he's never made a decision in his life. You're fixating on him because he stole the Subaru but remember he did it under orders from his boss. What we need to work out is who pulls Billy Peters' strings.

'No rest for the wicked.' The desk sergeant greeted Coupland as he and Oldman entered the main door of the station. 'You've to go to Topkapi Fast Food Restaurant on Pendlebury Road.' It was the place Coupland had taken Oldman for lunch, where the rookie had confessed to being a vegetarian.

'What's happened?' Coupland asked, perking up at the thought of a meat feast snack.

The desk sergeant scanned through the message: 'Owner's gone missing.'

Chapter 28

The sign in the shop window had been turned to closed but the door was unlocked. Coupland and Oldman entered, moving towards the voices behind the beaded curtain which separated the living quarters from the restaurant.

When Osman hadn't returned to the shop in time for the evening shift the night before Kamal thought at first his brother was on a winning streak at the casino they frequented regularly and had lost track of time. Fatima, his sister in law, used to her husband's late night shenanigans had already gone to bed. It was the following morning, when neither hide nor hair of Osman had been seen that both of them started to worry. Kamal would have expected at least a text from his brother, either bragging about his winnings or the woman he'd bunked up with. It was so unlike him to not keep in contact; a quick call to the casino made his heart sink: Osman hadn't called in there last night yet he still wasn't answering his phone. It was only when Kamal drove over to the Cash 'n Carry to be told by the manager his brother had never arrived that he decided to call the police.

Osman had been missing for over 24 hours.

Fatima was sitting on a cottage style armchair dabbing at her face with a tissue. Kamal alternated between trying to reassure her and swearing into his phone when each contact he called told him they'd not seen Osman in ages.

Coupland crouched so he was the same eye level as Fatima: 'We'll need a photograph, love,' he said gently, 'we'll need to get it copied but we'll bring you the original back.'

'Here,' Kamal said briskly, lifting a photograph down from the shelf behind him. 'It was taken a month ago at a cousin's wedding,' he added. In the photo Osman was standing in the grounds of a manicured garden, clean-shaven, dressed up in a dark suit jacket with a white mandarin collared shirt beneath. He was smoking a cigarette, the corner of his eyes wrinkled at the pleasure of it.

A knot began to tighten in Coupland's stomach.

'What about his car?' Oldman asked, 'Ford transit van,' Coupland replied, 'uniforms have radioed details in.'

His gaze fell from Kamal to Fatima, 'We'll pull out all the stops.' He said to them, hoping to convey a confidence he didn't feel.

Alex had spent the afternoon conducting background checks on Angela Louden. According to the Family Liaison Officer attached to Rebecca's parents the couple got on well enough; relatives arriving at the family home to pay their respects after their daughter's shooting made no mention of any trouble in the marriage and if there had been any tension it would have surfaced by now.

Career-wise Angela had been at the accountancy firm since returning to work when Rebecca started school. Yet the feedback Alex got from the firm's managing partner, Mike Rogers, was far from complimentary. 'I'd rather not discuss this over the phone,' Rogers had bleated in a tone too close to condescending for Alex to ignore. She'd been prepared to drive over and speak to him but if he was an arse over the phone he'd be even more of one face to face. Men like him usually baulked when they saw a pregnant woman, like she'd over stepped her place and should be barefoot in the kitchen baking scones. Damn, just the thought of cake made her hungry. There was a bakery just down the road from the station; she'd have time to call in if she got a move on.

'That's absolutely fine,' she'd purred, all sympathetic, 'There's a quiet room we can have a chat in at the station, can even send a car to pick you up if you like…'

A sigh.

'Fine,' Rogers said irritably, 'what do you want to know?'

Chapter 29

Coupland had been watching from the canal bank for over an hour. He'd been called out of his bed at an ungodly time following the sighting of a body floating face down in the Bridgewater Canal. Standing beneath the footbridge for shelter against the wind he lit his second cigarette of the day, paying particular attention to the top of a uniformed officer's hat as it bobbed up and down while he prodded at the surface of the foul smelling water with a long pole.

'Let me know if you need a hand, Derek.' He called out between drags, missing the officer's terse reply, carried away by the wind. Grinning, Coupland was sure he'd heard the word 'Cough' but he couldn't be sure.

The canal was separated from Bridgewater Road by a grassy bank and pavement, where several policemen were busy cordoning off the area with blue and white tape, cracking jokes about the couple that had called it in. It was well after closing time; the couple had been returning home from an evening drinking in the Barton Arms when they'd taken a detour along the lonely canal path.

'What I don't understand...' One officer called out to another '...is how only the bloke saw the body at first.'

'She was obviously busy at the time.' replied his mate laughing. The other men standing within earshot chuckled. Coupland shot them a dirty look. It had been a while since he and Lynn had got busy with each other, he thought gloomily, what he wouldn't give to be sliding up to her in bed right now...but after her operation she seemed so fragile, besides, he didn't want to come across as insensitive. *Christ,* he grumbled to himself, *you've been reading too many self-help books; you'll be growing your hair long and chanting next.* His stomach gave an involuntary churn as the still water cast up the smell of decay, he took a couple of steps back so he was no longer down wind, glancing at his watch for the umpteenth time wondering what time the café over the road opened up.

The water in the canal had a distinct orange tint because it came from old mines containing traces of Iron Ore. Coupland stared at the stagnant water, wondering how desperate someone would have to be to want to fill their lungs with rust coloured liquid. Of course it may not be suicide, he reminded himself. It was more than likely some unlucky drunk lost their footing as they staggered home. The officer hooked the pole onto the top of the object, prodding and poking it until it worked its way towards the canal bank. He turned and shouted to his colleagues, calling for them to help him pull it out of the bloody water. Coupland watched as the officers who'd been laughing earlier ran down the bank and grabbed at the bundle of wet clothing, lifting and swearing, one lying on his front to get a better grip at the water's edge until the body was out of the canal sprawled out on the grassy bank. Coupland moved towards it, pushing it onto its back with his foot. Grey waxy skin with wide-open eyes stared back at him.

'He's dead then.' One of the men said to lighten the mood. A couple of the others grunted, hacked off they'd be finishing their shift smelling of piss and fetid water and oil. The body was male, middle-aged, with hair as black as soot flattened against its skull. His lips were mottled blue and the whites of his eyes stained orange from the water, giving him the appearance of being coloured in by a pre-schooler, a colour blind one at that.

But it was something else entirely that made Coupland suck in his breath.

The CID room was busy when Alex arrived. Oldman, who'd been sitting at her desk jumped to his feet the moment she lumbered over rubbing her back. 'I'd love to tell you not to bother, Kiddo,' she muttered as she smiled at the eager young cop, holding the chair steady as Alex lowered herself into it, 'but right now I've got bunions where you don't even know exists yet, so all acts of chivalry are gratefully received.' She looked at the small group of officers huddled around Coupland's desk, inclining her head in their direction. 'What's going on?' Her aches and pains now forgotten.

'Pulled a body out of the canal early this morning,' Oldman informed her, 'Sergeant

Coupland's assembling officers to take statements from staff at the Bridgewater Hotel and Barton Arms to see if they saw anything suspicious.

'Have we ruled out a suicide..?'

Alex didn't wait for an answer, instead she moved closer to the team assembled around Coupland, listened as he assigned tasks to each officer: collecting witness statements, chasing forensics. He was on edge, barking out orders as though the shit had hit the fan. She only ever saw him like this when there was a problem at home or he had to go on a course.

'Can I help?' She asked when the last of the men had filed out. Coupland shook his head; rubbing at the spot where his spine met his neck, pulling a face that indicated he wasn't making it any better. 'Got it covered for now.' He sighed, giving up on the neck ache, deciding instead to seek relief from his cigarettes. He motioned towards the corridor with his thumb and Alex followed, grabbing her coat on the way. Sheltering in the doorway that led to the car park Coupland replayed for Alex's benefit the morning's gruesome find.

'It was Osman.' Coupland informed her.

'The MISPER from yesterday?'

Coupland nodded.

'I was only bloody with him the day before.' He admitted, throwing his arms open wide as if he couldn't quite believe it.

'What, you knew him?'

'In a way,' He replied, 'He owned the kebab shop just off Pendlebury Road, had run it for over 25 years. I should know, I owe my Cholesterol level to him.' The laughter in his voice didn't quite make his eyes and he shrugged his head into his chest.

'Isn't he a witness to Rebecca Louden's shooting?' Alex asked slowly.

'*Was.* He'd seen the car the shooter used, hadn't seen the driver or the passengers as they were driving away from him, but his description of the vehicle was able to corroborate Abby Marlowe's.' As Coupland spoke an electrical charge ran up and down Alex's spine, and for once it wasn't junior's high kicks.

'OK,' she began slowly, 'It's rotten coincidence but it could still be a suicide.'

Coupland shook his head. 'I'd be with you on that Alex apart one little detail I haven't mentioned yet.'

She raised an eyebrow in enquiry.

'He had a bullet in the top of his head.'

'Shit.' Then, 'Have you told the boss?'

'He's talking to Curtis now.'

Mallender waited while Curtis digested the contents of the file he'd handed over. The details of which suggested a link between the killing of the kebab shop owner with the arson attempt on Abby Marlowe's home. He'd thought twice about briefing Curtis so soon, had been tempted to hold off a while longer but he was a newly appointed DCI - the last thing he wanted was his senior officer losing confidence in his ability to judge a situation, sending up a flare when guidance was needed. Recent events had sent this case spiralling out of shape and Mallender was more than happy to seek as much guidance as he could.

'They both witnessed the same crime, albeit from different angles,' Mallender summed up to Curtis, 'and someone out there knows that.'

'If this was a low level gang covering their tracks then they've just called in the big guns, haven't they?'

'Possibly.'

'The nightclub owner checked out?'

Mallender nodded. 'His father, Omar Zadawi, pulls his strings, but we checked him out too. He's amassed a fortune through several businesses but it's all legit.'

'No other witnesses?'

'Nada.'

'So all you've got left is this girl,' Curtis concluded, 'who had to be relocated due to an arson attempt on her home. Following the death of this shop owner we're potentially looking at a severe threat to her life. Does she know any of this?'

Mallender shook his head. 'Not yet,' he began, 'but what we tell her depends on what action you intend to take with this information, Sir.'

Curtis studied Mallender's face so intently the inspector had to fight the urge to wipe his mouth and nose.

'I think you're right to be concerned,' Curtis concluded, 'but you need to show me the cause of that concern. I need names, Stuart, and if the name is big enough we can make it like this girl has never been born.'

Chapter 30

Abby's eyes registered recognition the moment she opened the door. She smiled uncertainly.

'Hello!' She greeted him. 'I wasn't expect-'

With a gentle push he was inside the bedsit, closing the main door firmly behind him. 'Where are the others?' he asked urgently, it was vital that their conversation wasn't overheard.

'Mum's new carer takes her to the community centre every day – gets picked up first thing, the boys are at school.' Abby sat down on the bed-settee the boys had been given to sleep on, offering him the only other chair. Coupland remained standing.

'What's wrong?'

'Your boyfriend, where is he?'

'He's at work.' She answered warily, 'What's going on?'

Coupland walked towards her, placing a hand above each elbow to hold her steady. 'Remember I told you there was a shopkeeper who could corroborate your description of the car used the night Rebecca was shot?'

Abby nodded.

'He was found dead this morning. We need to move you for your own safety.'

The colour drained from Abby's face. 'Jesus…How did-' but Coupland was already shaking his head. 'Now's not the time, Abby,' He gripped hold of her upper arms preventing her from looking anywhere else in the room bar his face as he spoke, 'but believe me, it wasn't pretty.'

'Oh, God,' Abby felt the room spin but Coupland

held her firm, staring into her eyes as though searching for something her face wasn't telling him.

'We need to work out who knew about the shopkeeper,' he began, 'but first we need to make sure our one remaining witness is safe.' He paused to let that sink in.

'You mean they want me dead? You told me they just wanted to scare me.' Abby's voice was low, as though fearful her assassin had already tracked her down and was listening in another room. Her eyes darted to the corridor. 'Where..?'

'We don't know that. But we need to move you to somewhere safe straight away.'

She looked around the flea-bitten room that had become her family's home since the arson attempt. 'Well,' she shrugged, 'we won't be sorry to leave this place behind, that's for sure.'

'Just you, Abby.'

She stared at him as though she couldn't quite understand the language he was speaking, hoping she'd misunderstood in some way.

'The twins?'

Coupland shook his head.

'It's safer for everyone if we just move you. You'll be easier to spot if you move somewhere else with a disabled woman, two small boys in tow.' Abby shrank away from him, wriggling free of Coupland's grasp and getting to her feet as though he'd suggested something indecent.

'But what about *their* safety?'

Coupland paused. 'At the moment, the biggest threat to them is you.' He said quietly.

Abby visibly paled.

He could understand now why the Witness Protection Team took over at this point; it was harder to argue with a stranger. He thought it was only fair to be the one to tell her, in some perverse way he'd imagine that telling her himself would soften the blow but who was he kidding? He was about to pluck her from the centre of her family, in what way did he think he could stop that from hurting?

'Can I ring mum? I'll need to let the school know-'

'We'll take care of all that. But we need to leave now.'

'Can I at least ring Aston?'

Coupland stopped. 'Abby, listen to me. Do you want to bring the person who killed Rebecca to justice?'

A nod.

'Then we need to keep you safe so that no one can get to you before the trial. That means when we move you today, you won't be able to speak to your family, or Aston.'

Coupland locked eyes with her, dipping his head till it was level with hers, the way he did with Amy when he was making a point. 'Listen to me Abby,' he said carefully, 'The less *anybody* knows about where you are the better.'

He checked the time on his watch, 'I'm sorry,' he said, 'but we need to make a move. Just pack a few clothes-'

'I've only got a few clothes!' she spat angrily, 'Someone set my home on fire, remember?'

He said nothing more, waited while she threw several items into a holdall.

Chapter 31

Oldman could barely contain himself. One look through Dale's phone and he'd found a timeline of car thefts and drug dealing that would guarantee even a first offender a custodial sentence - if it wasn't for one little detail. The evidence, because of the way Oldman had gained it, was inadmissible. He pictured Sergeant Coupland's face if he told him what he'd done and shuddered; on this occasion honesty was definitely not the best policy.

He still couldn't believe Dale didn't automatically delete his texts. What kind of a criminal did he think he was, leaving footprints for all and sundry to find? He'd be posting photos on Facebook next – a selfie of him in front of each stolen car. In amongst the messages from his regular druggie clients were texts from *Billy P* - no prizes for guessing who that was - dating back several days with clear instructions: addresses, dates and times that cars would be available for him to 'lift'. And there, slap bang in the middle of them, was a text from Billy on the night Rebecca Louden was shot:

Blue Subaru. Pawnbrokers. Pauly needs it now.

Oldman closed his eyes, savouring the moment. The evidence he held in the palm of his hand may not be any use in a court of law but it sure as hell proved he was on the right track. All he had to do was show a direct link between Dale and Pauly that *was* admissible then maybe Sergeant Coupland would take him more seriously. Dale may only be guilty of stealing the Subaru and passing it on but there were hundreds of messages on the phone that proved he was dealing as well. Either way you looked at it, he was a killer. Dale's phone continued to beep with orders for weed and crack with such regularity Oldman reckoned he must produce the stuff at home. Maybe he was a much bigger player than anyone had originally thought.

It was the last text that Dale had opened before Oldman had taken his phone that made his pulse quicken. The one from 'P', which was probably as clever as the dozy dealer could get at disguising Pauly's identity. The message had summoned him to a meeting this evening, telling him to make sure he wasn't fucking followed. The best bit, the bit that would have made Oldman laugh out loud if he didn't need to keep his mouth shut right now was that Dale had entered it into his diary, and better still logged the address. *Coupland will love this*, Oldman thought; *he'll absolutely bloody love it.*

And now, clinging to the shadows in the back yard of a Swinton drug den, Oldman could see Dale Brown talking to a man he kept calling Pauly, the gang leader whose photo now graced the incident room wall.

A low watt light bulb flickered on and Oldman could make out through the grimy window that they were standing in a kitchen. Several sets of weighing scales were assembled on the worktops. The window was slightly ajar and their voices carried across the yard to him where he'd found a hiding place behind a wheelie bin.

'You let us down, Dale.'

'You wanted a fast car, I got you one.'

The sound of air being sucked through teeth. 'We didn't expect fuckin' go faster stripes down the side.'

Another voice, deeper: 'Half of fuckin' Salford saw us, man.'

Oldman's pulse quickened. He was listening to Rebecca Louden's killers.

'Yeah, but the shopkeeper's been taken care of-'

'And that cost serious money,' The voice turned cold, like steel.

'-and we've still got problems,' the other voice

chimed in, 'The main fuckin' witness who can eyeball everyone for all I know.'

'So you'll take care of her too.' Dale's voice was low, emotionless. Either he saw the trouble ahead and was trying to head it off or his go-slow brain really couldn't pick up the tension around him.

'Pauly...' Dale's voice, more urgent.

Oldman's brain was racing. This Pauly had power, lots of it. What had compelled him to shoot a teenage girl? He thought of Julia, another girl in the wrong place at the wrong time. If he'd gone to that party with her, maybe she wouldn't have tried that first line of coke...

'Pauly...I gotta tell you something.' Dale sounded frightened; the fear in his voice put Oldman on alert. 'I've lost...' Someone closed the window cutting the conversation so abruptly Oldman thought he'd gone deaf. He computed the distance from his hiding pace to the back door, which was slightly ajar, reckoned he could make it in a couple of strides; if he kept his head down no one would see him from the window. Two strides and he was just outside the door, could make out that Dale was being given the third degree over something.

'...I don't remember, Pauly!' he snivelled like he was about to burst into tears.

'Wha' yi mean yi cyan't remember?'

Oldman recognised the next voice, calmer than the others but just as threatening: 'Why the fuck didn't you say?'

'I'm sorry Billy.'

'Have you tried ringing it...?'

And before Oldman realised what the hell was going on the phone in his pocket began to ring out.

Coupland was getting to grips with the report Turnbull and Robinson had placed on his desk. An empty can of lighter fuel had been found hidden in a bin at the back of the flats where Abby and her family used to live. A fingertip search of the area had failed to add anything else. Whoever had started the fire must've been fast on his feet, he wouldn't have risked taking the lift, would have had to run down the flight of stairs before anyone heard the kitchen window explode.

The Fire Officer had given the council the all-clear to begin clearing up and redecorating throughout. The fire had spread quickly along the hall, where the accelerant had been poured through the letterbox. Jackets and coats hanging from pegs along the wall had caught light sending flames licking up towards the ceiling.

It had been Jordy who'd dialled 999, repeating the words he'd heard so often on the medical dramas his mother and sister liked to watch. Thank God the boys hadn't tried to hide, had stayed where their mother could see them. If the fire crew had had to search for them for one more minute it might have been a different outcome entirely.

Try as he might Coupland couldn't erase the look on Abby's face from his memory when he'd left her at the new address. Standing in the centre of the living room that was to be her home until the trial, she'd looked so young, so bloody vulnerable.

She'd stood there, not challenging him, not throwing a hissy fit because he'd taken her to a shit hole, a shit hole far away from everyone she'd ever known or cared about. Instead she'd waited quietly, *accepting*, as though this was all she'd come to expect from him.

'Thanks.' Was all she'd said.

And as for the public, would they even give a toss about the sacrifice she was making? Coupland wasn't so sure. Though there was outrage at the felling of a local girl outside a nightclub, that's all it was. Outrage and a general acceptance that these things happen as long as they happen to someone else. Coupland blamed the media for demonising young people – painting a picture of binge drinking and ASBOs, removing all traces of sympathy as people consoled themselves that any tragedies were in some way deserved. He grimaced as though he'd caught himself in his fly. Abby trusted him. She'd said so in as many words: '...If you're telling me this is the only way to get justice for Becca, then I'll do it...'

He'd merely nodded, fearful that if spoken aloud, his words might just stick in his throat.

Mallender found it nigh on impossible to look at the photo of Abby Marlowe and not see the girl Joanne could have been. There was no striking resemblance to his twin, more a downright stubbornness that reminded him of long ago disagreements – that Jo always won – and her absolute conviction about right and wrong. She'd have made a good cop, he knew that much, and the bittersweet thought made him smile. His mobile buzzed loudly interrupting his train of thought, *Dad*, flashed up on the display screen. He pushed the hands free button. 'Mum OK?' he demanded, his insides tightening.

'She's fine, son.' His father reassured him, then a pause as he exhaled the smoke from his cigar. 'Listen, a neighbour's coming round to sit with her tonight; I thought maybe you and me could go for a bite to eat.' It was the last thing Mallender felt like doing but his father seldom requested his company. He couldn't deny he was more than a little intrigued. 'I'll pick you up.' he said, pulling into the nearest side road so he could turn the car around.

At his parents' home he took a breath before knocking on the double-fronted door. Time alone with his father usually resulted in trading insults followed by contrition as they kept their distance for several weeks. He hoped this wasn't going to be one of those nights. He heard footsteps moving along the hall, a voice calling out 'I won't be a minute, love.' as the door opened.

'Hello Dad.' He said simply.

Inside the sitting room Mallender stroked his

mother's hand, planting a kiss on her cool cheek before joining his father by the window overlooking the well-stocked lawn. John moved over to the coffee table, held up the tea-time edition of the Evening News. Rebecca Louden's face still made the front pages. Mallender didn't need to read it to know his name would be there too.

'Joe Public's getting restless Stuart, have you really not got anything to give them yet?'

Mallender sighed inwardly; it was like an audience with Curtis.

'There is a name.' Mallender conceded as the photo of Paul Constantine on the Incident Room wall came into mind. 'I can't actually link him to the crime,' he admitted, 'It's just a feeling. He keeps cropping up, local hood done well.' He looked over at his father, 'Seems to have made it into the bully boy league.'

'So why haven't you brought him in?'

'I've got nothing to go on,' he shrugged in reply, 'other than supposition.'

John snorted. 'Since when does that stop you lot?'

Mallender exhaled heavily, ignoring his father's sarcasm as he edged his way back towards the hallway. 'Will she be OK?' he asked, glancing over at his mother, wondering if she was keeping up with their conversation or did it wash over her like a foreign language.

'Will any of us?' John answered darkly.

It had always been his father's rule never to discuss business at home. He asked Mallender to take them to his favourite restaurant, a family run affair in the centre of Worsley that had a large room in the back that was available to only a handful of customers. His father followed the same process when he worked through a problem – always over a full stomach with a good glass of red and a cigar in his hand, as though the smoking ban was a figment of the Government's imagination.

There was little conversation during the drive. For one thing, neither of them felt like talking, instead they sat in silence allowing the passing scenery to distract them, so that the small talk they made never had a chance to become too volatile, too involved.

'What's eating you?' Gibson asked.

'Nothing. Everything.' Mallender shook his head, 'Ignore me; you've caught me at the end of a bad day. At least driving gives me the space to look at things from a different angle.'

''Cept you'll never get your head around the thought processes of a con, that it?'

Mallender nodded slowly. 'Partly.' He conceded, 'I mean, what you've said before is right, we might spend every day keeping the streets clean but we never really understand what make someone choose crime over...' he searched for a tactful way of saying it.

'Over an honest day's graft, eh, son? Is that how you see it?' John shook his head indulgently as though Mallender was eight years old and he'd recounted a fanciful story about aliens or ghosts or some other far-fetched phenomenon.

'*Keeping the streets clean.*' Gibson mimicked. 'I love it. Do you really think that's what you do?' he challenged without waiting for an answer. 'To you the world is black and white son, a key requirement for a copper, I accept. But it isn't real. Take a look outside.'

The car turned into Bridgewater Road. Office cleaners were making their way into now empty buildings, a few after work drinkers weaved their way to a couple of pubs further up the canal. Posters of Rebecca Louden had been pasted on lampposts and in shop windows, asking for anyone who saw anything suspicious outside Ego nightclub on the night of her murder to call the police incident room, or Crimestoppers.

The city seemed to be holding its breath, as though uncertain how the evening would unfold.

'Have you learnt anything over the last couple of years?' John goaded, 'White-collar crime goes on under your nose day in, day out. The system's about as honest as an MP's expense sheet, yet you have the nerve to talk about keeping the streets clean!'

What his old man said was true; bankers with knighthoods had brought the country to its knees. Mallender acknowledged the point with a nod of his head.

'Is it really any different from the guy on the street flogging knock off gear from the back of his van?' John persisted. 'He doesn't wear a shirt and tie, doesn't drive a flash car – does it make his crime any worse?'

'Counterfeit goods fuels terror-'

'And we've been selling arms to our enemies for years,' John interrupted, 'where's the logic in that?'

He had him there. 'Look, I'm no politician,' Mallender sighed. 'I don't make the laws, I just uphold them.'

John shook his head. 'And that makes it alright?' he asked, 'Do you remember when I ran my business? The people I employed? I provided more work than the local bloody job centre.'

Mallender recalled the respect – and fear – his father's name brought when he was growing up. The people who looked after him purely because he was his father's son. He never had to put his hand in his pocket for anything on the high street – if his father didn't own the business then he'd lent money to the people who did – people the banks had refused to help. At times it was like being the son of the lord of the manor.

'I gave jobs to people who couldn't read or write, who wouldn't get a look in with a normal employer. Through me they became self-sufficient, could look after their own.'

'You make it sound like working for Disney.' Mallender retorted. 'You forgot the part where if anyone crossed you they'd lose a kneecap.'

Gibson's laughter made his eyes crinkle in the

corners. 'Happy days.' He reminisced, catching but ignoring the scowl on Mallender's face.

'There was respect for the old values in those days, son. All that changed when the drugs started coming in. Foreigners telling us there was a fortune to be made for very little effort – placing an order or making a delivery – but I wanted no part in that. It would have been easier, granted. At the end of the day by the time you took into account the premises I owned and the staff I employed I was running the equivalent of a major corporation – but the guys moving in with drugs had no interest in the community other than making a fast buck – they sure as hell didn't give a shit about what happened to their customers. It's the drugs that have given criminals such a bad reputation, son, and was the reason I got out of the game.' There was a flaw in his logic somewhere, Mallender was sure of it, but his head was too full right now to get into semantics. There were things about his father that would never change, like the way he mapped out the exit routes when he entered a room. Mallender remained silent, preferring to watch his father exchange pleasantries first with the owner, Cal, then Cal's demonstrative wife, Gill, hair newly coiffed and fully made up, clothes perfectly coordinated if a little young.

'So what's tonight all about, Dad?' Mallender asked abruptly.

Gibson smiled appreciatively at his son's candour.

'It's about the latest killing.'

'What about it?' Mallender asked sharply. 'The body's barely cold.' Osman's death hadn't made the lunch-time news, although it was sure to get top billing during the evening broadcast. He was quietly relieved; the media had less time to fuel the public's fears, though he was sure they'd make up for that tomorrow.

'Is it the same killer as the girl?'

They were interrupted by Cal who batted not one eyelid at the topic of their conversation. Murder and weapons were discussed as frequently on his premises as bags and shoes might be in some gastro pub at the Trafford Centre. He came armed with a bottle of red, 'this is so good I don't include it on the menu.' He said as he placed it on the table between father and son so they could ogle the bottle before he made a show of opening it. Mallender's father nodded appreciatively while Mallender tugged at his collar. The temperature in the back room was ambient but he still perspired when he knew he was about to be offered a drink. It wasn't so much the humiliation of having to refuse that rattled him, more the fear of saying yes. Instinctively he put his hand over the wineglass. 'Fraid not.' He said as cheerfully as he could muster. 'Driving and all that.'

'Thought you boys looked after each other.' Cal said, bemused, but a look from Mallender's father discouraged any further discussion, instead Cal called over to Gill to fetch a bottle of spring water. 'I'll leave you gents alone.' He said picking up Mallender's empty wine glass and replacing it with a tumbler. 'Let me know if there is anything else I can get you.'

There was never a menu; it was whatever their chef took it upon himself to cook. Would have earned himself a Michelin star if he wasn't here illegally. Mallender wondered how many times he'd have to turn a blind eye to maintain the rocky relationship with his father. It was like walking a constant tightrope, one wrong move and his career would come crashing down around him.

Mallender's father picked up the thread of the conversation.

'The dead girl. You think a hitman shot her?'

Mallender shook his head. 'From the witness description we're pretty sure it was a kid – a member of a local crew but a kid all the same.'

Mallender relayed the facts of the case as he knew them; pausing once in a while to check his old man was keeping up.

'The shooter that killed the shop owner was brought in to clean up the amateur's mess then.' Gibson summed up with an authority that made Mallender shudder. The manner of Osman's shooting bore all the hallmarks of an execution, but again, at the moment this was conjecture, a pathology report and the results of a fingertip search would provide the investigating team with something more concrete to go on.

Mallender listened as his father warmed to his theme. 'Booming business.' He said matter of factly. 'There's no shortage of work for a good hitman.' What his old man said was true. It never made the news because one thug wiping out another didn't have the same appeal as a sports star blasting his girlfriend to death through a toilet door. One more criminal off the streets was hardly a bad thing. But this was different; witnesses to a crime were being hunted down.

'Look son, crime is this country's third biggest industry.' Gibson held his hands up in mitigation, 'I know it's not an easy concept for you to handle, but that's the way it is.' His old man shrugged helplessly, as though the thought never occurred to him that he'd been instrumental in this very industry for the best part of thirty years.

'Gangsters bring more cash into this country than almost anyone else, and when they spend it, they keep legit businesses afloat too. Son, we've done more to help keep the economy going than the Chancellor of the fucking Exchequer.'

Jim carried a selection of Moroccan dishes to the table. A tagine of lamb, fragranced couscous and a selection of breads and pastries and pickles and meats that made Mallender's mouth water. He raised his hands in mock surrender. 'Get to your point, Dad.' He said, eyeing the banquet appreciatively.

'Things are heating up,' Gibson warned, 'I worry

about you.'

'Is that it?' Mallender smiled at his father's sheepish face. 'Don't get me wrong,' he said, scooping large spoonfuls of lamb onto his plate, 'I'm flattered, *really*, but I'm a big boy now.'

'And these are even bigger boys you're dealing with.'

'Do you know who they are?' Mallender asked sharply, hating himself for mistrusting his father but doing it anyway. John shook his head. 'What do you take me for?' he asked angrily. Mallender glanced over at Cal and Gill as they busied themselves with customers front of house, 'I don't know who it is but I know the type, and they'll remove anyone who gets in their way. Your investigation is stirring up a hornets' nest-'

'-You think I don't know that!' Mallender spat back.

'All I'm saying is if you need my help-'

'-I don't.' Mallender retorted, 'I can't believe you'd even think of offering.'

His old man grimaced before taking a generous gulp from his wineglass. 'It's
something you do when you when you want to protect the ones you love.' He said simply.

'What?' Mallender asked.

A pause. 'The unthinkable.'

Time seemed to stand still for the few seconds it took for Oldman to locate the phone and silence it.

Dale's gormless voice: 'Did you hear that Billy?'

Oldman didn't need to wait for his reply as Billy Peters yanked open the back door and locked eyes with him, a Cheshire Cat grin spreading right across his face. 'It's a fucking cop!' Peters bawled out to the others in the house, causing a collective response of 'fuck' and 'shit' and toilet flushing. Oldman started to back away but collided with a young black teenager who appeared behind him. 'Hey, watch it!' Earl grunted.

Peters, fast on his feet when he wanted to be grabbed Oldman's arm and pulled him into the terraced house, dragging him into the kitchen where Dale and half a dozen or so dealers turned to stare at him. 'Looks like we've been Gulfed, lads!' Peters said sarcastically, referring to the National Crime Agency's *Operation Gulf* that was specifically targeting Salford gangsters and their associates. 'I know with the austerity measures and all there have been cutbacks but a one-man surveillance unit is taking things a bit far!' The others started laughing, relaxed that Oldman didn't pose a threat to them. For now.

Peters let go of Oldman but held out his hand: 'Phone.' he barked.

Oldman did as he was told, passing the smartphone to Peters who in turn threw it at Dale. 'And this time keep fucking hold of it.' he warned.

Oldman, sensing the danger he'd been put in now he'd seen all their faces raised his hands in the air. *You'll get no trouble from me,* he tried to convey. He thought of Coupland's warning not to work alone, wondered what the hell Coupland would do now.

'This is one of the coppers who raided the garage.' Billy Peters explained for Pauly's benefit. Pauly, still seething over Dale's fuck up, didn't need the details. The trespasser was a cop; that was all he needed to know. He lifted a hand to Kester to signal he was to stay put; he wouldn't be needed for this next task.

'Dale,' he commanded in his low growl, 'appears you bin granted a life-line.'

Dale blinked. He slid his gaze from the cop to Pauly, waited for him to repeat his comment in words of one syllable. 'We got a problem, Dale.' Pauly said slowly, slipping his hand inside his leather jacket and pulling out a knife. 'And I want *you* to clear it up for me.'

'No!' Earl gasped from the doorway. The word

had slid out instinctively; Oldman got the feeling the boy would be punished for speaking out of turn. 'No more killing,' the boy persisted.

Pauly's look silenced him; even so Oldman had to admire his courage. 'Either he does it,' Pauly barked, inclining his head in Dale's direction, 'or you do.' The boy dropped his chin to his chest, shame preventing him from looking Oldman in the eye. Oldman knew he had to act fast. 'Please,' he began; fear rising from him in waves, 'my colleagues know that I'm here. They'll be sending back-up if I don't radio in.'

'Show me your radio then,' Pauly invited, his grin indicating he knew Oldman was bluffing. Oldman's crestfallen face gave him away.

In the moments that it took for Dale to take the knife from Pauly, Oldman found himself kicking Billy Peters and wind- milling his arms as though this act alone would keep him safe. An image of Julia's coffin slid into his mind, the photograph their mother had placed on top of it. It hadn't been a recent photo; a lank-haired, pasty-faced scowl wouldn't have evoked so much emotion. Instead a bright eyed girl grinned at the camera, one week into sixth form and yet to go to the party that would be her undoing.

He always knew it would skew his decisions, that not every dealer was to blame for Julia's overdose but they were to blame for someone else's. All he'd wanted was to take one off the street. And now his obsession with Dale had led him to Paul Constantine, a criminal so ruthless his men would rather be sent down than cross him.

'*Bastard.*' Oldman shouted, as he threw a punch so hard that when his fist connected with Pauly's face something in his wrist cracked, and he looked on in fascination as the gangster spit out stringy blood and a tooth. Oldman tried to laugh but the sound was trapped in his throat, and the kitchen turned on its side as the young cop fell to his knees. He looked on in surprise as Billy Peters and Pauly and his henchmen, instead of retaliating, took a step away from him; cursing and shouting at Dale that he was a stupid fucking deadleg, look at the fucking mess he'd made. The kitchen was all red, and they were red too.

In that soft focus reality that buffered life and death Oldman raised his hand to his throat, felt the void that used to be his carotid artery. At least he'd see Julia again.

Pauly looked over at Earl, who'd remained rooted to the spot beside the back door. 'See what you started,' he said viciously, anger pouring off him like a vapour.

'I'm sorry.' Earl muttered, turning on his heels and running for his life. Pauly didn't respond. As far as he was concerned Earl was dead to him.

His murder just hadn't happened yet.

Chapter 32

Hannah Baptiste wrung out the old man's washcloth and patted his hand. 'That feel better?' She asked, zipping back up his toiletries bag and reaching for his teeth which she placed over his gums. She leaned into his good ear: 'You look so handsome that daughter-in-law of yours will think she married the wrong man!'

The old man chuckled, rewarding her with a boyish grin. Hannah loved caring for the elderly, you could learn a lot if you took the time to listen to their stories. It surprised her how often she found herself defending her job - people pulled a face when they learned she worked on a geriatric ward. Might as well say she worked in a mortuary, the way some folk responded. God's waiting room, some called it. So what? Hannah shrugged; all the more reason for her to make that wait as pleasant as it could be.

She enjoyed visiting time, watching the patients' relatives arrive, seeing so many generations crowd around one bed. It made her think of her own family, her eldest son now grown, his brother not far behind, not forgetting little Arlene who made even the hardest days seem better. Their fathers may be long gone but they were the losers, missing out on the lives they'd created simply because they couldn't keep their trousers zipped up. A knot of fear began to pulse beneath her ribs, Earl hadn't come home last night, hadn't tried to call her either. It wasn't like him, he didn't like her worrying, so much so that when Aston was in prison and money had been tight Earl had found himself a part time job, one that fitted round his schoolwork and looking after Arlene. It had eased the burden, and brought them closer too. There was money to be made in distributing leaflets it seemed, as long as he distributed enough of them. She thought he might have eased off the hours he worked once Aston came home, especially with exams looming but he'd carried on as normal, 'I'm used to the extra money, Mum,' he'd tell her.

Tipping soapy water down the sink she placed the washbowl back on the trolley, straightened the sheets over the old man's chest. 'I'll bring you a nice cup o' tea,' she informed him, pushing her fear to the back of her mind, 'and a biscuit if you're lucky.'

Halfway towards the sluice room a voice behind her made her jump. 'Mum!' Hannah turned quickly to find Earl making his way towards her on the ward, 'What in heaven?' she gasped, looking round quickly to see if Sister was nearby, 'Is everything OK?' Earl didn't answer but the slump of his shoulders told her something was wrong. 'Come into the staffroom.' She piped, looking at her watch, 'I'm due a break.' She wondered for a moment what the hell he'd done that made him look in so much pain. His eyes looked haunted, causing a spasm of anxiety to pulse through her colon and she had a sudden urge to open her bowels. Closing the staffroom door behind them she turned to her middle child:

'Earl, what's wrong, honey?' she asked, already dreading the answer.

Hannah's face did not register any emotion. No doubt there was shock, a dull presence of disappointment, albeit a slight one, as though the confession Earl made to her now was something she'd been expecting all his lifetime to hear. She clamped her hands over her mouth to stifle the moan that threatened to escape from her lips. All at once her second-worst fears had been realised. She listened intently, staring wide-eyed and open-mouthed until the light she held for him finally died in her eyes.

She'd slumped into one of the foam-backed chairs;

fearful her legs were about to give way beneath her. Still, she couldn't quite take it in. She wondered if it was a sick joke he was playing, or her hearing was playing her up. She struggled to make the connection between the reports of the shooting on the news and the slight boy in front of her who'd struggled with toilet training and had needed a night light for far longer than his siblings. She put her hand to her face as though trying to mask her reaction.

He'd shot that girl.

'Why?' Hannah asked him over and over but he shrugged his shoulders and stared at the carpet as though working out how best to clean it, 'because Pauly asked me.' He said feebly.

He was agitated, refusing to let her call Aston. *It's too late for that now,* he'd said simply. Things were getting out of control, he explained, *No,* he couldn't say what, it was better that she didn't know. '*You're gonna hear some tings,*' he warned her, '*please don't believe what they tell you, I'm...I'm not a bad boy Mum.*'

Hannah didn't know whether to laugh instead of cry. He'd just confessed to killing someone yet he might get the blame for something worse? He moved towards the door but she made no effort to stop him, it took all her concentration to control her breathing, to keep the emotion that threatened to rise to the surface buried, at least until she got home.

'*I have to go Mum.*'

There were people after him, he told her. He needed to leave. Hannah lowered her head in sorrow.

Even now, he wasn't bothered about forgiveness.

He was getting the hell away.

Chapter 33

Coupland had to remind himself that he was on his way home, that talk of victims and perpetrators would be suspended for the evening and normal service would once more resume. Whatever normal was. He drummed his fingers on the steering wheel, turning up the volume on the radio; Junior Murvin sang about Police and Thieves. Never had the lyrics of a song summed it up so well, tapped into the anger building within him. He'd seen close up the damage that guns can do; the power they wield in the wrong hands and the trail of devastation they leave in their wake.

He was just turning into his street when a call came out that a body had been found in Worsley Woods.

'All we fuckin' need.' he muttered sourly as the prospect of a decent night's kip disappeared into the ether. The entrance to the wood was only two streets away and he'd be there in less than five minutes. He fumbled one handed in his jacket pocket until he'd located his cigarettes, pushed in the cigarette lighter and wound down his window. Might as well settle his stomach with a smoke, he reasoned. He parked in the visitors' car park, nodding to the boys in uniform who were already cordoning off the entrance to the wood, then stepped into the darkness.

Mallender's phone startled him, its ring, shrill and insistent. For a beat he thought about not answering it. His instinct, his police sixth sense, told him, yelled loudly at him, that if he answered there'd be no going home at a reasonable hour. If the shit was hitting the fan let the next shift scrape it up.

He answered on the third ring, 'Hello?'

'There's been a stabbing.' Coupland's tone was clipped, as though he couldn't trust his voice not to give way part way through his sentence. There was something more his sergeant wanted to say, Mallender could sense it, but nothing could prepare him for what came next.

'Todd Oldman's been murdered.'

'Oh, Jesus,' Mallender whispered as he lurched to his feet, dropping the phone back onto its stand at the same time banging on the glass to catch Alex's attention. It was the end of her shift and she'd been about to leave with Robinson. They were sharing a joke, her head tilted back in laughter as she wriggled into her coat, Robinson pausing at the door to help guide an arm into an errant sleeve.

'Back here!' Mallender managed to splutter, fear and anger reducing him to simple words, as though he'd been struck by the same affliction as Coupland.

Alex and Robinson – indeed the other stragglers remaining in the CID Room were regarding him strangely, as though he'd shouted out something foreign or obscene. He needed to tell them quickly, soon it would be all over the station – and the news – there would be reporters camping outside and there was the family still to tell. Mallender lurched out of his office and snapped his gaze onto Alex, moving forward quickly he pulled out a chair, saw fear and uncertainly flash across her face. 'You need to sit down for this.' He began.

A canopy had been erected around Todd to protect him from view; lighting rigs provided artificial light enabling forensics to comb the area for signs of disturbance. As word spread around the division officers swarmed to the scene in droves, there were so many uniforms it was as though the area had become the venue for a macabre police reunion. Patrol cars raced to the entrance to the wood, the drivers parking haphazardly at the crime scene tape before running from their cars, shouting to colleagues on the other side of the tape to tell them what the fuck was going on.

Coupland sat twenty yards from the body, slumped on a patch of grass, his back supported against a gnarled oak tree stump jutting out from the ground. A paramedic had tried to cajole him into an ambulance but on seeing that he was wasting his breath had returned with a blanket, which he draped awkwardly over the bulky sergeant's shoulders.

Coupland had recognised Todd instantly. Although an attempt had been made to sever the rookie's head from his shoulders, his face remained intact. Already his skin had taken on the waxy pallor of the dead, his eyes, staring ahead but sightless. Despite this, and despite all his training that told him to preserve the locus at all costs, Coupland had still tried to cover the gaping wound on Todd's neck. The flow of blood had diminished long since, but there was something inhuman, indecent, about the level of damage that had been inflicted on him. He'd finally moved when the pathologist arrived yelling obscenities at him for contaminating the scene.

With traces of Oldman's blood on his hands Coupland had retreated to the edge of the cordoned off perimeter, awaiting the arrival of his DCI.

You're a bloody vegetarian aren't you? He'd accused Todd only days before, and now his butchered body lay yards away, attracting flies like offal on a meat counter. He fished in his pockets for his cigarettes, attempted to light one with shaking hands before giving up and tossing his lighter to the paramedic. 'Make yourself useful.' He grunted, clamping the cigarette between his lips.

Chapter 34

Earl's legs shook as he walked through the car park towards the hospital's exit. He forced himself not to turn round and look up at the third floor window his mother would be staring out from watching him leave, willing him not to. He'd told her everything. About doing jobs for Pauly when Aston went inside, how the jobs had got bigger and more important since he'd come out. How on the night of the shooting they'd been driving around mucking about, he'd didn't for one moment think Pauly'd been serious when he'd given him the gun.

'But why shoot her, den?' his mother had asked, and he'd looked at the floor as he'd answered. 'Because Pauly told me to.' It was the lamest answer in the world and here he was using it, hiding behind it to justify his actions. 'But you had a choice...' She whispered, more to herself than to him, and in that moment he knew that he'd lost her. Oh, he'd had a choice all right, and even then he'd fucked it up. 'The redhead,' Pauly had whispered before lowering the passenger seat window. Earl had nodded, took his aim. But in the seconds it took him to pull the trigger the girl had seen him, had locked eyes with him, knowing in that instant the bullet was intended for her. If she'd dropped to her knees her friend would still be alive, instead she'd pulled her into the trajectory of the bullet. After that all hell had broken loose, Pauly calling him a stupid fucker, Kester laughing out loud because he'd screwed up yet again.

'Can't you see he's a fucking liability?' Kester had spat as they'd screeched along the back roads until they'd pushed a trembling Earl out of the car. '*One* little ting,'

Pauly had hissed, shaking his head like a disappointed head teacher, jabbing Kester's shoulder, ordering him to get them the hell away.

This was why, despite his mother's pleas to hand himself in, Earl had to get away and fast. He'd give anything to talk to Aston, tell his older brother the truth, in his own words. He owed him that much. Earl shook his head, he wasn't stupid, he knew enough about his brother's rages to know he could never tell him face to face so he'd written him a note, placed it in the outside pocket of the rucksack he'd left with his mother, instructing her to take it home and keep it safe. The note, and the ID he'd found at the house the cop was killed in would expose Pauly and his henchmen, what Aston did with the note was up to him. It seemed fitting his fate should be decided by the people he'd wronged. If Aston chose to say nothing then Pauly would make sure Earl was fitted up for the cop's murder. If Aston handed Earl's note to the police it would clear him of that crime but in it he'd confessed to shooting Rebecca Louden - either way he was screwed. He cursed himself for the hundredth time.

He was a loser all right. Took after the dad he'd never known. The man his mother referred to as *that jerk*, as though his name wasn't worthy of being uttered. Yeah, he'd fucked up, got more backs up than he cared to acknowledge because he'd done the wrong thing badly. Not only had he killed someone against his better judgement, it turned out he'd killed the wrong girl.

He saw the car as it mounted the kerb alongside him. Watching as if in slow motion as the passenger jumped out of his seat and moved in his direction.

Chapter 35

'Officers are carrying out a fingertip search of the area where Todd Oldman was discovered.' Mallender began, 'We're waiting on the pathologist's report but early indications are he died from a single wound to his carotid artery.'

'The bastard tried removing his fucking head.' Coupland simplified, showered and changed after a brief visit home but still as angry. He'd insisted he was up to accompanying Superintendent Curtis to deliver the death message to Todd's parents. He now sat towards the back of the room, every nerve in his body jumping.

'Lack of blood at the locus tells us he was moved from the original crime scene after his death.' Mallender continued. The incident room was packed with off-duty officers and civilians awaiting orders. Standing room only as they crowded into the small workspace to hear how a young rookie in their care was snuffed out and disposed of so callously. Alex perched a buttock on the edge of a desk, sitting in her own chair would have seemed disrespectful. Twenty four hours earlier she'd resented Todd for symbolising her departure from work, now she'd give anything to see him taking her seat, rearranging her desk top into some semblance of order.

Curtis was standing at the front of the incident room with Mallender, staring past the sea of faces. No manual prepared him for this.

'I know this won't be easy,' Mallender continued, 'but we want a lid keeping on this for 24 hours whilst we gather as much intelligence as we can.'

Coupland looked around the incident room, studying the reaction of those present, confusion followed by disbelief: local residents would have had to be blind and deaf not to notice the sea of yellow high visibility jackets that had descended upon the town in the moments following the call, the number of off duty officers reporting to the scene, anger and distress etched into their faces.

'What about the Press?' he spat suspiciously.

'We've obtained a news blackout,' Superintendent Curtis stepped in, 'both at national and regional level. It is hoped the killer or killers will be lulled into thinking Oldman's body hasn't been discovered yet, giving us more time to establish who they are and where the murder took place.'

It was feasible, Coupland supposed, that those guilty of the crime had got the hell away as fast as their stolen motor could take them, they couldn't rule out someone skipping the country – port authorities and airports had been warned to look out for last minute tickets purchased for immediate travel. If the suspects thought the body hadn't been discovered there was more chance of them making a mistake that would lead to their detection. They needed to feel they were above suspicion.

'What about the member of the public who found the body, sir?' Alex asked.

'A local prostitute found him.' Coupland informed her. Animals had already started to pick through the plastic bin liner Todd had been wrapped in, leaving his face and upper torso exposed. 'She'd gone there with a punter who took off when she started screaming.' Coupland explained. 'We tracked him down though, he's cooperating fully with our investigation,' he added ominously.

'Just tread carefully,' Mallender muttered, swiping his fingers through his hair, 'keep it above board,' he warned, shooting Coupland a look. He was conscious of Curtis' eyes burning into his neck. 'The last thing I need right now is a visit from Complaints.'

Coupland forced his left hand down by his side; his right hand had formed into a fist. He thought of the utter bollocks he'd fed Oldman about biding their time and doing things by the book. The kid was impatient when they'd been staking out Billy Peters' garage; it was obvious he thought Coupland was past it. What if Oldman had decided to take things into his own hands? Followed up his own lead because Coupland hadn't been willing to. He pictured Billy Peters' smug fat face covered in hundreds of bruises. He ground his teeth together, willing his fingers to relax.

'Kevin?' Alex whispered beside him, 'You OK?'

He nodded without meeting her eye.

Alex groaned at the MISPER report left on her desk. *Haven't we got enough to do?* She muttered, her eyes following her colleagues as they moved with purpose from the CID Room to the incident room to collect car keys and files, before heading off to complete tasks Mallender had allocated to them during the briefing, actions over and above their tasks on the nightclub shooting but no one complained, each officer keen to do their bit to nail the bastard who thought it was OK to kill a cop, one wet behind the ears at that.

Mallender had turned her away, point blank, when she'd asked to be part of the investigating team, 'It's not up for discussion.' He'd said curtly before delegating tasks to the officers around her. Coupland had gone off like a shot, Turnbull and Robinson in tow, their voices low like distant thunder. Officers staying on from the night shift made a quick detour to the canteen for a takeaway breakfast before going back out on the streets, civilians returned to computers to carry out searches and input reports. Mallender had followed Curtis upstairs to his office, for a private briefing or a bollocking Alex couldn't be sure, neither face gave anything away.

Alex had been left behind. At least the others could concentrate on catching Todd's killer if she helped pick up the slack, she consoled herself, quickly followed by *Who am I kidding?* She was angry with herself for being so self-centred, for thinking of Todd only in relation to what his arrival had meant for her. She'd been so keen to get him out from under her feet; she hadn't taken the time to really get to know him. If she'd spoken to him more, maybe he'd have confided in her what he'd been planning to do last night, assuming he'd been planning anything. Some officers liked to live close to the wind, priding themselves on their personal knowledge of the local low-life but Oldman hadn't seemed like that. She couldn't imagine him hanging out in bars and clubs with mates that walked on the wild side, he was too…well, fragrant and clean-cut for that, which left only two other options: A random tragic act of violence, which was possible even if unlikely, or his killing was related to the case he'd been assigned – Rebecca Louden's shooting. Alex placed her head in her hands. If the latter was the case then she *was* to blame, she was the one who'd thrown him in the deep end just to keep him out of her hair. She sighed deeply, placing a hand protectively over her stomach as she thought about Todd's family. How could she ever begin to make things right?

She picked up the missing person file half-heartedly and flicked through the two-page printout. A fourteen-year-old boy reported missing by his mother, a nurse at the local hospital. The woman had last seen him when he came to see her on the ward yesterday during her shift. He'd told her he was going away – which piqued Alex's interest – what would have made a fourteen-year-old boy want to leave home in the first place? What mitigating reason could he have given his mother that she didn't try to prevent him from going? Alex quickly scanned the address, then sat bolt upright in her chair. She'd already called at this address once this week, when she went looking for Abby Marlowe's boyfriend – the missing boy was Aston Baptiste's brother. She remembered the edgy young man waiting on the stairs the first time she'd gone round to Byron House; he resembled the photo attached to the file – what was troubling him so badly that he had to get away? At that moment her mobile began to vibrate, moving around on her desk like it was in a demolition derby. She glanced at the display screen but it was a number she didn't recognise, 'Alex,' she said briskly, staring at Earl's photograph for clues to what had driven him away.

'It's Aston Baptiste,' the caller informed her, 'I…we…need your help,'

'I know,' she said quickly, pushing herself to a standing position. 'Your brother's file's just landed on my desk, are you at home?'

'Yes.'

'I'm on my way.'

Alex arched her back, pressing her hand over the base of her spine, moving it in a circular motion. 'Ooh, that's better,' she said aloud, allowing her eyes to close just for one minute. When she opened them again Coupland was studying her with concern,

'You OK, Alex?' he asked.

'Still shell-shocked. How about you?'

The rising body count following Rebecca Louden's shooting seemed to have aged him, his skin looked pallid, weary eyes peeped out beneath heavy lids. Coupland pulled a face, 'What do you think? The guy who ran off after discovering Todd's body has got no previous, just panicked at the prospect of his wife finding out what he did on the nights he was supposed to be at a photography club,' Coupland sighed, swiping at his eyes with the back of his hand. 'I…I should've seen it coming.'

'You can't blame yourself, Kevin; I couldn't wait to get him out from under my feet.'

'Even so.'

'Let's apportion blame later.' Alex said briskly. 'I'm going out on a MISPER interview but there's something about it that's set the alarm bells ringing already.'

'What is it?'

'The missing boy's brother is going out with Abby Marlowe.'

'I'm coming with you.'

Aston Baptiste met them as they emerged from the lift at Byron House. His normally angry face was drawn, as though fear had replaced injustice. He ignored Coupland, preferring to speak to directly to Alex. 'I didn't know who else to call,' he began, 'when she told me…I just wanted to…*Jesus*, it's just as well he's nowhere near.' Below the surface simmered a tide of emotion he was trying to suppress; Alex wasn't sure how best to get him onside. 'I'm glad you called me, Aston,' she said softly, 'Shall we go and see your mother?'

'She's in bits,' he warned, then, 'there's something I need to tell you.' Alex glanced quickly at Coupland, unsure whether he wanted to take over or not.

Coupland shook his head.

'Aston, what are you waiting for?' Aston hadn't moved, had remained rooted to the spot like a toddler in a sweet shop, Alex wanted to at least get him inside his flat so they could talk without being overheard.

'He did it,' he said quietly, 'He shot Abby's mate…' His lips trembled as he spat out the words, but Alex understood that he needed to do this much, say the words out loud to them, tell them so his mother didn't have to.

'How do you know this?' Coupland said harshly, wondering if Rebecca and Todd's killer was one and the same. He pushed thoughts of Osman's professional style execution to the back of his mind.

'My brother told Mum last night at the hospital.

He wanted her to understand why he couldn't stay around. She tried to talk him into handing himself in but he was scared, not just about what would happen to him but I think he was scared of how I'd react. I mean, it could have been Abby…'

'C'mon,' Alex said briskly, aware that each minute they wasted was a minute further Earl had had to get away.

Hannah was waiting for them in the doorway of the flat, her eyes staring ahead, looking over the balcony but seeing nothing of the movement below: teenagers scratching their names on the children's see-saw in the playground, a man pissing in the bus stop on the ring road. At the sound of their footsteps tapping across the balcony she turned her head in their direction, nodding at Alex and Coupland as though their visit wasn't out of the ordinary.

Aston took his mother's arm and helped her into the cramped front room. There was a heaviness about her, as though her limbs were pushing their way through treacle. Her shoulders sagged too. She gave the impression she was holding her breath, taking in air only when she had to and then only in a rapid series of little gasps followed by an occasional yawn, not through exhaustion but her body's attempt to get the oxygen it needed.

Hannah pointed Coupland towards a sofa that had seen better days, invited him to take a seat. All offers of tea or coffee refused she flopped into the only armchair as though her legs had suddenly given way. Aston remained standing, taking up position behind his mother's chair, placing a barrier between him and the detectives. 'It saps you, you know,' Hannah began, 'wondering where the hell he is, what the hell he's doing, what more damage he can inflict.' She pointed to a collage of photographs strewn across the coffee table, Earl at different stages: chubby baby, inquisitive toddler, angelic schoolboy. Large brown eyes stared into the camera, a smile playing on his cherubic face.

'I can't stop looking at dem,' Hannah explained to no one in particular. Coupland had seen it countless times, parents combing over family photographs, looking for tell-tale signs to warn them of what was to come. Hannah looked over at him helplessly, her eyes shiny, lips trembling as she spoke. 'How come I was so blind?' she asked, 'Was I a bad parent?'

'No, Mum!' Aston reassured her, 'You were the best, stop thinking that way!' He looked as Alex helplessly.

'So how come I couldn't see what was happening?'

Alex remained silent, but her mind formulated its own reply:

Because if we knew, we'd give up, throw the cards in because the emotional investment was too much. She placed her hand protectively around her bump; she'd seen enough to know that upbringing alone wasn't the over-riding factor, that this baby of hers already had his own personality, his own trip switch when it came to common sense, all any parent could do was deal with the cards they'd been dealt.

Hannah held up a framed photograph taken in a studio, a close up of Earl's upturned face looking off into the distance. 'What was going through his mind? Was it all a lie?' she shook her head as though remembering every interaction she'd had with her boy, dismissing them as a waste of time. 'How could he reject the life I made for him?' Although she spoke aloud, Coupland knew her questions were no longer meant for anyone in the room. Guilt enveloped Hannah like a fast approaching tide. When had it happened, the mistake she'd made that sent Earl on his path to destruction? What crime against motherhood had she committed that could explain away his actions, for isn't that what some shrink would be assigned to do, to whittle away at his childhood until they found the moment that cleared him from blame?

All these years. All the time and energy and sleepless nights spent protecting him from the horrors of the outside world. How could she have known that the biggest threat he needed shielding from came from within.

'C'mon Mum,' Aston soothed, laying a hand protectively on her shoulder, 'It'll be alright.' His eyes locked with Alex as he said this, as though saying it aloud would make it so. Alex looked away.

Coupland had witnessed scenes like this before over the years: bewildered parents wondering where they'd gone wrong, blaming themselves for the way their offspring had turned out. Every so often the papers would campaign that parents should be punished for the behaviour of their children but they didn't see the emotional meltdown following the actions of a wayward teen, the parents' hurt and anger, the sheer bewilderment as their flesh and blood ran headlong towards a life they'd done everything to shield them from. No, Coupland concluded, those parents had been punished enough.

'Any idea where your son could have gone?' he prompted. He tried to reign in his frustration but while Earl was missing they were back to square one.

Hannah moved her head from side to side. Aston leaned in closer, wrapping a crocheted blanket that had been draped across the back of her chair over her shoulders. 'We're not a large family,' she said quietly, holding on to the blanket like a life raft. 'There's my sister in Birmingham, but he hasn't seen her in years, so I don' tink he'd go there. There's no-one else...'

'What about his father?' Alex asked gently. Aston sucked air through his teeth in disgust. Hannah patted his hand to quieten him, 'He still thinks he's a rolling stone,' she said simply, 'he's never been one for hangers on, even if the hangers on are his kids.'

'So you know where he moved to?' Alex asked hopefully.

Hannah pushed herself to her feet, shuffled slowly to a sideboard behind the sofa, pulling out drawers until she found what she was looking for. She handed a tartan address book to Alex, opening it at a certain page. 'Good luck with that.' She muttered, returning to her seat.

Coupland crouched down in front of Hannah, placing his hand on the exhausted woman's arm, 'I need to look around his room, don't get up again,' he insisted, 'Aston can come with me,' he glanced over at him as he said this, daring him to argue, 'Try and get some rest.'

'How can I?' Hannah sighed. She leaned back in her chair, eyelids drooping; the strain of the last 24 hours beginning to take effect.

Aston followed them across the hall; hovering in the doorway to the room he shared with his brother. 'The shit tip belongs to him.' He said matter of factly, pointing to the half of the room crammed with items of clothing hanging from every possible surface: tracksuit bottoms draped over the head board of an unmade bed, sweatshirts on hangers all along the curtain rail, jackets looped over the wardrobe doorknob. Trainers heaped in the corner of the room like a modern art installation, fast food wrappers scattered along every surface.

'Drives Mum mad,' Aston offered, 'that 'im reject Jamaican food for burgers served in cardboard.' Alex smiled, appreciating the effort he was making. Aston moved towards her, his face a mass of frowns, 'You told Abby?' he asked quietly. Alex watched Coupland get down on his hands and knees to look under the bed, pulling out odd socks and school books, old mobile phones. 'Not yet,' she began, wondering how much she should tell him. 'But she will need to be told, Aston,' she reminded him gently. His young face was guarded; he had frown lines on his forehead that shouldn't be there. He'd taken it badly, the news that Abby had gone into hiding. Saw it as a reflection on him that he couldn't be told where she was.

'Can I call her?' he asked, 'I need to explain…she might think I knew about it or that I was even involved,' his voice rose several octaves causing Coupland to look up in alarm. He pushed himself to his feet and came to stand between Aston and Alex. 'She has an officer assigned to her, who keeps her informed of any developments in the case. It's that officer's job, not yours, not mine, to tell her.'

'But what if she blames me..?' His voice trailed off as he searched Alex's face for a sign that she'd help him. Coupland's attention had been caught by a rucksack sitting atop Aston's bed; he distanced himself from the discussion going on and held it up. 'Is this yours?' He asked, Aston shook his head, 'No, it's Earl's, Mum said he wanted me to look after it.' Coupland unzipped the bag carefully, peeking at the contents before pulling them out one by one: sweet wrappers, a bottle of Lucozade Sport, a contraption that looked like a mobile phone until the keyboard slid off to reveal miniature weighing scales.'No need to ask what these are for…' Coupland grunted.

Alex placed a hand on Aston's arm as though sensing his anger. 'My brother's not a dealer!' He spat, 'No way!' Coupland continued to stare him down. 'He moves supplies around for Pauly when stocks are running low, that's all.'Coupland glanced at Alex; she'd clocked Pauly's name too.

'It's my fault,' Aston told them, 'this wouldn't have happened if I hadn't been sent down.'

It seemed to Coupland that people could be split into two types: The life long victims who never took responsibility for their own actions, blaming others for the choices they made, and those hell bent on wearing a hair shirt. Aston seemed to fall into the latter group. 'You're not responsible for the company he keeps,' Alex soothed, 'remember that.' She looked at the bag in Coupland's hand.

'Wonder why he didn't take it with him?' She asked, the words catching in her throat when Coupland pulled out the envelope addressed to Aston along with a torn photograph of Abby Marlowe, except the name on the back of it wasn't hers.

Chapter 36

Angela Louden sat across the desk from Coupland. If she was put out that he'd summoned her to the station she didn't show it. She sat before him composed, if a little curious; happy enough to help with his enquiries. Beside Coupland sat a WPC Angela remembered from the hospital the night Rebecca was murdered.

'How are you?' Coupland asked, conscious that whatever crime she may be guilty of, she'd still lost her child.

'Shell-shocked,' she began, 'but we have good people around us, making sure we're never left alone with too many sleeping pills.' She laughed, but it was hollow. 'I went to the supermarket the other day and the girl at the checkout had the cheek to say she couldn't sell me more than two packets of Paracetamol, yet for five pence she offered me a plastic bag to carry them home. "So I can suffocate myself instead?" I joked, though strangely enough she didn't see the funny side.'

Angela eyed Coupland steadily. 'I'm sure you didn't send a car for me just to find out how I'm keeping,' she stated shrewdly, 'So what is it?'

'Tell me about the money you've been syphoning from Rogers and Black,' Coupland replied, deciding to get to the point.

Angela didn't even blink.

'I don't know what you're talking about.' She answered, picking fluff from the smart trousers she had on. She wore a plain yellow gold band on her wedding finger; on her other hand a striking solitaire set in platinum.

'During your absence the senior partners at your firm have noticed certain, shall we say, irregularities.' Coupland expanded further: 'Several transactions involving the movement of substantial sums of money to offshore accounts they knew nothing about.' Coupland paused, 'The books aren't balancing Angela, any idea why?'

'They must be mistaken,' she replied confidently, 'they're not familiar with all the systems I put in place when I became Office Manager-'

'-Angela, they interviewed the staff, then called in accounting regulators when they still couldn't make sense of it, the regulators sent in a team of forensic accountants to conduct a full audit. They wanted to be certain before speaking to us but their fears have been confirmed now.'

Angela swallowed before replying: 'I think I need to speak to a lawyer.'

After stopping for a short spell to locate the duty solicitor and arrange refreshments for Angela the interview commenced once more, this time with Alex by Coupland's side. After checking the tape machine was working and confirming everyone's presence Coupland began his line of questioning once more.

'Were you embezzling money from Rogers and Black, Angela?'

'No.'

'Did you set up dummy accounts?'

'No.'

'Do you think your activity could be linked to your daughter's murder?'

'No!'

'How can you be so sure?' Alex asked softly, pushing across the torn photograph found in Earl Baptiste's rucksack. 'This was found in a bag belonging to the person we believe shot Rebecca. Can you confirm whether this is a photo of your daughter?'

'You've caught her killer?' Angela gasped, looking

first at Coupland, then Alex for corroboration.

'We're gathering evidence,' Alex said softly, 'but he's an important suspect.'

Angela sat forward in her chair, barely glancing at the photograph before glaring at Coupland accusingly: 'Why are you showing me this picture?' she spat angrily, 'If this is some kind of game you're playing, it's sick.' She slumped back in her chair and folded her arms. Alex waited for Coupland's signal then turned the photograph of Abby Marlowe over to reveal the name scribbled on the reverse.

Rebecca Louden, it stated simply in black ink.

The colour drained from Angela's face as the truth dawned on her. 'Oh God,' she whimpered, covering her mouth with her hands, '*Sweet Jesus.*'

'Angela,' Coupland persisted gently, 'Why don't you start from the beginning?'

Angela nodded, ignoring a suggestion from her lawyer that she might prefer another break, instead, shaking her head wildly she insisted on continuing. 'I've been so stupid.' She whispered in such a tiny voice Alex had to ask her to repeat it for the tape. 'Most people hanker after the good things in life, don't they?' Angela asked. Coupland said nothing; it was that hankering, in his experience, that got folk into so much bother.

'Go on,' Alex prompted.

Angela sighed, 'We hardly ever had money the first few years of our marriage but that's only to be expected, isn't it? John started climbing the ladder soon enough and was keen for me to stay at home with Rebecca, which I was happy enough to do. When the time came for her to start school I had itchy feet and longed to go back into the workplace but didn't really have anything to offer an employer. I went to night classes at the local college and twelve months on secured an admin job at Rogers and Black,' a year after that I was awarded my diploma and they promoted me to Office Manager. I'd been bitten by the learning bug then,' she said proudly, 'decided to study on-line for a degree.'

'Life was good, we enjoyed great holidays, went out for meals in smart restaurants, we couldn't have been happier - then just like that John lost his job. I was so confident he'd get another but I hadn't anticipated the blow it was to his confidence. ' Angela smiled at Alex as though seeking out an ally. 'It was like treading on eggshells each time I talked to him about our future. I missed the fun we had, I suppose.'Angela confessed. 'I got this idea in my head that I was valued at work,' she added bitterly, that they actually gave a damn. By then I'd been there fifteen years, thought of the firm as an extension of my own family. I asked for a meeting with the partners, asked if they'd considered making me an associate partner.' Angela paused, the memory of it still raw. It really hadn't been that much of a stretch but do you know what they did? They laughed. They actually laughed at me, said they didn't know what I was thinking of! I hadn't graduated from a top university; I hadn't spent my traineeship with a blue chip organisation. To top it off they claimed the part time degree I'd got was second rate…'

'Well, you can imagine how I viewed our relationship after that. I'd developed all these systems, introduced a new client database they hadn't a clue how to operate and it occurred to me that I could use that to my advantage. Any loyalty I'd had towards them had gone.'

Angela paused, as though summoning every ounce of willpower to continue. 'So, I started moving money about, small amounts at first, just to see if anyone noticed but they never did – I was their control mechanism, I was the person who signed cheques and oversaw the juniors' work, double-checked for errors – or foul play. No one bothered to oversee what I was doing.' Angela shook her head at the simplicity of it. 'I was never greedy.' She said in her defence.

'Didn't John wonder where all the extra money was coming from?' Alex asked. Angela lowered her head, 'He thought I'd got the associateship,' she confessed.

'Then one day John telephoned me at work to tell me he'd got a job!' Angela smiled at the memory but it died on her lips. 'That should have been the end of it shouldn't it? No more deception… Then one day Mike Rogers stopped by my desk and asked if I could stay behind that evening. He told me one of the partners was due to retire and they'd be happy to discuss an associate position with me. I couldn't believe it, after all this time they were offering me what I'd asked for but I'd backed myself into a corner - once someone else took over my old post there was every chance they'd uncover my secret. I had to rectify what I'd done – and fast.'

'I couldn't take out a legitimate loan – how would I have explained that to my husband? Instead,' another pause as though choosing the right stream of words, 'I made the worst decision of my life.'

Angela stared at Coupland, shame and despair etched into her face. 'I went to see a moneylender. I'm sure he thought his Christmases had all come at once.'

'How much did you ask for?' Coupland asked.

'Twenty thousand.'

The room fell silent as the detectives contemplated the financial abyss Angela had leaped headlong into.

'I began to pay back the firm's money,' Angela picked up the story once more, 'and no one was any the wiser. I kept up with the repayments, and life returned to normal. Then after about six months I got a visit from a very unpleasant man who said that he'd recalculated my loan and I needed to increase my repayments by two hundred percent. I'd already paid back half the original amount; they were now expecting me to treble that in the same period of time. I couldn't do it, which I now understand was the whole point.

"Perhaps there is another way you can repay your debt." He said when I objected, and went on to explain that occasionally he needed to move large amounts of cash in a hurry, and that not all of his outlets were secure. If there was a way I could take some of this money and…'

'…launder it,' Coupland completed her sentence, 'he'd wipe out the interest payments on your loan.'

Angela nodded. 'A year passed by and he was still bringing me money. I'd repaid the original twenty thousand plus the original amount of interest and moved over four hundred thousand pounds through our books. I was terrified I was about to be discovered, my tenure as associate partner had been confirmed and I just wanted to put an end to it all, so the next time he came round I refused, told him I'd more than fulfilled my part of the bargain.' Angela shuddered.

'He just looked at me and laughed. "It isn't over until I say it is." he warned me before walking away. A couple of weeks later my purse was stolen while I was out having coffee with a friend, apart from the inconvenience I thought nothing of it until that creep turned up at work. I took him into one of the meeting rooms – I didn't want anyone getting suspicious; put it this way, he didn't look like our usual type of client.

'He held up a photograph which I'd kept in my purse,' she pointed to the torn photograph on the desk, 'told me I must be very proud of my daughters. "I just have one daughter," I corrected him naively, and his face broke into a grin. "What's her name?" he asked, and I was too frightened to lie, besides, I didn't want him causing a scene where I worked. "Rebecca." I told him, hoping like mad that he'd leave.'

'"Which one?" he persisted, holding the photo in front of me and I finally understood the threat.'

Angela looked at Coupland, then Alex, before spreading her hands on the table top between them. 'You

have to realise I was desperate for him to leave me alone,'
she begged them; 'I was scared and just wanted it to end.'

'What did you do?' Alex asked softly.

Angela couldn't meet her eye: 'God forgive me,'
she whispered, 'I pointed at Abby.'

'I think we need a break now.' The duty lawyer
insisted.

*

'So what do you make of that?' Alex had
accompanied Coupland to the canteen where she'd
ordered a bacon roll with the lid dipped in fat. Coupland
called out to the woman behind the counter 'make that
two,' before carrying their tray with coffee and sauce
sachets to the table.

'I think that Angela was quite happy to offer up
her daughter's best friend as a target,' he said sadly, 'she's
now got to live with the consequences.'

'Why the hell didn't she report it when their
demands got out of hand?' Alex asked in frustration. So
often tragedies could be headed off at the pass.

Coupland shrugged. 'Pride? Greed even? As she
said herself, she'd finally got what she wanted…'

They ate in silence, each trying to imagine how
desperate you'd need to be to do business with the
moneylenders around the city. Their reputation for
violence was well documented in any local news rag, yet
still people used them. 'It's easy to condemn going to
them,' Coupland observed, 'but for some people it's the
only option open to them if they want to buy presents for
their kids at Christmas.' Alex considered this, picturing
Ben's face the year before when he'd found an Xbox
sitting under the Christmas tree. 'But access to credit
wasn't Angela's problem,' She countered, 'She could've
got the money from anywhere she wanted.'

'Pride's a funny thing though. Why confess her
mistake to her hubby or fabricate a reason for the loan to
a bank manager when she could do business with

someone outside her social circle, someone who, once the loan was repaid, she'd never have to see again?'

'Fair point.' Alex conceded, licking the grease from her fingers and taking the paper serviette from the tray.

'Thinking about booking a holiday,' Coupland said out of the blue, 'you know, after Lynn's treatment has ended. With Amy too. This time next year she'll have sacked us off good and proper, thought it would be good to have one last holiday before she flies the nest.' Alex imagined Ben leaving home and her insides tightened. 'So where do you fancy?'

Coupland pulled a face, 'That's the bloody problem, none of us can agree. Amy's after us going to Ibiza, like that's gonna happen, and Lynn fancies somewhere spiritual, like India.'

'And you?'

'I've always fancied Vegas…'

Alex laughed, 'Who do you think you are, George Clooney?' Coupland sat back in his chair, a faraway look on his face. 'I can see myself at the roulette wheel, wearing a tuxedo and sipping a cocktail…'

'More like slumped in front of one of those slot machines in your joggers, bitching about all the money you've pumped in and the price of the beer.'

'Christ,' he grumbled, 'I might as well be at home, the sympathy I get from you. Aren't we all allowed to dream a little?' Then all at once they found themselves thinking of Todd Oldman. Alex knew he was telling her this in an attempt to waylay her, put her off asking how his meeting with Todd's parents had gone. She'd tried asking earlier, all she'd been able to get out of him was a tight-lipped 'Grim.'

'Just make sure you book something.' Alex told him softly.

'C'mon,' Coupland said, getting to his feet, 'Let's get this show back on the road.' He looked at Alex and laughed. 'I think you've been working with me for too long.'

'Why?'

'You've got brown sauce on your top lip.'

By the time they'd returned to the interview room Angela had calmed down, although her face was still drained of its colour. 'My client is willing to make a statement.' Angela's lawyer informed them. Coupland nodded. 'There's something else I need to know before we begin,' he said. 'I need the name of the money lender you went to'

Angela looked stricken. 'I-I don't know his name!' She replied, 'The name of his company is Corden Holdings, but I only saw him once. He was foreign, well-spoken, but once I'd signed the contract and began repaying the original loan it was a regular stream of young men who'd turn up at the door. That was, until the guy who demanded a change in the terms took over the debt, he became the regular face after that.' Mallender suspected both men worked for the same company but didn't see the point of going into that right now.

'OK,' he conceded, 'can you tell me anything about the last man that came to see you?' Angela shook her head. 'Only that he wasn't polished like the other man, far more threatening, otherwise I'd have never taken out the loan. He was a brute, largish, but not fat...hands like shovels, oh, and there was a tattoo on the back of one hand, a bird of some sort...'

Coupland stored the description away whilst Alex made notes to be included in the statement Angela would sign at the end of the interview. He studied her as she answered Alex's questions, the stoop of her shoulders as she leaned forward in her seat, the tremor in her voice and her sudden inability to look either of them in the eye.

Coupland suppressed a sigh.

Pride.

In his experience it always came before a fall.

Every single time.

Chapter 37

Alex had finished updating the incident room board. A photograph of Angela Louden and Earl Baptiste had been added to it, with arrows pointing from them to Rebecca, more arrows still leading from their photographs to a large question mark with the words *moneylender with bird tattoo* in brackets.

A crowd of officers joined her while she brought them up to date with the investigation. Earl Baptiste didn't own a passport but they weren't taking any chances: his photograph had been circulated to all UK ports and airports; all stations had been alerted that he was on the run – possibly armed and certainly desperate. Robinson studied the board. 'So this kid, Earl Baptiste, he confesses to shooting Rebecca but not Todd's murder. Can we trust him?' he asked, not unreasonably.

Alex shrugged. 'Why confess to one killing and not the other?'

'Because one involves killing a cop,' Coupland responded, 'and whoever did that knows they're not gonna see the light of day for a very long time.'

'I still don't buy it,' Alex persisted, 'this kid's gone to great lengths to finally confess to shooting Rebecca Louden – he's running the risk of the members of his gang catching up with him before we do – going inside would have been safer.' Even as she said it she knew that wasn't quite true. Aston had already told her about Paul Constantine's connections in jail; it wouldn't take long for those with a grudge to reach him.

'To be fair, I think his confession is on the level,' Coupland stated, 'the way he tells it is that he thought the order to shoot someone was some sort of initiation, rite of passage, I don't know…call it what you will. Either way he thought they were testing him. That at some point along the route there they'd tell him they were winding him up…but they didn't. Instead, they handed him a photo of the girl, even pointed her out in the line, only in his panic his aim faltered and he shot her mate.'

Alex ran through the content of Angela Louden's interview, her admission that she'd been blackmailed into laundering money.

'It seems that the shooting wasn't as random as we first thought,' she added, 'Rebecca Louden was the intended victim all along. Angela was up to her ears in a scam that meant threats were being made against her family; she deliberately made the thugs think that Abby Marlowe was her daughter.'

'Charming!' Turnbull muttered, 'So when this lad killed Rebecca by mistake, he'd hit the rightful target all along.'

Robinson whistled through his teeth. 'What tangled webs we weave…'

And then, 'But how did they know the girls would be at the nightclub?'

Alex shrugs, 'I'll bet one of the gang members had been following Abby Marlowe for a couple of days. Maybe they saw her queuing for tickets, maybe it was something else *mommy dearest* let slip, all they had to do after that was circle the nightclub every half hour or so after the doors opened until she appeared in the line.'

Robinson: 'So does this kid mention *any* names?'

Alex shook her head. Reaching behind her to a chair piled high with files and reports she retrieved a photocopy of Earl's crumpled note, passing it round for the officers to study.

'As you can see he's keen to make it clear about his own guilt,' she observed, 'but he's chosen not to name the driver or the other passenger. His brother is convinced Paul Constantine is involved somewhere along the line – Earl had agreed to do a job for him on the night of the shooting – it is possible that Constantine would've wanted to be up close to the action, getting his thrills at someone else's expense.'

Coupland banged his fist on the desk. 'Shit, something Angela said when we interviewed her has been bugging me but I remember now – I'm certain the bloke visiting her at work to pile the pressure on was Billy Peters,' he piped up, pointing to the photo of Paul Constantine then moving his finger along to where Alex had written up the description of the man who originally persuaded Angela Louden to launder money, 'he's in cahoots with Paul Constantine, *and* he has a tattoo of a swallow on his right hand.'

Earl's heart thudded from exertion and fear. When the 4x4 mounted the pavement outside the hospital he'd turned on his heel, running back the way he'd come, cutting through the hospital car park to the area reserved for consultants' cars. It was down an unsignposted ramp where a sharp turn was required by those in the know. Kester, still circling the perimeter of the visitors' car park, had no idea about the narrow access road reserved for senior medics. When Earl was small his mother used to bring him here, show him the smart cars the consultants drove. Together they'd look at the Porches and top of the range beamers, 'Maybe you'll drive cars like that when you grow up.' She'd say to him. Fat chance of that now, unless he stole one. From the parking bay a narrow walkway led to the hospital's main entrance and the cluster of bus shelters across from it. Earl ran towards the nearest bus stop, jumped on a bus that was just pulling out.

He was hungry. He had fifty pounds in his pocket but was too scared to stop to get anything to eat in case he was still being followed. The bus's final stop was the railway station at Manchester Piccadilly. Seemed like fate was helping him along, Earl thought, immersing himself in a crowd of commuters beginning their journey home. All he had to do was work out where to go. He had an auntie in Birmingham but the first thing she'd do was ring his mother and although he didn't want her to worry, he couldn't go home just yet, especially when going back could mean she and Arlene were in put in danger.

Going to jail didn't scare him half as much as trying to live on the outside now Pauly wanted him dead. He'd killed a young girl for him then witnessed a cop being murdered on his say-so. He was a threat to Pauly and both of them knew it. He wasn't like the other members of Pauly's crew. They were hard men, career criminals who thought nothing of killing someone if they got in their way. He was just a stupid boy, he saw that now, a stupid, gullible idiot boy who whichever way you cut it was guilty of killing someone too. Dale might be stupid, but everyone knew that was the drugs. God knows what Earl's excuse was; his shoulders drooped when he realised there was none. And now, as well as the police he had Pauly on his tail. Pauly, who would stop at nothing to keep him quiet.

Earl sighed. He deserved his punishment, he'd done a terrible thing and he needed to pay for that. What stopped him from handing himself in was the pressure the cops would put him under to grass up the others. All he had to do was bide his time, a cop had been killed and the police would be pulling out all the stops, or so he hoped - once the main players were rounded up he could hand himself in without any fear of reprisals to his family. Family came first. He'd been too busy running around with the wrong sort of guys to realise what mattered most. He thought of Aston, hoped to hell his brother didn't hate him. *I need him to be in my corner;* he thought sadly, *I need him to hear my side of the story.*

While Aston was inside money had been tight,

their mother had taken on several jobs while Earl looked after Arlene. Only it was never enough. Then Pauly came calling, claiming he was asking after Aston but he had spies inside jail that he could have used for that. It was like he had a sixth sense, a way of sniffing out desperation, offering him money, substantial amounts that meant their bills would be paid on time, that their mother wouldn't need to work so much. Aston and their mother would never have approved. *Our secret,* Pauly'd soothed. *There might be a time when I need you to do a job for me...* Only one job kept leading to another, and look where that had got him.

The station tannoy announced the London train was due to leave in five minutes. Earl didn't know anyone in London, and right now that appealed to him. He ran towards the platform, jumping onto the last carriage just before the conductor blew his whistle.

Coupland opened his front door, calling out automatically for Lynn. It sounded daft but he liked her being around more, since she'd reduced her hours it meant she was home several days in a row and he enjoyed the evenings they spent together, whether talking about Amy or staring at the TV they shared moments together that twenty years of shift patterns had denied them. He wondered quite when they'd turned into Howard and Hilda, two halves of a psyche that performed more effectively together than alone, but he wasn't complaining. He only wished they'd had some choice in the matter, that Lynn's health hadn't been the cause of it.

There was no reply.

He called out her name again whilst moving through to the kitchen on automatic pilot, switching on the coffee machine and scanning the garden through the patio doors: Autumn bulbs lying beside empty pots, a large bag of compost left unopened– no sign of work being done today.

Coupland tried to quell the unease that engulfed him whenever Lynn wasn't where she was supposed to be. He knew it was selfish but their routine reassured him. It was as though the cancer had stripped them of the right to be spontaneous; so much of their life revolved around hospital visits and chemo that nights out and weekends away had to be pre-planned with care. Since they'd got the diagnosis he'd been watching Lynn like a hawk, looking for any sign he was losing her.

'Kev?'

Coupland followed Lynn's voice, found her lying on the sofa in the front room, a fleecy throw tucked around her, a pile of cushions supporting her head.

'What are you doing there?' he had to clear his throat several times; his voice came out high pitched, as though someone was strangling him.

'Oh, I was tired,' she answered sleepily, 'the weather's not been too clever today and the bulbs can wait,' She inclined her head in the direction of the kitchen and the garden beyond. 'Thought I'd put my feet up, have forty winks before you got back.' Coupland sank onto the footstool so he could lean in close. Burying his head into her neck, he closed his eyes. His heart pounded beneath his ribs. He was still reeling from visiting Todd Oldman's parents.

Curtis, already writing the eulogy for the rookie's funeral, had wanted to try a couple of sound-bytes out on him during the drive over. 'It's essential we convey words of comfort to his parents,' he'd stated, as though anything else was an option. Coupland had merely nodded. He'd felt guilty, his insistence on accompanying the Super was partially a selfish one, a way to road-test someone else's grief, try it on for size, see if when the time came he would sink or swim.

It was Todd's father who'd answered the door, but within seconds his wife had joined them in the hallway; a mother's instinct that all wasn't well. Afterwards, they had driven back in silence, Coupland staring out of the window at a city oblivious to the turmoil going on within it.

'What is it, Love?' Lynn whispered into Coupland's hair, her hands already moving to his face, lifting it so she could look him in the eye.

'I'm tired too.' He said evenly.

Carl was having a rare night out with the boys. It was late, Ben despatched to bed hours earlier was spark out in the land of nod, eyes shut tight against the world outside. What did he dream of, Alex wondered as she smoothed his fringe away from his forehead. Dragons? Demons? The latest computer war game that everyone in school seemed to own bar him? Unable to settle she pottered from room to room taking solace from the photographs that adorned every surface: Ben taking his first steps on an Easter trip to Legoland; holding aloft a rubber dinosaur; taking his first swimming lesson.

It was impossible these days to look at the snapshots of her life with Carl and not reach out, touching each one as though making sure every image was real, not an illusion, an imagery of the life she thought they had. She found herself plumping cushions in the living room and straightening tea-towels in the kitchen, lining up pens on the hall table so they were in line with the writing pad beside them. Each piece of furniture she passed received a tender stroke. What was she so frightened of, she wondered, that she found reassurance in rituals? She worried for the baby inside her, for the world she'd resigned him to. Was she tempting fate, pushing her luck; was her family's good fortune about to come to a sudden and violent halt?

Todd's murder had made Carl jittery. Most of the time he managed to push fears for her safety to the back of his mind but during her pregnancy his imagination seemed to go into overdrive; Todd's killing proved his worries were justified.

Alex had finally persuaded Coupland to open up about Todd. On the first day he'd partnered him the rookie had mentioned a sibling at university. Turned out this was wishful thinking. Todd's parents informed Coupland that their oldest daughter had got caught up in drugs in the sixth form. Suffering from bouts of paranoia and becoming increasingly more violent she'd been expelled from school and was in the process of being thrown out of the family home – the couple had been at the end of their tether, had thought tough love would shock her into seeking help.

She died from an overdose of Heroin and diazepam following an argument.

Her death had changed the course of Todd's life; before she died he'd wanted to go into teaching. He'd have made a great teacher, Alex thought, one of those trendy high school types all the kids wanted to be like. Instead drugs had killed him too, albeit in a round-about way.

Once the news embargo on Todd's murder was lifted there'd be uproar on the streets, the media would feed on the public's constant fear of crime, it would be an all-out invitation to the lawless to up their game.

A superbly executed tumble-turn from junior startled Alex back to the present. She placed her hands protectively around her bump. 'Be patient,' she whispered to her unborn child, 'you'll have me to yourself soon enough. Just let me deal with this last case; let me do this one last thing for Todd.'

Earl's first impression when he got off the train at King's Cross was how busy the station was. Imagine how big the city must be, he thought, to have this many people coming in and out of it each day, how easy it will be to get lost. He smiled his first smile in days; the prospect of being anonymous soothed him. Pushing all thoughts of his family to the back of his mind he followed the exit signs, found himself passing a Burger King reminding him he hadn't eaten since the night before, hadn't wanted to waste the money he had on the rip-off prices on the train. He walked up to the counter.

Chapter 38

'Press restrictions are to be lifted on Todd Oldman's murder this afternoon so we need to be prepared for the media circus.' Mallender surveyed the room as he said this, his eyes resting on those he felt needed it spelling out to them, 'All questions must be directed to the press office and on no account do you express anything other than your condolences to the family. Preferably don't even say that, I know Superintendent Curtis has been drawing up a statement in readiness, we don't want to send out any contradictory messages.'

'I'd like to send out a message.' Coupland murmured to the detective beside him, catching Mallender's glare but ignoring it. 'C'mon, boss,' he said defensively, 'I think Joe Public'll understand we're not too fuckin' happy at the moment.'

Mallender raised his hand in mitigation, 'I get it, but can you imagine how we'll look when all reasonable comments have been edited out and the six o'clock news is full of knuckle grazing cops swearing revenge. It'll hardly do anything to reassure the public; just convince them we're not capable of being impartial.'

'How can you be impartial when they've come after one of your own?' Coupland demanded. 'That's the point!' Mallender said animatedly. 'We need to reassure the public we get fired up over every case equally, not pick and choose who we care about.' Coupland could feel his throat contract, he always tied himself in knots when he tried to get his point across, either that or he ended thumping someone. He decided to keep his mouth shut. For now.

'Alex,' Mallender said, moving the briefing on, 'what've we got back from the PM?' Alex sucked in a breath. 'Todd's throat was cut using a kitchen knife,' she said slowly, 'it had some sort of serrated edge, which explains-'

'-Why the bastard made such a mess of trying to take off his head.' Coupland finished for her, 'I was the one who found him, remember?'

'Easy now,' someone muttered behind him, which had the effect of lighting touch paper. 'Are you having a laugh?' he exploded, getting to his feet and turning around to glare at the roomful of officers behind him. 'You didn't see how they left him...'

'Coupland...' Mallender tried to bring him back but he was already at the door, arms raised as though wafting away a swarm of angry bees, 'I'm done!' he snapped, storming out. Alex caught Mallender's eye, waited for his permission to slip out of the room. Permission granted, she nipped out of the room discreetly, or rather as discreetly as she could for someone who looked like they'd consumed their own bodyweight and then some.

Coupland was standing outside in the smoking bay that someone from health and safety had insisted on erecting given the number of fire doors that were being wedged open so staff could have a sly smoke. Resembling a Perspex bus shelter with lean-to seats it provided much needed protection from the elements now the weather was turning. Only there was something wrong with the setting. Alex had to study the scene for a moment to realise what it was. Coupland wasn't smoking. Instead, he leaned against the shelter staring out into the car park like a shepherd surveying his flock. He'd had his back to her but the tap of her heels on tarmac made him turn round.

The look on his face told her she wasn't welcome.

'Leave me be, Alex.' He said as she approached him.

'Now why would I do that?'

'I just need a minute, OK?'

'For what?'

'Just leave it, yeah?'

Alex considered Coupland's request. It wasn't like him to keep his grievances to himself, he could be a narky so and so at times but he liked to snipe to an audience, was never one for keeping his cards close to his chest. Something was wrong.

'Is it Lynn?'

Coupland bent forward as though he was going to be sick, holding onto the side of the shelter for support.

'Kevin?'

The sound he emitted was low, like an animal in distress. He couldn't bring himself to look at her. Up until now Alex had kept her distance, had stayed a good arm's length away but she moved to him now; placing both hands on his arms she drew him to her.

'I'm gonna lose her.' Coupland whispered into the gap between them, so softly she had to strain to hear him.

Alex looked at her friend, feeling useless in the face of his misery. How would she feel if she were in his shoes? How would *she* deal with it? Tightening her grip on Coupland she searched his face for some hint of what he wanted from her; what he needed.

'Not yet.' She said firmly.

Coupland looked down at his shoes, as though checking them for dirt. 'There are days she looks so vulnerable, like a puff of wind could blow her over…and I get so angry. She works on a baby unit for Christ's sake, cares for sick little scraps like each one is her own, how the fuck did she deserve to get cancer?'

'It doesn't work that way, Kevin.' Alex said softly, though she knew what he meant.

Coupland shook his head in wonder. 'She rules the bloody roost at home, keeps me and Amy in check…I wouldn't know what day of the week it was if she didn't tell me.'

'I always suspected as much.'

Coupland paused, as though weighing up his next words. 'We had a good life before, now everything has changed; I have to pitch in more, and it's not about that, don't get me wrong, but Lynn's always looked after me in ways I can't ever do back; she has a knack of knowing things…things that don't even register on my wavelength…I just feel if it had been me that was sick our life wouldn't be so different, that she'd have carried on caring for me and I'd have carried on being the one who was cared for. Now…well, she has to depend on me more and more and you wouldn't wish that on your worst enemy would you? I mean, what kind of bedside manner do *I* have?'

'A crap one, probably,' Alex answered truthfully, 'but a funny one, too. You make her laugh, right? And trust me that's worth a hell of a lot more than plumping up pillows just right. Besides, if it had been the other way round you'd have been a grumpy git, admit it - you'd have made all your lives a misery so how would that have been any better?'

'Maybe.' Coupland conceded.

'So do what you're good at, Kevin, because that's what Lynn needs right now.'

'DS Coupland! DS Moreton! Boss wants you back!' Turnbull shouted down from a second floor window, closing it quickly in case Coupland retaliated with a mouthful.

Alex looked at her friend, inclining her head in the direction of the station's automatic doors, 'You ready?' she asked anxiously.

'As I'll ever be.' Coupland quipped, unsure whether Alex was asking about returning to the incident

room or coping with his world as it crumbled around
him.

Mallender had returned to his office by the time
both detectives made their way to the second floor. 'The
PM report is back about Osman.' he informed them
before sitting behind his desk. He'd allocated actions to
the other officers before dismissing them from the
incident room.

'It confirms it was a professional hit.'

Coupland nodded, the clean shot to Osman's head
had made it clear it was no lucky amateur.

Mallender repeated the information they'd missed
while Coupland had gone to cool off. 'Witnesses saw a
dark coloured 4x4 driving away from the locus at speed
shortly after the estimated time of death.'

Coupland already knew this much. It irked him
that door to door enquiries along the canal where
Osman's body had been found had failed to gather
anything else. Most people only wanted to engage with
the police if they themselves were the victim of crime;
when the crime happened to someone else the urgency to
find the perpetrator was gone, along with their memory.
It was amazing really, how many folk suffered from
amnesia.

Alex moved into the only other available chair.
'What does the Super say?'

'He's alerted the NCA, but for now they're happy
for us to do the grunt work.'

'Right up until we make progress and they come
over the hill to take the credit. 'Coupland sniped.

'Pretty much,' Mallender conceded.

'Look, I'm not sure that we should fight to keep
this,' Alex objected, 'we're overstretched as it is with
Todd's murder, I don't know how many plates we can
expect to keep spinning in the air.'

Mallender nodded, 'Normally I'd agree, but in the

space of a week we've had three murders, and thanks to Earl Baptiste's hand written witness statement we now know Todd's murder is linked to the killings of Rebecca Louden and Osman Afram, but we need evidence the CPS will accept and the say so of a killer doesn't cut it.' Mallender paused as though weighing up his words. 'And I think we've got more chance of gathering that evidence if we have some level of autonomy over all three investigations.'

'You mean the NCA won't share information with us even if it's crucial, so we need to go find it ourselves. 'Coupland could be relied upon to tell it like it was. If Mallender harboured any doubts about the sergeant's ability to cope during his wife's illness he had no such doubt about his commitment to do the right thing.

'I think it's fair to say you've hit the nail bang on the head, Kevin.' He said.

Abby glanced around the characterless room and sighed. How the hell had it come to this? To have to hide from view because there were people out there who wanted her dead. She shuddered as she recalled the sight of the twins lying side by side in hospital. She had brought danger to their door simply by telling the truth and now all their lives had changed. Three months ago she'd baulked at leaving them to go to university, what kind of fate was she resigning them to now? At best a foster home, at worst they'd be placed in care with occasional visits to an immobile mother.

If she could she would undo it all, claim she hadn't seen a thing, let the cops do the donkey work finding out who'd pulled the trigger. As far as she could see they were no nearer catching the culprit despite the description she'd given; and here she was, separated from her family while she waited to be sent to a new town or county where she wouldn't know a soul – wasn't that a form of punishment in itself?

From the sofa in the living room Abby watched

the two officers assigned to protect her move about the flat as though it was perfectly normal to bunk up with a stranger, a maudlin stranger at that. They offered her tea and endless biscuits, making small talk like being on the Witness Programme was no big deal. She waited for them to go into the kitchen to prepare the evening meal before slipping out her phone.

Moving into her bedroom, she hit the speed dial then waited for it to connect. She let it ring twice before ending the call. She counted to ten before ringing once more. This time the call was answered immediately.

'Hello babe,' she said quietly into the receiver.

Chapter 39

Abby's breath came in gasps, forced, as though each one was her last.

'I have to go and say goodbye, she was my best friend!' She argued, pulling at her clothing as though the neckline was too tight. She was angry that no one had informed her Becca's body had been released for burial, thank God Aston had told her that the funeral had been arranged for tomorrow.

'It's too dangerous,' Coupland objected, knowing it wouldn't be that simple. 'You've seen what these people are capable of, you'll be a sitting target the moment you go anywhere near the place.'

'I need to pay my respects.'

Coupland sighed. 'I know.' And then she rounded on him. 'When were you going to tell me that Aston's brother had confessed to shooting Becca? Surely that means I'm no longer needed as a witness? That I can come home?'

Coupland was at a loss for words, unsure which answer would cause least hurt.

How could he tell her that by sticking her head above the parapet she was a dead woman walking, that Earl's confession didn't protect her from harm?

'Your statement corroborates Earl Baptiste's confession,' he agreed, 'it confirms that he's telling the truth when he says there were two other people in the car with him. He doesn't name them, but we're pretty certain we know who they are-'

'So why can't you take them off the street?'

It was pretty much what Abby's boyfriend had

yelled at him the night Earl had been reported as missing, when he'd asked to see Abby and Coupland refused to tell him where they'd moved her to. He could understand their logic, but they were applying common sense, not the law. 'We have warrants for the arrest of Earl Baptiste *and* Paul Constantine,' he said slowly, 'but until we have identified all the main players in this gang and lifted them at the same time, there could be reprisals.'

Abby studied his face.

'Something has happened, hasn't it? *It's not my-*'

'No,' Coupland reassured her, 'your family is safe.' He sifted through the information he could trust her with, mindful she was still in contact with Aston despite warnings not to speak to anyone. 'One of our officers was killed.' Coupland paused to give Abby a chance to take the information in. 'We know there's a connection - can you see now why you're in the best place, that until we know what the hell we're dealing with you need to remain out of sight?'

Abby's breath came out in a sob but no tears followed; instead she pushed herself to her feet and began to pace around the room. She moved towards the window.

'What are you doing?' Coupland swallowed back the alarm in his voice.

'I need air,' she gasped, 'can't breathe.'

Fearful in case anyone had followed him there and was studying each window from a car below he pulled her away, guided her towards the back wall separating the kitchenette from the bedroom. 'Here,' he said, 'do this.'

He folded his arms before resting them on the wall in front of him, just above his head. Abby stared at him as though he was crazy, but her breathing was so erratic it was like she'd forgotten how to do it at all, so she gave it a go. She copied his stance, her forehead touching the cool wall.

'It opens your diaphragm see,' Coupland

explained, 'so with each breath you take in more air.' It was a coping mechanism the nurses had shown him when Lynn went into hospital for her mastectomy. He'd spent many an evening, in the first weeks after her diagnosis, standing facing a wall.

'Now, breathe out to the count of five, your body'll do the rest.' Within a couple of minutes Abby's breathing returned to normal. She turned towards him, her eyes asking if this was what her life had been reduced to.

'I still need to be there.' She said stubbornly, reminding him of Amy when she wanted something he'd already said no to. 'I'm sorry.' He said, moving purposefully towards the door before he could change his mind.

Earl walked into the pub behind the boy he'd met in Burger King earlier. The kid was the same age, shorter than Earl with a bottle scar just below the hairline on his forehead. *Mates call me Vinny,* he'd said, promised Earl a night on his sofa in return for a Whopper n fries. They'd turned left when they'd come out of the restaurant, away from the bright lights of the station; instead the road they were taking was dimly lit and uneven. A shabby pub stood at the centre of what looked like a condemned row of shops. Vinny paused at the door to usher Earl inside. 'Gonna introduce you to a mate o' mine.' He told him.

A smartly dressed man leaned against the bar reading a paper. He looked about forty, dark hair already balding on top. Tig, Vinny said his name was. Tig nodded, taking in Earl's dishevelled appearance.

'On the run?' He asked, not unkindly.

'No.' Earl replied.

Tig smiled, like he was used to being lied to and it didn't bother him one bit. 'Here,' He said, his hand already inside his wallet, lifting out a couple of twenties that he pushed in Earl's direction.

Earl's heart sank. Easy money and a bed for the night. By tomorrow they'll have him dealing, either drugs or sex it made no difference.

He'd left behind everyone he cared about for what?

Another bully boy calling the shots.

Alex stared at her reflection in the compact mirror. Miss Piggy stared right back. She was red faced and bloated; the make-up she'd applied so meticulously that morning had all but slithered off. She snapped the compact lid closed. 'Where the hell did my cheekbones go?' she asked Coupland as he shut down his computer. 'Same place as my six-pack,' he quipped, patting his stomach for effect. 'It's baby weight, Alex, stop fretting. It'll fall straight off once you've had the nipper. At least you've got an excuse.'

Alex smiled, 'I take it all back, you can be quite nice at times. Just hope I can find something smart that I can fit into for the funeral tomorrow.'

'I didn't know you were going.' Coupland turned off his desk light, checking his pockets for car keys and mobile before moving over to Alex's desk.

'Think the boss wants someone to go with him.'

'Which boss? I thought Curtis was going.'

Alex shook her head. 'He wants Mallender to go, said there should be someone with operational responsibility present now Abby's going to attend.'

Coupland thought he'd misheard her. 'She isn't going Alex, she asked me if she could attend but I told her it was too risky.'

Alex frowned. 'Sounds like she wasn't taking no for an answer, then. Kevin..?'

Coupland was already out the door.

'You're having a laugh, aren't you?'

Mallender's door was ajar and Coupland stomped over the threshold without waiting for an invitation.

'You're letting Abbey Marlowe go to Rebecca's funeral?'

Mallender looked up from the report he was reading; pushing back from his desk he leaned back in his chair as though he'd been waiting for Coupland to show himself. 'I took a call from my equivalent in the protection squad,' he said, holding a hand up to silence Coupland while he explained, 'he said he'd had a call from one of the officers assigned to Abby, told him she was kicking off, wouldn't put it past her to slip out and go anyway.'

'And they can't handle a teenage girl?' Coupland spluttered.

'Seems not.'

'Look,' Mallender placated, 'I ran it by Curtis-'

'-who no doubt ran it by the ACC,' Coupland interrupted, 'So now the general arse covering has been carried out, has anyone given thought to this girl's safety?'

Mallender ignored the barb. 'It's a done deal, Coupland,' he said, adding, 'Curtis did a risk assessment...'

Coupland had heard it all before.

'We'll all sleep better for that then.' he muttered sourly.

Chapter 40

The mourners gathered at the entrance to the chapel, moving forward at a snail's pace, eyes downcast, tissues gripped tightly in fists that shook as they took their places inside. Once the pews were filled the overspill of friends and acquaintances assembled at the back, shifting their weight from one leg to the other as they waited for the service to begin.

Mallender had travelled in Alex's car, the low-slung seats in his own MG not suitable for a heavily pregnant passenger. 'I could get in,' Alex observed when they'd considered which car to come in, his smart MG or her battered Fiesta, 'but I'd never get out again, not until my waters broke anyway.' She'd added, that last sentence convincing him her car was the better choice on this occasion.

They'd parked along the track leading to the crematorium, walking the final two hundred yards or so passing a memorial garden with several rows of small brass plaques dedicated to loved ones, mounted on plinths. Small posies had been left here and there, an occasional teddy bear forcing Alex to look away. She found it hard during her pregnancy to control her emotions, felt one blink away from tears at a moment's notice.

Although Mallender had said that Abby could attend the funeral, he'd made it clear there were conditions. The conditions came in the form of the two armed plain clothes officers assigned to her - they would accompany her to the service and not let her out of their sight. It was the best he could arrange given the short notice, normally a patrol car would have been deployed to drive around the perimeter but there wasn't time – nor resources, Curtis reminded him – to coordinate this. Mallender was there to make sure that Abby's attendance went without a hitch. He could understand Coupland's nose being out of joint but that was because he was caught up in the thick of it, couldn't see the wood for the trees; the least they could do, given that she was their chief witness, was let her say goodbye to her friend.

There was a moment's hush as Rebecca's parents paused at the mouth of the chapel. They looked hollowed out, like empty versions of their former selves. They'd learnt the hard way there were no certainties in life, other than the certainty nothing in the future would ever surprise them again.

'Angela!'

Angela's head lifted meerkat-style as she searched for the person who'd called out her name. Abby propelled herself forward from between her two minders, hair tied back into a simple ponytail; she wore a dark raincoat over work clothes. Angela held out her free hand, forcing the corners of her mouth into a smile as she did so. Scanning the sea of faces as she walked towards the pews at the front of the chapel Abby locked eyes with Mallender, briefly nodding her thanks.

An hour later mourners filed out of the chapel, returning to cars that would ferry them to a local hotel where food and drink had been laid on. Abby stood back as Angela and John thanked people for coming, shaking hands and listening politely to mumbled platitudes. The Special Branch officers stood directly behind her, heads bowed but eyes trained on her, careful not to let her slip from sight.

'Thank you,' she whispered to Mallender as he made his way over to her.

'For what?'

'For making it possible for me to come. I know it

won't have been easy.'

She didn't know the half of it. No other services had been permitted that morning, allowing officers to search the chapel with a fine tooth comb. Sniffer dogs had worked their way along the pews, looking for concealed weapons or explosives. Abby had been categorised a Priority 1 witness, which basically meant after the trial she'd be offered plastic surgery to alter her appearance. Mallender studied her flawless complexion; she wore contact lenses now and her hair had already been dyed, yet even that couldn't detract from her beauty. He thought of a surgeon being given the task of removing a stunning girl's looks, wondered for the thousandth time what the hell the world was coming to.

The chapel had emptied; work colleagues and neighbours hung around, not wanting to appear keen to get away. Smokers lit up for want of something to do. Mallender moved to Abby's side. 'Has Rebecca's mother said anything to you?' he asked. Abby looked over to where Angela and John stood talking to the minister who'd conducted the service.

'No,' she said simply. 'Not directly, but she sent me a letter.' Abby's relatives and close friends had been given a P.O. Box number to write to, which her assigned witness protection officer visited on a regular basis and brought directly to her so that her new address was not written on anything that could give her location away.

'I was so angry when I first read her letter, I mean, how could she knowingly let a thug think I was her daughter? But then, after a while I figured my anger was pointless. Not like it can change anything. Besides, her deception back-fired big time didn't it? And I wouldn't have wished that on her, no matter what. In a way she's serving her time now, isn't she? Seeing me today must have killed her inside, a reminder of what she's gambled, and how much she's lost.

'You know it's funny, I keep thinking back to how

she was in the office – so efficient, so self-assured, when all the time she had her hand in the till. In her letter she explained the reason behind staying in their home rather than moving to a bigger, more expensive property was because she didn't want to draw attention to her spending. Meals and holidays can be obscured, and when, like me, you've no money at all, when someone tells you they're going out for a slap up dinner that could have meant anything upwards from a Little Chef and I'd have been none the wiser.' Mallender nodded, although he couldn't help but notice Angela's expensive watch and dress ring; thinking she wasn't as modest as she liked to make out.

'We'd better go,' the officer nearest to Abby instructed. Abby looked at her watch.

'We're going to the hotel though?'

The female officer shook her head.

'But I was hoping to see Aston there!' Abby looked at Mallender for backup but something in his face told her she was on her own with this one. Besides, the fewer people she saw from her previous life the easier it would be when the time came to relocate her.

'Better do as you're told, Abby.' Mallender said simply but Abby was having none of it. 'For Christ's sake,' she cried, backing away from them, 'how much more of my life do I have to give up?' Frustrated at no longer having the power to make decisions over the simplest of things Abby ran away from the crowds and into the memorial garden where council workers were tidying away old wreaths. Mallender called out to her to stop playing silly beggars when one of the gardeners caught hold of Abby's arm and at first Mallender thought he was trying to help but instead of staying put he dragged her towards a van concealed by overgrown shrubs. Abby struggled against him but the van doors opened revealing two men in black balaclavas who reached out to bundle her inside.

Mallender glared at the plain clothed officers in disbelief. 'I thought you'd checked the whole area!' he yelled.

'They had ID!' one of them yelled back as they ran towards the van just as the back doors slammed shut and the driver started the engine. Mallender followed, throwing himself at the side of the vehicle, banging his fists on its side all the while shouting for the officers to draw their weapons. At the sight of the first officer's gun the crowd began screaming, Alex, who'd been talking to mourners had to shout to be heard over the screeching of tyres:

'Everybody get down! Please! Now!'

Most folk did as they were told, grabbing small children and pushing them down on the ground, those who weren't shouting whimpered.

All Mallender achieved by hanging onto the side of the vehicle was obscuring the officers' line of vision. The van began to increase its speed, swerving sharply, making him lose his grip as it made its escape through the crematorium's exit.

Chapter 41

Coupland's heart hammered in his chest. Of all the stupid cock ups he'd ever had to clear up after, this one beat the lot. Every one of the rank and file who had decided Abby Marlowe could attend Rebecca's funeral needed their head feeling good and proper; this was a first class fuck up and no mistake. The mourners, still pole-axed by the shock of it all were proving to be the best part of useless when it came to providing details. Those who had done as they were told and got themselves out of harm's way during Abbey's abduction had precious little to add to what Coupland couldn't have worked out for himself just by looking around the place. He could see there'd been a struggle in the memorial garden, the discarded shovels told him the kidnappers had probably posed as gardeners.

He'd said that much to Mallender already, only the DCI had stuck by his original view, didn't seem to share Coupland's opinion that this had been a fuck up waiting to happen.

Pride.

Police vans arrived to cordon off the crime scene, Robinson and Turnbull were taking witness statements. Coupland walked Alex back to her car, telling her to go straight home. Although visibly shaken she was reluctant to leave, 'Go, please,' he'd urged, he was keen to be on his way himself, needed to know Alex was out of harm's way first. Something in his face must've told her that the last thing he needed was resistance so she conceded defeat, agreeing to go home on condition he call her the moment there was any news.

You mean if we find Abby's body.

Coupland turned away abruptly, marching over to Mallender who was standing by a squad car; he looked shell shocked, his clothes were dishevelled as though he'd rolled around the grass verge in them.

'I can take it from here, Sir,' Coupland said, his politeness saying more than a string of expletives ever could. He opened the car door, nodding to the PC at the wheel to start the engine.

'I want to stay and help.' Mallender objected.

'You've done enough,' Coupland stated, 'besides, Curtis has been trying to get hold of you.'

'I bet he has.'

With Mallender dispatched Coupland turned to a middle aged man nursing bruises from throwing himself to the ground with force. He'd already drawn a blank with the description of Abbey's kidnappers; they were wearing balaclavas, which was the only thing on which everyone agreed. Even the number of assailants was sketchy. 'Can you at least give me a description of the van?' Coupland asked.

'There was writing on the side.' The man said helpfully.

'What did it say?'

'Not sure,' the man said sheepishly, 'Wasn't wearing my glasses.'

'Give me strength.' Coupland sighed.

The Incident Room appeared to have shrunk in size, either that or the personnel milling around it had multiplied. There were uniforms and plain clothes officers Coupland didn't recognise; another white board had been erected with Abby's photograph placed at the top of it. An Asian man stood in the centre of the room, his eyes lit up when Coupland entered the room.

'DCI Amjid Akram, National Crime Agency.' He said, hand outstretched, pausing while they both shook hands.

'DS Coupland. No need to ask what brings you here,' Coupland said sourly, though fair play; the officer outranked him yet had taken the time to shake his hand. 'I take it you're new?' he added drily. Amjid was medium height with short-cropped hair; dark rimmed glasses framed a young looking face. He seemed pleasant enough, not his fault he was treading on Coupland's toes.

Coupland looked around the incident room; there were barely any faces he recognised. He regarded Amjid suspiciously, 'Where's Curtis?'

'Ensconced in his office with a DCI Mallender...'

'Hmmm...No surprise there then.'

'Sorry?'

'It doesn't matter,' he said briskly, the clock was ticking and he didn't intend to spend it babysitting visitors while Curtis and Mallender slugged it out in playing the blame game. 'But if you wouldn't mind telling me exactly why you're here?'

Amjid nodded, 'A Crown Prosecution Witness has been kidnapped,' he began, as though spelling out the blinding obvious were needed, 'my team is here solely to track down...' he glanced over to the incident board and the large photo that had been pasted onto it, read the name scribbled underneath, '...Abby Marlowe, the missing girl.'

He caught Coupland's look of impatience. 'Look, I've been brought in to do a job,' he said simply, 'not to get in the way. I can help you find her.' He moved towards a map of Salford that Coupland had used to mark the location of each incident relating to the case – Rebecca Louden's shooting, the canal where Osram Afram had been found and the wood where Todd Oldman's body had been discovered.

'You've got a spiralling body count,' Amjid added, 'You need us in your corner right now.' 'If you can spare me the time to bring me up to speed...fill in the blanks your senior officers aren't able to help with?' Amjid asked, 'then you can carry on with your own line of enquiry. I can see you feel I'm holding you back.'

Coupland nodded, 'You are,' he said honestly, but if it helps us find her...'

'Just give me five minutes of your time...' Amjid coaxed.

'OK...'

Mallender found himself turning off the slip road that led to his parents' home. He sped down the leafy suburban street where the houses were a respectable distance apart, lawns not overlooked, gravel paving wide enough for several family cars. Pulling in behind his father's Jaguar he rapped quietly on the oversized front door before he could change his mind.

Swallowing his guilt he waved away the invitation to come in for a drink, instead he asked his old man to get his coat.

'This isn't a social call, 'he blurted, believing he stood a better chance if he was upfront from the beginning.

'I can tell.' John said simply.

Mallender glanced at his father sharply, he wasn't in the mood for another confrontation, his run-in with Curtis was quite enough for one day. He'd learned a valuable lesson though, that while the senior ranks might approve your decision they retain the right to apportion blame when it goes wrong, and shit only ever runs downhill. There'd been no sighting of the van that had driven Abby away from the crematorium two hours earlier, and thankfully no bodies. Curtis had appointed a DCI from the NCA to lead on the abduction. *This has got the propensity to turn into a bloodbath,* he'd said simply, glaring at Mallender as though he alone were to blame.

His head was still reeling, Abby had been snatched away right before his eyes. He felt twelve years old again, watching helplessly as his twin sister was carried out of his life, her eyes boring into his soul. He gripped his hands around the steering wheel, watched as his knuckles turned white. They were several miles out of the area before Mallender realised his father hadn't asked him what the hell he was doing, he'd merely climbed into the passenger seat leaning back into the head rest. Maybe that was the benefit of living life in the fast lane, or rather on the other side of the tracks, Mallender mused. You learned to deal with whatever life threw at you.

'So, care to tell me what's going on?' his father asked.Mallender sighed, 'I'd need to make sense of it first.' He replied, shaking his head, 'One of our officers was taken down yesterday. A kid still wet behind the ears.'

'I didn't hear anything.'

'News blackout. We asked for 24 hours to give us a head start. There'd be panic if the public thought they were caught up in the crossfire between two warring gangs.'

'And you think that's what it is?'

'It's more than that.' Mallender tried to hide the catch in his throat. 'Our chief witness in the drive-by went missing this afternoon.'

'The girl?'

Mallender nodded. 'It smacks of someone going out of their way to cover their tracks. Someone with local pull but resourceful enough to keep one step ahead of us. Three dead bodies in the space of a week – no obvious connection but there sure as hell is one I'm sure of it.' He looked at his father hoping he didn't have to beg but prepared to do so all the same. He hoped to God he wasn't wasting his time; that he'd not embarked on some fool's errand while Abby was in danger. It pained him to think that his father could be right, that there was no such thing as a random act of callousness where executions were concerned. 'Someone's trying to cover their tracks, son; they must be pretty big tracks if it's worth committing murder for.'

The proximate cause had been Angela Louden's deception. She'd embezzled her employer's funds to live a lifestyle she felt she deserved, and before long became embroiled in a lucrative money laundering scam. But who was pulling the strings? The shell company, Corden Holdings, had a derelict lock up as a registered address, and so far attempts to trace any of its employees had been met with defeat.

'I need your help,' Mallender said simply, 'I need to know who's really behind all this…I need to find Abby.'

'What makes you think she's still alive?'

Mallender's blood ran cold through his veins at the prospect that it was already too late.

'So I sit back, wait until she becomes another statistic before I lift a finger?' he demanded. 'Another dead girl?'

Mallender's father said nothing, letting the silence give them the space they both needed to gather their thoughts. 'I've been thinking,' he said after a while, 'since the other night when you were telling me about that shop keeper's execution. There was a guy…Cal reminded me of it later, nasty bastard in a suit, a foreigner, one of the first to bring drugs into the manor. I kept him at bay for a long while…but the truth was he was offering easy money.' His father sighed, as though some things were beyond his control. 'It was like Wall Street had come to Salford, and before long cons were smuggling gear in and buying and selling like they were on some stockbroker's trading floor, was it any wonder they began to turn their noses up at honest crime?'

'Anyway, this bloke, he had a bit of money already, from shady property deals he'd headed up in Spain, he moved onto importing goods, only everything he shipped in came via Amsterdam or Morocco, know what I mean?'

Mallender nodded. He knew the type well enough;

only there were hundreds of them now, each responsible for bringing millions of pounds of Class A substances into the UK every month. The depressing fact was that the Drug Enforcement Agency was struggling to keep up, confiscating only a fraction of the supplies reaching UK soil. And now with the advent of so-called legal highs the force was entering a political minefield – pressure from parents to respond to their concerns but a legislative process that couldn't keep up. One minute industrial cleaners are the substance of choice, the next an extract from plant food – how were they ever going to stay on top of that? And all the while the money from this trade fell into the same old greedy hands.

'Anyway this guy's sons have taken over the family business, so to speak, and rumour has it it's the worst decision he's made.'

'How come?'

'They can't keep their hands out of the till. Bleeding the business dry with their fancy cars and lifestyles to match, they're constantly on the lookout for ways to make money while barely lifting a finger.'

'Money laundering?'

His father nodded.

Mallender shrugged, 'So where's the connection?'

'Their right hand man is a thug called Paul Constantine-.'

'-Jesus,' Mallender said eagerly, 'I know all about *him*.'

Mallender stared at his father as he spoke. All these years he'd spent keeping his distance when the old man knew the pulse of the city more than any specialist crime agency. He could do a lot worse than invite his old man into the station to run a briefing; he stifled a smile as he imagined Curtis' reaction to *that*.

'The brothers rule half of Salford. Their territory runs from Manchester's City Centre to Salford Quays.' This made sense, both ends of the patch included wealthy clients looking for relief from their highly paid jobs in the city's financial and media districts, the area in the middle belonging to those whose habits were paid for by the welfare state. Mallender thought about Amjid Akram coordinating data back at the station. He should really call this in. He turned to his father. 'Can you take me to them?' he said instead.

Gibson directed Mallender to a café on Pendlebury Road. It was small; resembling a converted terraced house with a large front window, a sign on the door stated *Halal food served here.*

They parked across the road; Gibson pointed to three big men dressed in traditional Muslim clothing sitting in the window. They broke pieces of bread before dipping it into oil, talking animatedly with Paul Constantine.

'The Mossbank Team, in all their glory.'Gibson muttered.

The brothers were dark skinned with short wiry hair beneath cotton Kufi skullcaps. All three wore smart cotton Najib shirts. Two of the brothers sported trimmed beards, the youngest, still in his teens, hadn't sprouted anything worth trimming yet.

'So, Pauly answers to them.' Mallender muttered as he watched him get to his feet and touch fists with the trio before leaving. No sooner had Pauly set one foot on the pavement, a blacked out 4X4 pulled up outside, engine purring as it waited for him to climb into the rear passenger seat before speeding off. Inside the café the brothers had got to their feet.

'Let's follow them,' Mallender instructed his father.

Gibson shook his head. 'No point.' He said, nodding in the direction of the town centre where the Call to Prayer carried over the loud speaker from the minaret atop the mosque, watching as the brothers joined the throng of worshippers that seemed to gather from nowhere, as they set off to pray. 'No guesses where they're going.'

Mallender nodded, rubbing his eyelids with the heel of his palms while trying to work out what the hell to do next. He had no evidence yet to link these men to Abby's kidnap, other than the company they kept. He needed to speak to Superintendent Curtis, get him to find out from the Drug Enforcement Agency surveillance unit following Pauly that it was safe to lift him. It occurred to him that if the DEA had been as conscientious about keeping Curtis informed of *their* operations Todd Oldman might not have put himself in danger but it was a painful thought, one better pushed to the back of his mind for picking over later.

'Apparently the boys rediscovered their faith after a trip to Pakistan.' His father piped up, still watching the brothers' retreating backs. 'Came back spouting all sorts of fundamentalist stuff, rumour has it their money laundering scams are funding extremist cells already set up over here, biding their time until given the nod.'

Mallender closed his eyes. It would explain the urgency to remove anyone who could lead the police to what was really going on here – the funding of a terrorist group already living in the community.

After making a brief call to Curtis about Paul Constantine, Mallender started up the MG, heading back the way they came so he could drop his father off at home before returning to the incident room. He may have pieced together more links in the chain of events but he was no nearer the whereabouts of Abby. The longer the silence the less hope there was that this was a ransom and the chances of a passer-by stumbling upon her body increased hour by hour.

'Who would they use to make a professional hit?' he wondered aloud. Whoever had executed Osman Afram had access to weapons and cars not available to the ordinary hard-nosed criminal. The shooting had been close range and deliberate, with no prints left behind at the scene. This killer knew their stuff.

'He'd need serious bank-rolling, but-'

Mallender turned to look at his father, Christ, what more could he know?

'But what?' he prompted.

'There's a guy from Amsterdam, Jon Bujak, he's at the top of his game right now...'

They slowed at the traffic lights, Mallender drumming his fingers on the steering wheel while a group of school children took their time at the crossing, swearing and flicking chips at each other.

'He's pricey, but then money's not an issue here is it? The Zadawi brothers come from expensive stock-'

'What did you say?'

'That they come from expensive stock, their old man's mint-'

'Not *that*.' Mallender butted in, 'what did you call them?'

'The Zadawi brothers.'

'Omar Zadawi's their father?'

'You betcha.' Gibson chimed, 'You've come across him then?'

'You could say that.' Mallender said grimly, pulling in sharply against the kerb.

'You'll need to get a cab from here,' he said abruptly, looking around to see they weren't far from Swinton precinct, a cab firm operated from a unit across the road, around the corner from a massage parlour and sauna that had been the cause of a Scottish politician's fall from grace a couple of years before. His father would be home in less than ten minutes.

'Where you going, son?' His question met with a squeal of tyres as Mallender executed an illegal U-turn, going back the way they had come. He wondered when he'd ever learn. He hadn't liked Omar Zadawi from the moment he met him yet still he had chosen to believe the man, thinking his only crime was giving life to a feckless son. Just how much of Rebecca Louden's shooting had been staged? Given the intended target had been Abby, was it still a coincidence that both girls had become separated from their other two friends right at the entrance to the night club? The bouncers had let two of the group enter the club but Rebecca and Abby had to wait.

Another of life's crazy coincidences?

Mallender hit the speed dial on his hands-free kit and waited for the recipient to pick up. He needed someone skilled at extracting truth with the minimum of time.

'Coupland…' the familiar voice barked into the receiver, prompting Mallender's first smile of the day.

Chapter 42

The Sportsman's Bar was a recently refurbished bar on Swinton Precinct. A wall mounted plasma TV permanently tuned into the Champions League; signed replica football tops provided the only décor. The smokers standing outside were old enough to drink there but it was a close call; Tattoos were mandatory going by the number of bare arms on show; the air reeked of cheap cologne and attitude, and that was just the women.

A dumpy woman too old for the leggings and low cut top she'd squeezed into that morning allowed herself to be felt up by the doorman unaware of the man who'd stopped just behind them looking on as the bouncer's hand worked its way inside the woman's tunic.

'I'd be wanting danger money for that Warb,' Coupland cautioned, 'or at least a safety harness.'

'Cheeky bastard.' The woman retorted, then, when she saw that the bouncer wasn't going to defend her honour she tutted before stomping back into the bar.

Warby exhaled slowly. 'What d'ya want?'

'Sorry for spoiling your fun.' Coupland lied.

Warby shrugged, not quite hiding a smirk. 'Lucky escape.'.Coupland looked up at the sign over the door. *No baseball caps or trainers,* wondered who the landlord was trying to kid.

'How did you know I was here?'

'Your wife told me.'

A blush spread along Warby's neck.

'Moonlighting?'

'Need the money.' Warby replied truthfully.

'How come?'

'Shelley's pregnant again.'

Warby stepped back into the doorway, placed a hand in the middle of a punter's chest. 'Not tonight, mate.' He said authoritatively, standing his ground until the man slunk away. 'What was wrong with him?' Coupland asked, 'IQ in double figures?' He shook his head, the world kept on turning as long as there was someone you had power over.

'I'm sure you've not come here to watch me work.' Warby muttered as he returned to Coupland.

'You got that right.' Coupland responded. 'I'm here about Ashraf Zadawi, your boss at Ego, you ever collect money for his old fella, Omar?'

Warby sighed.

Coupland kept on staring.

'Look,' he began, 'I asked Ashraf for an advance on my wages. He said he couldn't do that but said I should have a word with his old man; he was always looking for people to collect his loan repayments. All I had to do was call at a few houses the same time every week; pick up their cash, that was it. Easy money.'

'Should imagine it was for a big guy like you.' Coupland observed.

'Fair enough.' Warby conceded with a roll of his shoulders.

Coupland changed tack.

'The night the young girl was shot outside Ego. You were one of the fellas on the door, right?'

'You know all this; you saw me there, one of your lot took my statement.'

'Bear with me Warby,' Coupland placated, 'It's been a long day. Sometimes I need things spelling out for me.' He pulled a cigarette pack from his pocket, offering one to Warby before lighting it then his own. He inhaled slowly.

'Who told you to separate the girls when they got near to the front of the queue?'

Warby looked shocked. '*What?*' he shook his head wildly, 'I have no idea what you're talking about.'

'A group o' four girls arrive at a nightclub, two are let in, two are left standing in the queue. I want to know why.'

'One of them wanted the toilet.'

'And that would be a good enough reason for you to let them queue jump?'

Warby nodded but said nothing.

'So in your operating manual or whatever you call the bouncers' code of conduct, you are expected to let every Mary, Jane and Fanny in who can't control their bladder?'

'Well, when you put it like that…no, we'd be expected to use our judgement.' Coupland tried but failed to keep his face straight.

'How many others asked if they could jump the queue-?'

'-It was only by a few minutes! They'd have got in soon enough.'

'You didn't answer my question.'

'I don't know! There's always a few try it on I suppose.'

'So why relent with these girls? What made them so special, and why leave their two mates outside?'

Warby waved his arms in frustration, 'Jesus, I don't know…it's just a job, you know, I just do as I'm bloody told.' He touched his earpiece, pausing to listen to the hiss that travelled down the wire. 'I'm on my way.' He spoke into the microphone wire just visible beneath his lapel.

To Coupland: 'Look, I'm needed in there,' he nodded towards the pub's entrance, 'it's kicking off inside the ladies toilets again.'

'What's the range on those things?' Coupland asked, pointing to the radio transmitter inside Warby's jacket pocket.

'Up to 100 metres I think.'

'So,' Coupland paused to take a final drag of his cigarette before crushing it underfoot. 'You didn't make the decision. You followed orders that you got down the radio.'

Warby studied his steel toecaps.

'Christ man, we're talking *Accessory to Murder* here, *Joint Enterprise* if the CPS have the stomach for it,' Coupland threatened, 'You need to start looking after your own arse rather than covering someone else's.'

'I didn't know she'd get shot!' Warby hissed, 'I swear it.'

'So who gave the order?' Coupland persisted, staring at Warby until eye contact was re-established. 'Who told you to let two of the girls in but keep the redhead and her mate outside?'

'Omar Zadawi.' Warby muttered.

Chapter 43

Abby blinked and looked again. The room she'd been bundled into earlier looked down onto the valley of Irlam, which meant she was half a mile from home. She felt overcome with joy, but then it occurred to her that if they wanted her dead they didn't need to take her far in order to kill her.

She'd feared for her life when they'd bundled her into the back of the van and sped away from the officers who'd been assigned to protect her. She could still see the look on the inspector's face when he realised what was happening. He'd looked genuinely afraid, as though his worst fears were about to be realised which had frightened her all the more. One of the kidnappers – she still wasn't sure how many had been involved – had clamped his hand over her mouth before replacing it with tape smothering the scream that had risen in her throat.

'Don't make it any fuckin' harder than it needs to be.' Someone hissed as he grabbed at her legs, tying them together with something thin and sharp, making her suck in her breath.

Something that felt like a pillowcase was slipped over her head, secured around her neck with more tape. She hadn't seen any faces, just blurs of black balaclavas pulled down low. Someone jerked her arms back holding her wrists together while they were also secured with twine. She tensed her body, ready to receive whatever blow was coming but none came, instead she found herself being pushed onto the floor where she lay quietly, trying not to knock into the legs of the men around her as the driver crunched through the gears making sharp turns as they made their escape.

After what seemed like an age the van came to a halt and someone banged on its two rear doors. Abby felt herself being lifted out feet first; the crunch of gravel underfoot the only sound she could make out. No one spoke, which she took to be a good sign. If they were going to kill her they wouldn't care what she heard, what she saw for that matter. They carried her up a flight of stairs which made her feel quite out of sorts by the time they finally let her stand, like the first few moments when a theme park ride comes to an end. One of her captors removed the twine from her ankles; another stood behind her and began to unravel the tape securing the pillow case to her head. No attempt was made to free her hands. Only when the door shut once more did Abby dare to turn her head to check she was alone. She cocked her head; raised voices were coming from the floor below.

Coupland's call to Amjid in the Incident Room had been brief. Long enough to tell him where to assemble the Firearms Unit, and to learn that an assassin known to the security services had flown into Manchester Airport from Amsterdam seven days earlier before disappearing off the radar. The next day Osman Afram, the kebab shop owner, had been executed.

'And we're only just hearing this now?' Coupland barked.

'They're not going to advertise the fact they'd fucked up, are they?' Amjid said simply, 'We've only found out this much because your DCI had a tip off from an informant.'

Just as well, given *this* fuck up was down to him, Coupland thought sourly.

A pause, then: 'How long till the T.U. are in place?'

'They were already on stand-by, but this property's near a busy road so we need to put road blocks in place first, my guess is half-hour tops.

Coupland prayed that wasn't half an hour too long.

'Why the hell did you not follow orders?' Omar Zadawi demanded, glaring at Billy Peters like he was something he'd stepped in, 'Can you not do this one simple thing?'

'Your sons told to me to bring her here and await further instructions!' Peters yelled back, 'Which is what I've done.' This seemed to stop Omar in his tracks, 'Even Ashraf?' he asked, 'Are you saying Ashraf contradicted me?' Billy sensed the answer he gave now was important to the old man, besides, he knew enough about family dynamics to not get caught up in them if he could help it.

'Not Ashraf,' he said honestly, 'the others.'

'Bah!' Omar seized on this admission, tried to turn it to his advantage. 'Don't you see they are not to be trusted? What kind of boys try to set their own father up?'

Billy didn't answer; the men he came across in his line of work would sell their granny and their first born if they had to; instead he tried to look sympathetic. 'If you could just pay me what you owe me, Mr Zadawi…'

'You need to move her to the nightclub, like we agreed. Look, I'll even pay you for your trouble, isn't that fair?'

Though the prospect of extra money appealed Billy knew the chances of moving the girl across the city without discovery now the cops were looking for her were slim. He cursed himself for telling the other lads to bugger off; he'd thought all he had left to do was collect the money and he hadn't needed anyone else for that.

'*I don't think so.*'

Zadawi and Billy Peters turned in unison to stare at Jon Bujak. Neither had had the opportunity to meet the trained killer before, his credentials had come recommended by a far higher link in the chain, one that neither of the men wanted to get on the wrong side of. Especially not now, the older man thought to himself, for in Bujak's right hand was a .5 calibre gun.

'The girl's upstairs.' Zadawi informed Bujak, his reluctance at having Abby here now forgotten. She'd be easier to move once dead, he reasoned, which he hoped Billy fuckwit could handle on his own.

Billy didn't seem as convinced as Omar that the cavalry had arrived. In fact since Bujak had turned up he hadn't been able to tear his eyes away from the assassin's gun.

'Show Mr Bujak where the girl is.' Zadawi instructed Billy, like he was a bell boy in some 1950s movie. Billy didn't move. Zadawi turned to him, irritated by his lack of drive.

'What is it?' He snapped, conscious that all the time they spent staring at each other the higher the chances Sofia would walk in on them and how the hell could he explain away Bujak's gun? Or the girl tied up in the bedroom, for that matter.

'It wasn't supposed to happen this way.'Billy said slowly, stepping away from Zadawi.

The old man stared at him. 'What are you talking about?'

Bujak moved closer. 'He means that I've been hired to kill you, only he's starting to wonder what's taking me so long.' He turned his attention to Billy. 'Am I right?' Billy gulped a yes.

Zadawi wasn't a stupid man, had already computed his options. His own gun was kept in a drawer in the study and it was clear Billy would offer no protection.

He started to back away. 'My sons, they are behind this?' he asked, already knowing the answer. 'Not Ashraf, though.' Billy piped up like it mattered now.

Like any of it mattered.

By the time the message was patched through to Mallender that shots had been heard coming from Zadawi's property he had already turned into the slip road that led to Zadawi's house. Two cars and the van that had been used in Abby's abduction were parked on the gravel drive. Leaving his car out of sight behind the garage Mallender ran around to the back of the house, remembering the large patio doors that looked out onto the lawn when he'd visited the property with Coupland.

The scene that met him as he looked through the window caused him to catch his breath. Two bodies sprawled on the floor. He clawed at the window, his heart pounding wildly as he took a step back to work out how he could get in. Running like a mad man he found a side door slightly ajar which led into a garden room. Moving from one room to another he re-oriented himself with the layout of the house, locating the large sitting room where he and Coupland had waited for Zadawi.

His first thought when he discovered that it was Omar Zadawi and Billy Peters lying dead on the floor was relief. It wasn't Abby. He let out a long slow breath, fearful that even that could be heard from another room. Then another thought chilled him – what if Abby had been left for him to find in one of the other rooms? He shook that thought right out of his head, he had to stay focussed. He decided against using his phone – the Tactical Unit was on its way, nothing he could say or do now would change how quickly it'd get here.

Mallender crept into the hallway.

Chapter 44

Coupland arrived at Zadawi's home in time to find Mallender looking through the large window into the sitting room and whatever he'd seen there made him enter the house without waiting for back-up. He knew better than to call out to Mallender, alerting him – and whoever else was in there –to his presence.

He decided to follow him instead.

Once inside the house he found the bodies of Omar Zadawi and Billy Peters. He felt nothing at the sight of their shattered faces, at least, no pleasure that they were dead. He'd always hoped to cross paths with the gob-shite garage owner, but in his mind's eye it was in in a dark alleyway with no CCTV at its start or its exit, just him and the dumpy con man knocking seven shades out of one another. As it was, the end result was better than he'd hoped, just without the satisfaction.

Taking the stairs two at a time he stood on the landing unsure which way to go next. The first floor split in two directions with a number of rooms leading off it. Damn. The same feeling of helplessness had overwhelmed him after speaking to Warby outside the Sportsman Bar. The bouncer, once he'd started talking, developed verbal diarrhoea, telling Coupland of the growing unrest between Zadawi and his sons who seemed intent on taking over the reins of the family's business empire with, or without, his blessing. It didn't take a genius to work out that returning to Ego, the nightclub where Rebecca Louden was shot, would provide him with missing links to the chain. It was there that Coupland had spotted a surveillance van parked close to the entrance, decided that the boys inside might want to share some of their *intelligence* with him, save him having to ask questions that had already been answered.

Twenty minutes later and he'd emerged from the van with the missing names from the chain of command and the knowledge that Abby Marlowe had been taken on the orders of the Zadawi family. Seeing the DCI's car speeding towards Omar Zadawi's house told him the boss had worked it out too. The only thing he didn't understand was where the hell he'd got *his* intel from.

As he crept along the landing a feeling of unease settled upon Coupland's shoulders; the dead bodies downstairs and a van out front told him two things.

Abby Marlowe was definitely here.

But so too was the assassin hired to kill her.

Mallender circled the rooms downstairs; instead of a long hallway each room led into another: the sitting room led into a grand dining room, beyond that a family room with a state of the art kitchen leading off it, each room impeccable, no sign of a struggle or of occupation for that matter. He entered Zadawi's study which was situated towards the rear of the house, moving towards a large oak desk he searched through a couple of drawers when he heard a floorboard creak above him.

Whoever was in this house was upstairs.

Abbey stared wildly at the man who'd walked into the bedroom she'd been left in trying to work out whether he was friend or foe. When she'd heard the gunshots downstairs she'd harboured the hope that the police had arrived, that any minute now they'd rush in and untie her, take her *home* to her mum and the twins. Instead this man had sauntered in casually, staring at her for the longest of moments as though checking her face against the one he'd consigned to memory.

Then he pointed a gun at her.

Coupland edged along the landing in time to see a broad shouldered man open a bedroom door. The contract killer, he assumed, given the man pulled out a gun and pointed it at Abby who was tied up on a bed.

Coupland swallowed.

This should be the point where *his* job ended and the tactical team's began, where he could stand down and wait as the specialist marksmen got into position. He thought of Curtis and his sodding risk assessments. It was easy for the higher ranks to hide behind procedure; his Amy was the same age as this tied up girl and if she were in danger he prayed that someone with big enough balls would step up to help her. To him it was that simple; you can't want it for your own yet not be prepared to do it for someone else's.

It was a no fucking brainer.

Of all the thoughts that raced through his mind at that moment the irony of leaving Lynn a widow when she needed him most loomed largest.

He blinked it out of the way as he ran towards the killer's back.

As he mounted the stairs Mallender saw the tactical unit through the large galleried window. His heart sank. They were taking instructions from a senior officer but the fatal flaw in whatever plan Amjid Akram had put together was blindingly obvious now they were here. Zadawi's property overlooked the valley of Irlam which meant there were no properties or even trees opposite for the marksmen to use to get into position, nowhere for them to take aim at Bujak once they'd located him. The best they could do was wait on standby and charge into the building when what? When Abby had been shot and all that was left to do was apprehend the killer?

He'd been too late once before, when he'd watched dumbstruck from the landing as a kidnapper abducted his sister. He wasn't going to put himself – or another girl - in that position again. He ran up the remainder of the stairs two at a time.

The scene ahead of him stopped him dead in his tracks.

Coupland was clinging onto the back of Bujak as the killer tried to shake him off. Panting for breath, Coupland shoved Bujak into a wall, causing the killer to use both arms to buffer the impact. At least for the moment Abby was no longer in his line of fire.

Mallender saw his chance. 'Police! Drop your weapon!' He knew it was like standing in front of an oncoming train but once Bujak saw him he would have no choice but to deal with him first, for Coupland, though closer, didn't pose the same threat at all.

For Mallender was holding a gun.

Ahead of him Bujak smiled, as though this kill was an unexpected bonus, as though he'd worked out he was on a losing streak so he might as well take as many with him as he could. He raised his arm, hand steady, finger squeezing the trigger. Coupland's reaction was super-fast, kicking Bujak's arm so that his shot would not be a fatal one. It was then that all hell broke loose. The landing exploded into gunfire as marksmen stormed up the stairs shooting Bujak in the head when he refused to put down his weapon. The tactical unit lined up on the landing moved in quickly, securing the scene before untying Abby. Through the crackle of static a message carried over the radio: *Urgent assistance required, officer down, repeat, officer down.*

'Officer Down.' Alex adjusted her earpiece, holding her breath while she waited for more news. Sat in the control room she studied the expressions on the faces of the officers around her, registered the shock, the moment suspended in time while they awaited confirmation of the officer's I.D. and condition.

'Who is it?' she blurted into her mouthpiece,

stomach griping with fear. Coupland and Mallender had both radioed in to say they were on their way to Omar Zadawi's home, she'd not heard from either man since. She waited while the officer on the other end asked his colleague for an update; the sound of approaching sirens could be heard in the background.

'DCI Mallender.'

'Is he alive?'

She waited for a response, some reassurance that he was walking wounded. None came.

A wave of pain rose up from her lower back, coursing through her like an electrical overload causing her to jolt forward in her chair. Perhaps Carl was right, she thought suddenly. Who was she trying to kid, telling him the job wasn't dangerous while at the same time insisting on manning the control room from a surveillance unit at the scene of a hitman's killing spree. If you looked at it like that then she could understand his fear for her. But what else was she to do? Once they'd discovered where Abby had been taken to Alex knew that's where she had to be, not just for Todd, a rookie guilty of nothing more than being over-zealous in the hunt for a drive-by shooter, but also for Aston, a young man going out of his mind for a girlfriend he couldn't help anymore.

Being pregnant didn't stop her being part of a team she cared about, but Carl was right, she conceded, as the pain continued to rip through her; it did make you vulnerable. She gritted her teeth through the next contraction; she wasn't going anywhere till she knew Coupland was OK, and what the hell had happened to the boss?

'Sarge?' Robinson was the nearest one to her, placed an uncertain hand on her shoulder. 'Is it the baby?' Alex's head reared up incredulously, her eyes locked and loaded onto his own. 'You think?'

The entrance to the surveillance unit opened and

Coupland rushed in, accompanied by DCI Akram, keen to get a debrief before the stocky sergeant was sent home. Coupland was in one piece but shaken, his clothing dishevelled even more than was usual. He looked tired, but one look at Alex and he was over by her side. 'Who the hell authorised you coming here?' he demanded, glaring at Akram in case he was to blame.

'Never mind that Kevin,' Alex gasped, relieved he was safe, 'How's the boss?'

Coupland's face fell serious, his normally chirpy face creased into a frown, 'He's not great,' he answered looking from Alex to the other officers assembled in the small unit, 'He'd lost consciousness when he fell but the paramedics are with him now.' Alex groaned, both hands gripping her abdomen as she doubled over.

'He'll be fine, Alex, it's you I'm worried about now. 'Coupland helped her to her feet, by now several ambulances had assembled outside the property, most of the paramedics were standing around, waiting for confirmation as to the number of casualties. 'Good timing.' he observed, swallowing his fear as his gaze fell upon the pool of blood remaining on Alex's chair. Alex gripped onto her stomach as another wave of pain washed over her. 'It feels like I'm being ripped apart.' She whimpered.

Coupland looked over at the assembled emergency personnel waiting to clear the scene. 'Concentrate on yourself right now, Alex.' Then, 'Can you remember your breathing?'

'Go. Fuck. Yourself.' was all she said, but the corners of her mouth were turned up in an anxious smile. One of the waiting paramedics caught sight of Coupland helping Alex towards the first ambulance, nudged his mate who sprang into action opening the vehicle doors.

'How long have you been bleeding?' the paramedic asked, Alex looked down at the silky blood seeping through her trousers and moaned.

'A few minutes,' Coupland replied for her, 'that's all.' The paramedic said something in a low voice to his mate, who in turn spoke quietly into the radio.

'I'll see you there,' Coupland said to Alex brightly, giving her a grin he didn't feel, 'Not if I see you first,' she muttered before the ambulance doors closed. The driver turned on the siren, pulling out into the flow of traffic as it set off towards Hope Hospital.

Mallender was still being attended to at the scene.

Chapter 45

Alex's heart sank the moment she awoke and realised she was still in hospital. She'd been dreaming she'd been discharged, that she was at home in her own bed being waited on hand and foot by Carl and Ben when a baby's hungry cry awoke her. A searing cramp across her abdomen reminded her that she'd given birth too, her hand moved instinctively to the wound covered in a dressing following the emergency caesarean carried out when she'd been brought in two nights before. She looked about the room, startled.

'Ah, you're in the land of the living then.' Coupland hovered over her bed like a scary apparition, 'How're you feeling?'

'Like I've been run over by a bus,' Alex said groggily, 'every time I wake up I start to panic, keep forgetting they whisked him into the SCBU because he's so tiny.' She frowned at Coupland, disconcerted by the angle he was staring at her from, 'sit down for God's sake,' she ordered, 'you're making the place look untidy.' Coupland sat on the hard plastic chair causing it to creak under the strain of his bulk. 'These things aren't intended for people with generous proportions...' he grumbled, he didn't like hospitals as it was. 'He'll be OK though?' Coupland asked cautiously. Alex nodded.

'So, have you brought me anything?' she asked lazily, eyeing the plastic bag he'd brought with him. 'Tinned fruit,' he said eagerly, lifting a can of peaches out of the bag and placing it onto the cabinet beside her, 'at least that way you get to eat it before it goes off.'

'You shouldn't have,' Alex murmured, punching

his arm playfully, 'really…'

'And Lynn got you this.' He said, winking at her before lifting a teddy bear out of the bag and placing it on the bed beside her.

'Oh, I love it,' She said, wincing as she pushed herself into a sitting position. 'What are we waiting for; shall we go and give it to him, then?'

Coupland commandeered a wheelchair from outside the ward and helped Alex carefully into it. Just for a moment her smile faltered. 'How's the boss?'

'Bullet went into his collarbone, he'll live. It's his arsehole I'm worried about, what with Curtis ripping him a new one for brandishing a weapon.'

'I thought he found it in the house?'

'He did, in Zadawi's desk drawer. Lucky he thought to check in there…'

'If he hadn't you'd have been toast, Kevin. He saved your life.'

'I know, and I'm sure he'll live to regret it.'

'Anyway,' he said as he pushed her along a corridor he was all too familiar with, given the times he'd nipped along it when Lynn was on shift. 'What are you going to call him?'

'Todd,' Alex said, without hesitation.

Three Months Later

The cemetery was quiet first thing in the morning. Dead quiet, her dad used to joke. Abby paused a moment near his headstone to wipe cobwebs away from the inlaid vase before breaking off a lily stem from the bouquet she was carrying and placed it on the earth across his grave. 'From Mum.' She whispered before moving on in the direction of the new section of the graveyard, where a recently filled plot lay obscured beneath a mountain of floral tributes. A cold wind made Abby shiver as it rattled the layers of cellophane on the bouquet she was carrying.

'We need to go Abby,' Coupland said gently, mindful that what she was here to do couldn't be easy.

Abby nodded, placing the bouquet of flowers beside a large wreath in the shape of the word MUM. No one could be certain whether Marion's death was a result of the stress the family had been put under, or whether her condition had finally got the better of her.

Either way Abby hadn't been allowed to say goodbye, until today.

'I'll keep the boys safe.' She whispered. It was the one thing she wouldn't be talked out of, and Coupland didn't blame her – hadn't her family been fractured enough? Jordan and Findlay would be reunited with Abby after the trial, and where ever they were moved to, Coupland would not be part of the loop.

'What'll happen to Earl?' It was hard for Abby to care about him but when all was said and done he was Aston's brother and the outcome would weigh heavily on someone she cared deeply about. Coupland glanced at the officers waiting in the vehicle beside them. They shouldn't be having this conversation but in the grand scheme of things would it matter? 'Handing himself in certainly helped,' he said carefully, 'and thanks to him we've built a pretty strong case against three of Omar Zadawi's sons together with Paul Constantine who we can also prove instigated the murder of a serving police officer and a local shopkeeper.'

The gun that had been used to kill Rebecca had been found at the terraced property Paul Constantine used as a drug den, the place where Todd Oldman had lost his life. Dale Brown, the junkie who'd carried out the knife attack on Todd had been found dead following an overdose of contaminated Heroin. Coupland sighed, Abby had enough on her shoulders to contend with, she didn't need to know right now that Earl's elevated status to supergrass had resigned his own family to obscurity, that they too would be re-settled through the Witness Protection Scheme, although 'settled' didn't quite sum it up. Abby smiled at him nervously before climbing into the waiting car which would take her to court. Coupland knew, for all the right reasons, he would never see her again.

He settled into his Mondeo, turning the volume on the radio down while the DJ interviewed a boy band from the noughties no one gave a toss about. He turned to his passenger. 'How's the physio going?'

Mallender shrugged, accepted the cigarette offered him, 'It isn't,' he said matter of factly, 'but no need to tell Curtis that.'

'He'll hear nothing from me,' Coupland replied, patting his pockets. 'Here,' Mallender offered him his lighter, holding it steady while Coupland lit up. The DCI's phone beeped indicating an incoming text. He slipped his phone out of his jacket pocket. It was a message from his father:

Your mum's asking for you, son. Can you come round?

Coupland shrugged; the boss lapsing into one of his silences suited him just fine. He glanced once more at the holiday reservation he'd printed out that morning and placed on the back seat, already imagining Lynn's face when he showed it to her. He was taking her out to dinner, somewhere nice to celebrate her test results coming back clear.

He caught sight of his reflection in the rear view mirror and sucked in his cheeks. Might be worth losing a bit o' weight, he conceded, in readiness for the holiday belly he was bound to get.

THE END

Start reading the first chapter from the next book in the DS Coupland series, ONE BAD TURN, available now from Amazon…

ONE BAD TURN

Chapter 1

A proper little fighter this one. Didn't even scream when he jumped out behind her, just shoved him with both hands, sent him flying backwards while she tried to make a run for it. She had some speed on her; he'd give her that, shame about the heels holding her back. That was her biggest mistake, he reckoned, not taking them off before she tried to leg it. She'll pay for that, he smirked, just as her ankle gave way. He might not be athletic but he could outrun a fit woman in heels any day. He grinned as he began to catch up with her, grabbing her by the hair before pulling her into the bushes. She hit him then, a punch rather than a girly slap, and the shock of it sent him off balance. 'You can't win this,' he sneered as he righted himself, dragging her down onto the gravel path. He straddled her, yet still she struggled, as though there was any other way this was going to pan out. A pile of rocks were within arm's reach, looked big enough to do the job. He lifted one, felt the weight of it, cold in his hand. He held the rock above her head, staring at her features in the moonlight. He hadn't realised what a looker she was. 'Shame about that,' he whispered as he brought the rock down.

Coupland bounded through Manchester Airport, Lynn and Amy flanking him, a grin plastered across his face despite the flight's arrival being delayed by an hour. 'I tell you what,' he observed as they'd taken the green route through customs, 'that lot wouldn't dare search through my case, not without their bloody latex gloves, all the rich food we've been having.' He seemed disappointed no one had paid them any attention on their return journey. 'Kevin,' Lynn rolled her eyes at the back of his head as she tried to keep up with his cigarette starved pace, 'it's just routine when you go through security now, they were only doing their job.'

Even though two weeks had passed since he'd suffered the indignity Coupland was having none of it. 'You were giving them dirty looks, Dad,' Amy piped up between texting God knows who at this hour to say she was back and raring to show off her tan. 'I wasn't giving them dirty looks, it was my tired face.' Coupland reasoned, 'I just wanted to park myself down in the lounge and get some shut eye, which, might I add was impossible once they'd gone through my suitcase with a fine tooth comb. You'd think they'd offer to pack it back for you but no, you're on your own for that part.' Lynn pursed her lips, 'There was no need to make such a song and dance about it though; we only just made it to the boarding gate on time.' Coupland pulled a face, 'We were only late because Her Nibs wanted a bloody manicure she could have had on any number of the days she's not in college but no, it has to be this season's latest bloody colour,' his eyes widened as he said it, 'have you two heard what you've done to me?' he spluttered, 'You've turned me into Gok bloody Wan.' Even as he said it his chest filled with the sheer pleasure of moaning about normal things, inconsequential things that were no longer related to life or death. Or cancer. He caught Lynn's eye and smiled. 'All I'm saying is it's funny how they're not so eager to search through my scuddies now.' Lynn stared him down, 'I do your washing Kevin,' she pointed out, 'I wouldn't wish that on anyone.'

Two strides and they were through the exit, joining the cluster of nicotine addicts lighting up and sucking on cigarettes as though their lives depended on it. Coupland unzipped his rucksack, tore the cellophane wrapper from a pack of 200 Marlboroughs he'd bought in duty free. 'Why don't you have one of your electronic cigarettes, Kev?' Lynn cajoled. He shook his head like a crazy horse because he could do that and inhale at the same time. 'Are you serious?' he spluttered after the first hit reached his lungs, 'Ten hours suspended mid-air with nothing beneath you but a bloody great ocean, only the real McCoy'll do the trick right now, thanks very much.' Coupland held the first mouthful of smoke down in his lungs before slowly releasing it into the air.

'Does it not bother you, Dad,' Amy piped up, her attention momentarily distracted from her phone as she studied him, 'the horrible photos, all the stuff printed on those packets, showing the harm it can do?' Coupland stared into the distance, thought of the countless cases he'd worked on, the crime scene photos depicting the numerous ways each victim had met their untimely death. A cigarette didn't feature in any of them. He gave silent thanks that in Amy's world the greatest threat to his life was smoking, rather than the killers he came in contact with more times than he cared to ponder. The cocoon he'd created around his family remained intact; they worried about his lungs and his diet like they were a normal little unit. Like he was a bus driver or a teacher, rather than a detective sergeant in Salford Precinct's murder squad. He downplayed his role on every case that he'd worked on, did all he could to put their minds at rest. Amy's question told him it worked. 'It'll take more than a packet of cigarettes to finish me off, Ames,' he quipped, 'I'm like Wolverine, me, bloody indestructible.'

'You've got the werewolf bit right,' Lynn observed, brushing her hand across his unshaven face. The familiar buzz in his pocket took the edge off his mood. Pulling his mobile phone from his jacket he pulled a sorry face at Lynn as he barked his name into the phone. He hadn't switched it on more than two minutes since and already he was needed. His face darkened as he listened to the person on the other end, grunting a response before slipping the phone into his pocket. 'I'll walk you to the taxi rank,' he took Lynn's case from her and wheeled it with his own, his mood sombre, 'something's come up.'

Leaving the airport and driving along the slip road that would take him onto the M56 Coupland turned on the radio. More bad news about the refugee crisis, people trapped in a collapsed building in India. At least on the radio you were safe from the graphic images, the tragic photos and videos bandied about the internet like disaster porn. It didn't make sense why people clicked onto these sites, why folk would choose to look horror in the eye, experience close up someone else's tragedy. Coupland pulled the e-cigarette Lynn had bought him out of his pocket, eyeing it with suspicion. 'It's time you started to cut down, Kev,' she'd wheedled. It wasn't the first time she'd said this, but there was a steely look in her eye when she'd spoken, as though he wasn't going to get off as lightly this time around, 'especially now you're getting to that age.' He'd bristled at that. 'I'm at the top of my game,' he'd objected, but they both knew that wasn't true. His bulk was genetic, a bullying father who only stopped knocking seven bells out of him once he'd outgrown him. He'd never played sport, was an avid spectator though, rugby, football, pretty much anything that could be broadcast via Sky into his local. The pies and pints had taken their toll; his bulky frame was starting to soften. Lynn had put them both on a low fat diet, and to be fair he was feeling the benefit. He might not be able to take on Usain Bolt in a sprint but he could still hold his own in a dark alleyway if the situation called for it. There was a place for healthy living, he was sure of it, but didn't you have to believe the future was worth it? Coupland pushed the mawkish thoughts to the back of his mind; the jet lag had made him maudlin, his holiday already receding into the past. He took a puff on his vapour stick out of loyalty to Lynn. To think she worried about his health after all she'd been through…he puffed some more.

Coupland parked his car, shivering as he climbed out of it, whether from the change in temperature now he was back in Salford or from what he was about to see he wasn't sure. He stepped towards the cordoned off area where a uniformed officer stood guard. The officer nodded, lifted the cordon to let him pass. The information he'd gleaned from the earlier call had been sketchy, a body had been found in an area of woodland along the perimeter of a recreation park in Worsley. By the level of activity going on it had been discovered a couple of hours ago, that and the number of press cars circling the area like vultures smelling carrion.

The crime scene manager leaned against the driver's door of his car as he made a call. He nodded at Coupland, watching as the detective took a pair of shoe protectors from the open car boot and slipped them on. He clamped his hand over the phone, 'Didn't know you were back,' he tutted, 'no bugger tells me anything.' Coupland grunted, 'A bit of shut eye would have been nice.' A blond haired, slim built man appeared through a clearing, signalled for Coupland to make his way over. 'Good holiday?' DCI Mallender asked as a courtesy, already turning and heading towards the locus before Coupland had time to answer. Coupland grunted once more, his mouth forming a grim line. It never got easier, observing the dead. Especially when their exit had been violent. 'Looks like she was taken by surprise,' was all Mallender said before they stepped through the inner cordon. 'There's a bus stop a hundred yards or so further up, at a guess I'd say her attacker grabbed her from behind and dragged her into the bushes.' A tent had been erected to protect the body from prying eyes; it would also keep the rats at bay while the forensic team went about the business of collecting hair and fibre samples. Coupland stepped into the tent, nodded at the photographer setting up a tripod in the furthest corner. 'Can you give us a minute?' He waited while the man put down his equipment noisily before stomping out into the cool night air. We've all got bloody work to do, his body language seemed to say, but he'd been on the wrong side of the fat sergeant before and was in no hurry to repeat that mistake. Mallender stayed by the tent's entrance, he didn't need or want to survey the body a second time. Coupland let out a slow breath. There was no easy way to do this. When he was a kid he used to sneak in to the local cinema to see horror flicks all the time, his big build making it easier for him to be let into the 18-rated screens. If there was a bit that was too gruesome he could cover his eyes, wait for the camera to move onto a different scene. He wished he could do that now, shield himself against the worst bits, the bits that would come back to haunt him in the early hours. He let his gaze move over the victim's body. The woman was in her twenties. Black. Slim but not skinny, wearing a fitted business suit. Her skirt had ridden up over her thighs; her tights were torn in several places. Coupland turned to Mallender, eyebrows raised. The DCI answered his silent question. 'Her underwear's still on, so I'm guessing she's not been sexually assaulted.'

'Maybe not for the want of trying…' Coupland observed. 'Her bag was found beside her too,' Mallender added, 'a good one, by the look of it. Her mobile was inside it; along with a purse containing fifty pounds in cash, so the motive isn't likely to be a robbery is it?' The question was rhetorical; he'd already turned his gaze away from the tent's interior.

'What's her name?' Coupland asked.

'Sharon Mathers.'

Coupland had put it off long enough; he leaned over the woman's body to get a closer look, allowing his gaze to travel upwards. A halo of scarlet pooled around what remained of her head. Something foul tasting caught in his throat. The public seemed to think this part got easier, the more dead bodies you saw on the job the more immune you became to the sorrow but there was no truth in that. This woman had been loved, was still loved, Coupland may even have crossed paths with her at some point, sat beside her at the dentist, made small talk with her in a supermarket queue, she'd lived and breathed and cared for someone, yet had been discarded like a broken doll. It was the eyes that always did for him, the last fearful moments reflected in each victim's stare. Their faces were never at peace: they were shocked, frightened, or just plain sad. It was a palpable sorrow, one that weighed heavy on his shoulders every time. 'Jesus, have you seen what he's done to her face?' he whispered. There was a crater in the front of her skull; one eye socket was no longer visible. It seemed grotesque that the make up on the other half of her face was intact. From what remained Coupland thought she might have been pretty.

Once.

'Look at her hands,' Mallender prompted, and Coupland got down on his haunches to study them. Red painted nails were unbroken but her knuckles were swollen. 'She managed to get a punch in then,' Coupland muttered. All that fight yet it had still come to this. Coupland felt his hackles rise. He had a wife, a daughter, how often had he told them just to run away, put their energy into escaping rather than screaming for help, and failing that kick the bastard where it hurts and then run. But the truth was men were stronger than women, and a bastard hell bent on doing harm was nigh on unstoppable. Coupland stepped out of the tent, he'd seen enough. This young woman had literally fought for her life and lost in the worst possible way. He pitied the poor sod who'd stumbled upon her. He locked eyes with Mallender. 'Who found her?' he asked.

The DCI pulled a face. 'Boyfriend. Been living together for the past three years. She was late home from drinks after work. He'd started to get worried when she didn't answer his calls. Walked along the route she'd normally take when she got off the bus. Kept dialling her phone as he looked for her when eventually he heard a ring tone he recognised coming from the clearing.'

'Poor bugger.' Coupland muttered. He looked at his watch then realised he hadn't changed it back to Greenwich Mean Time. He pulled his mobile from his pocket. It was 3am. No wonder he was knackered. 'So the boyfriend found her about 1am?' Mallender nodded. The bus service was pretty regular until midnight, which wasn't a late night by many standards. Most people only considered cabs once the buses stopped running. Coupland ran a hand over his face. His euphoria on landing in one piece had long since evaporated; he felt like the walking dead.

'How did the boyfriend seem?' Coupland was referring to the defence wounds on the victim's hands. By the state of her knuckles her punches had found their target. Whoever killed her won't be looking too pretty by morning.

'He's clean by the look of it. No black eyes or bruises emerging but we'll carry out a full check on him.'

'Where is he now?'

Mallender inclined his head in the direction of a small development of houses beyond the bus stop. 'Back home, he's been assigned an FLO. I want you to go over there first thing. Get as much out of him as you can. Obviously until we get the all clear he's our key suspect.' Coupland knew the drill, not that it made it any easier. The fact remained that every week two women in the UK were murdered by their partners, so the process of elimination followed by the police during a murder investigation was not without just cause. 'I'll finish up here,' Mallender offered, 'Curtis will want a preliminary report on his desk first thing and you look ready to drop.' Coupland nodded, grateful to be making his way back to his car.

He'd intended to go home to grab a couple of hours sleep but found himself driving on autopilot, arriving at Salford Precinct station some fifteen minutes later. A bit like Coupland, from the outside the station seemed barely to have changed since it was built in the seventies, although the interior had had a major refurb over the last five years, firstly to bring the building in line with modern safety regulations, secondly to reduce heating and lighting costs, make it run more efficiently. Apart from five years spent at Stretford which he'd rather forget, Coupland had spent his entire career stationed here. Starting out as a young cop on the beat, in the days when that meant pounding the streets alone, never certain of what was round the next corner. Some of his contemporaries looked back on that time with nostalgia, reckoned it was better back then, safer, the public held the police in high esteem. Coupland wasn't so sure. Hard faced men have stared him in the eye for as long as he can remember, all that's changed are the fashions, not the attitude.

Coupland enjoyed one last cigarette before leaving the car. Yes, he was tired, he could sleep on a clothes line given the chance, but two hours kip wouldn't even make a dent in it. Might as well work through his exhaustion. They'd be setting up an incident room by now and he had a chance to read through the early statements that had been taken, get some momentum going under this investigation before he called it a night.

Or day, depending how you looked at it.

Want to read the rest? ONE BAD TURN is available to order from Amazon today.

READING GROUP QUESTIONS

A PLACE OF SAFETY

1. How sympathetic did you feel towards Earl and did your feelings change as the book progressed?

2. Would you speak out about something even though it could put your life in danger? Was Abby brave or foolhardy?

3. What do you think about the reasoning behind Todd Oldman joining the force?

4. Have you ever found yourself in a situation that has spiralled out of control? How did you deal with it?

5. Do you wear your heart on your sleeve like Coupland? Or do you prefer to keep something back?

Acknowledgements

To all the FRAGILE CORD readers who told me they wanted Coupland and Moreton to return – thank you for taking them to your hearts, I only hope I've done them justice.

It would be impossible to set a crime novel in Salford without touching on gangs – according to police sources there are over 25 crime syndicates running in the city at the moment - more than enough on which to build a series. In FRAGILE CORD the actions of a low level gang targeting drinkers in a Swinton wine bar have far reaching consequences for a young mother with a secret. In A PLACE OF SAFETY a planned execution goes badly wrong.

Thank you for buying A PLACE OF SAFETY, please post a review on Amazon if you have the time.

About The Author

Born in Salford Emma moved to the Peak District as a child, commuting into Manchester's financial district as a consultant for HSBC. Spells in Brummie beckoned (Selly Oak then Solihull) after winning a bank scholarship to Birmingham University before working out of bank branches in Castle Bromwich, Coleshill and Shirley.

Emma loved English Literature at school but studied Business and Finance in order to secure a 'proper' job. Other jobs have included selling ladies knickers at Grey Mare Lane Market and packing boiler suits in a clothing factory. "I did try for waitressing work at one point," Emma says, "but restaurants seemed to think I wasn't capable of carrying plates from one room to another."

After moving to Scotland Emma worked in the public

sector supporting socially excluded young men into employment which gave her plenty of material to work with.

Married with two sons Emma writes from her home in East Lothian which they share with their Jack Russell, Star.

Find out more about the author and her other books at:

https://www.emmasalisbury.com